Scandalous Kingpin

KINGPINS OF THE SYNDICATE SERIES

EVA WINNERS

Scandalous Kingpin
Playlist

https://spoti.fi/4fNxnkJ

Author Note

Hello readers,

Please note that this book has dark elements and disturbing scenes to it related to child abuse, torture, and foul language. Please proceed with caution. It is not for the faint of heart.

Don't forget to sign up to Eva Winners's Newsletter (www.evawinners.com) for news about future releases.

Kingpins of The Syndicate
series

Each book in this series can be read as a standalone. However, since this story takes part during the timeline of the previous books in the series, it might spoil some events.

The recommended reading order of books in this series is as follows:

Corrupted Pleasure (Davina and Liam), Prequel
https://bit.ly/3XayjIu
Villainous Kingpin (Basilio and Wynter), Book 1
https://bit.ly/4dRmqwJ
Devious Kingpin (Dante and Juliette), Book 2
https://bit.ly/3ZMRSpb
Scandalous Kingpin (Priest and Ivy), Book 3
https://bit.ly/3YTAUrU
Ravenous Kingpin (Emory and Killian), Book 4 https://bit.ly/4dRmqwJ

For more things Eva Winners,
please visit www.evawinners.com.

Blurb

Christian "Priest" DiLustro.
   A charming prince.
   Only when it suited him.

I had a taste of him and got addicted. But he was a heartless bastard and an arrogant mafia prince whose only goal was to ignore me after we scratched the itch.

Just when I thought we'd both moved on, he swooped in and claimed he made a promise that he intended to keep, even if it killed us both.

Ivy Murphy.
   An Irish mafia princess.
   Mine.

We might have started as a dream, but now I was her nightmare. I was damaged goods, scarred by my past. Still, I couldn't allow anyone else to have her.

So, I stole a marriage contract and her heart. It wasn't mine to own, but I took it anyway.

For better or for worse, in sickness and in health, I intended to keep her.

Until death do us part.

Prologue

IVY

"**W**elcome to Philadelphia!"
The radio announcer's perfectly timed words echoed through the speakers of Wynter's Jeep as we took the Benjamin Franklin Bridge across the Delaware River.

Wynter, Juliette, and Davina were my ride-or-dies from Yale. Wynter and Juliette were cousins, raised mostly together by Wynter's mother in California. Juliette was reckless but easy to love, and based on all the stories they'd shared over the years, she was the yin to Wynter's yang. Wynter, who'd been preparing for the Olympics since the day she'd slid her feet into her figure skates, had a single-mindedness to her that benefited from Juliette's wild ways.

Then there was Davina, who always made sure we

made the right moves and thought with our sensible brains rather than our lizard ones. We always joked that she was the mother hen of our group, but we wouldn't have it any other way.

And me... well, I was just me. Ivy Murphy, daughter of an Irish mobster. Both my father and Juliette's ran our families' parts in a much larger criminal organization. Her father ran the Brennan Irish mafia, their territory in Ireland and the States, and my athair—father—and my brothers ran the Murphy Irish mafia in Ireland only.

It worked for me—less chances of running into my brothers. Or, as they were known in the underworld, the Irish pricks. I hadn't been back to Ireland since I stepped foot on American soil, and even now with a Yale degree under my belt, I kept delaying my return to Ireland.

So here the four of us were, en route to carry out our heist—namely, rob one of the kingpins. How did this come to be, you might wonder? Well, it started with a house fire and Davina's ex-boyfriend blackmailing us. We followed one rule: never steal from the same place twice. So far, we'd robbed Juliette's father, a casino in Chicago, and now we were shifting our efforts to a club in Philadelphia. Diversity was important to us amateur criminals.

And something good had come out of it.

After Wynter's boyfriend assisted in erasing the evidence of our past operations, we decided to use the money to start a school. It was a school that would teach a regular curriculum supplemented with fighting, self-defense, and survival in the mafia world.

Before long, Wynter had parked her Jeep and we were strutting through the club like we belonged. On my left was the cloakroom, tinged in red neon lights, and a bar area with a dozen or so high-top tables. Some of the patrons had cleared a space for a dance floor, and behind it, on the farthest wall, hung a familiar sign.

Kingpins of the Syndicate.

Its large skull followed me as we passed through the dance floor, burning a hole in the back of my head.

Music blasted as we walked deeper into the club, vibrating the grimy floor beneath my feet. A few bodies writhed as we weaved between them toward another bar.

We ordered a round of sodas, and as we waited, my eyes traveled over the strobe-lit club. It was clearly catered toward the upper echelon of society—the people here were dressed so finely I could've sworn their clothes had come straight from the New York runways.

Juliette and I finished our drinks first, setting them down and moving on to the dance floor. We started swaying to the beat, laughing and shaking our asses like club girls trying to make a living.

Davina and Wynter joined us as "Morning After Dark" by Timbaland came on, and I craned my neck to spy the DJ, a stunning leggy woman with white-blonde hair and a pair of bubblegum-pink headphones. I made a mental note to slide her a tip on our way out.

The four of us laughed and shook our hips, letting ourselves forget the reason we were there. One dance turned into two, then three, and before long, it was time to execute our plan.

"Okay, be on alert, girls," Wynter said after she'd pulled us into a huddle. "The signal can't be far off."

We'd parked in the way of the money truck that was due at any moment. The plan was to go back to the car and follow the money truck out of here. Nothing could stop us now.

Well, *almost* nothing.

"I have to use the restroom." I glanced around, looking for a bathroom sign. "I'll be super quick."

"If you hear the announcement," Davina instructed, "don't come back here. Head straight to the car."

I scurried off with a jerk of my chin, leaving Juliette, Wynter, and Davina dancing. I waded through sweat-slicked bodies and dodged floating silver trays carrying drinks that glinted beneath the flashing lights. Once in the bathroom, I took care of business, washed my hands, and was about to make my way back down the dark hall when I collided with a man's hard chest.

He looked down, trailing up my bare legs before his emotionless gaze flicked up and caught mine. It was like he was looking straight through me. Goose bumps raised the hair on my arms, and I instantly knew who he was. Priest, the Syndicate's kingpin who ruled Philadelphia.

Instinctively, I took a step back, and something dark moved through his eyes.

"Now what have we got here?" he said softly. My stomach dropped like lead and a quiver started in my chest. Being alone with him made it feel like there wasn't enough oxygen in the small space. "You shouldn't be out here alone, angel."

He closed the distance between us in one powerful stride and a shiver ghosted through me. His eyes that locked on me were heartless. Invasive. Blue.

The moment stretched, stealing what little breath of air I'd managed from my lungs.

Just the idea of being this close to the man we were about to rob sent every nerve ending in my body tingling in expectation. I sensed danger, and I wondered how long it would be before my friends came looking for me.

Another step and I was cornered, his woodsy oak scent wrapping around me. His body singed as it brushed against mine, the heat powerful and impossible to ignore. My limbs felt heavy and light all at once, my skin buzzing like a live wire.

"I'm not alone."

I swallowed when he remained quiet. He was the tallest man I'd ever seen in real life, his blond hair a halo framing his face. Except there was something dark and unhinged in his blue eyes, and I found myself unable to look away. That full mouth of his probably had ladies falling at his feet, and judging by his smirk, he knew it.

His gaze ran down my bare legs like ice melting on my heated skin and he chuckled, making my cheeks flame with heat.

"You enjoying yourself, angel?" His voice was an elusive timbre, each word twined with an abrasive edge. It was sinful, inviting erotic images into my mind. The kind that you kept locked in the pits of your soul. I averted my gaze a little too quickly, making it painfully obvious that I'd been staring. "Don't be shy... I find myself quite fascinated by you too."

He touched my red locks and curled one around his finger.

"I wasn't... I'm sorry," I said with a shake of my head, then immediately winced. His grip tightened, and I wondered what it would feel like if he tugged. "I need to go."

It was like a magnetic field surrounded us, leaving us alone in the darkened hallway while hordes of people mingled only a few feet away. He was brimming with raw sexuality and masculinity, his presence inescapable, leaving me frazzled. Everything about him warned me to run away, yet my body refused to move and my pussy chose that moment to clench with need.

"Not so fast," he said, his voice low as he bent his head, bringing his mouth closer to my ear. "We should explore this."

I blinked, suddenly turned on like never before. "Explore what?"

"This." He nipped my earlobe and every thought I had withered away. *Oh, dear God.* This wasn't part of the plan. "You want it too."

I swallowed, shaking my head. We couldn't do this. He, of all people, was *not* on the agenda tonight.

"I don't think that's wise," I whispered.

"Then tell me to stop," he said, his voice dropping another octave. He placed a hand on my hip and my skin bloomed with heat. "You aren't even real, are you? An angel would never tempt the devil."

Both hands on my hips now, he pulled me closer to him, our bodies flush.

"I'm not... tempting anyone," I rasped. I couldn't let this man touch me—I had to put a stop to it. And yet... my body leaned closer to his, light drawn to darkness.

"You can't deny it, but something tells me you know that all too well."

"I don't even know your name," I protested, but my voice was so quiet it was barely audible. Yes, Wynter had briefed me on this man, but "Priest" couldn't possibly be his real name. "This is wrong."

"Forget about right and wrong," he commanded, ignoring my feeble reasoning. I nodded, almost as if in a trance. "Now look at me."

I lifted my head, staring up at him. His pupils were so wide, the blue hue of his eyes almost swallowed by the black. But it was the longing in his gaze that captivated me.

I opened my mouth to tell him to stop, but no words came out. All I could focus on were his strong fingers flexing on my hips. My core contracted, flooding with heat and making me suck in a stuttered breath.

I licked my lips, every cell in my body vibrating with sexual energy. I didn't know what it was about this man, but I wanted his hands on me, his fingers inside me. Just this once, I wanted to do something wild and reckless and let this gorgeous stranger ravish me and relieve this aching need.

"Now what?" I breathed out.

The man locked eyes with me as he trailed his hand up my thigh.

"Now I make you come," he grunted, his fingers reaching my panties and effortlessly sliding inside the flimsy fabric.

The music pumped, matching the anticipation buzzing through my veins. I wanted to touch him, rake my hands through his hair to steady myself as he slid his fingers through my folds, but intuition warned me he wouldn't like it.

So instead, I kept my thoughts away from my friends and tonight's mission, picturing eyes on us and being thrilled by it.

"Soaking wet already," he growled with a smirk.

"Don't let it go to your head," I told him, hoping he couldn't read the shock of it on my face. This *never* happened to me.

"So feisty." He let out a dark chuckle and circled my swollen clit with the pad of his middle finger, applying the perfect amount of pressure.

"Fuck," I breathed, my hands curling into fists and my knuckles turning white.

His lips pressed against my ear, his hot breath doing things to me. "An angel with the mouth of a sinner. I like that."

His lips skimmed down my neck, trailing a burning path over my sensitive skin as he dipped his hand further into my panties, pulling them down. Then he knocked my legs wider apart as he slid a finger inside me, easing in and out.

I bit my lip to stop from moaning or begging him for more. My hands flew to his hair, scraping my nails over his scalp. For a moment he stiffened, but I was too far gone to take note.

"Oh, fuck..." I moaned, gripping his short blond strands. "If you stop, I swear I'm going to murder you."

He groaned low in his throat, adding another finger, then resumed thrusting his fingers, my slick pussy dripping, coating my inner thighs. He nipped my neck and heat erupted inside of me, liquefying in my veins.

"Fuck, you're so tight," he growled. "You're not a virgin, are you?"

A wave of nervousness rushed in. I didn't want him to stop, and I definitely didn't want to be honest.

"You wish," I whimpered.

9

"Actually I don't."

There was a harsh edge to his voice, but there was so much lust in my veins I couldn't read between the lines. I rolled my hips, rubbing myself against him as he drove his fingers deeper, hitting my G-spot.

"Holy mother of fucking God." I clung to him, the sound of my arousal as he worked them in and out of me somehow audible over the din of the nightclub.

He lifted his head. A storm brewed behind his eyes, making me think he was about to stop. His lips curled into an arrogant, harsh smile. "I promise you, angel, God has nothing to do with this. By the time I'm done with you, we'll both get our salvation."

I found his words strange, but before I could ponder on it, he fell to his knees and dipped his head between my legs, licking me from my entrance to my clit. His growl of satisfaction shot straight up my spine and he ran a rough hand down my leg, hooking my thigh over his shoulder.

The move was obscene—him kneeling in front of me like I was a goddess and not a total stranger, the heady anticipation of being discovered here... It was all too much.

I ran my fingers through his hair and he pushed his tongue inside me. *In and out. In and out.* My back arched off the wall and my eyes rolled back in my head. He worked me like he'd known me for years.

I moved my hips as the familiar wave built, the pleasure rolling through my core. He nipped at my clit, then smacked me between the legs, and something dark crawled up from deep inside me. A fierce passion that had never reared its head before.

His blue gaze hooked on mine as he sucked at my clit, still throbbing deliciously, and the pressure finally exploded. I came so hard my ears rang, pulling all other sounds of the club underwater.

I closed my eyes, struggling to catch my breath as a languid sensation tugged on my muscles. My thighs trembled, and a peace unlike any I'd felt before washed over me.

He spoke, but the words didn't register. My eyes fluttered open to find him still on his knees, his eyes on me. My thighs were still trembling when the DJ stopped the music and spoke into the mic, piercing through the fog of pleasure.

"Will the owner of the red Jeep Wrangler please move their vehicle?"

I gasped, my hand coming up to cover my mouth. I turned on my heel and bolted away. I'd hear the rough chuckle that followed me for many months to come.

Chapter One

IVY

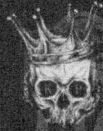

My athair's funeral came on a cold February day with a promise that things would never be the same. Athair—*Father* in Gaelic—had kept secrets, we all knew it, but some were inexcusable, even for him.

Such as his mysterious meetings with Sofia Volkov, a woman I'd met once years ago and who was now enemy number one among most criminal organizations.

How could he have left me with this mess?

All things considered, it was a beautiful day. Sunlight splayed onto the estate's immaculate grounds, where men in black suits guided women in black dresses and heels through to the burial spot. The Irish mafia and the kingpins had come to pay their respects as the cold winter air swept through Ireland, the frozen ground welcoming my athair's coffin as it lowered to join my mother's.

The black veil danced around my face while my brothers crowded me. Ever since Athair's death, they'd been even more protective than usual, almost like they were waiting for me to collapse in my grief. But, strange as it sounded, I felt nothing but numbness as I watched the coffin disappear.

Wynter squeezed my hand before drifting away with her husband, replaced by Davina and her husband, who wrapped their arms around me and said, "Want to come back with us?"

I barely had time to open my mouth when my eldest brother, Aemon, replied, "We'll need Ivy here with us."

Bren and Caelan muttered their agreement, sharing furtive glances with Aemon, and I sighed with resignation. Whatever they were hiding, those three would never share it with me, but little did they know how determined I was to find out.

"It's okay," I murmured, pressing a kiss on Davina's cheek. "I'll call you later."

Someone cried. A Hail Mary traveled in the wind like a caress. More weeping.

I watched my friend and her husband drift away when I noticed Juliette out of the corner of my eye, standing with her husband, Dante DiLustro. I frowned, surprised she hadn't come up to me. Usually she was the first one to comfort me and vice versa.

"You ready?" Bren asked.

"Just a moment."

Caelan took my hand before I could take a step and squeezed it gently. "Just remember, we need you home. We don't want you going off with your friends until we eliminate this threat."

"What threat?"

He winced like he'd let something slip. "Nothing for you to worry about. You just need to stay in Ireland and out of trouble."

Slipping my hands into my dress pockets, I headed through the cemetery, the frost crunching beneath my boots.

"Hey," I greeted, kissing Juliette's pale cheek, closing my eyes and breathing deeply as her dark hair curtained us in.

"I'm so sorry," she whispered.

"Don't be, we all know this life always brings death." My voice cracked, and I wiped a stray tear from my cheek.

"Not always," Dante protested.

"Maybe so," I said, flashing him a tight smile. There was a weight in my chest, something I hadn't been able to shake off since hearing of my athair's death. "Although, one could argue…" I gestured around at the funeralgoers but stopped short when I noticed the tears glistening in Juliette's eyes. The guilt instantly flared and I added, "Of course, none of this will happen to you."

"I have something to tell you," Juliette blurted.

I raised my brow, waiting for her to continue, when Dante wrapped his arm around her shoulder. "This isn't the time. We should be going."

He steered Juliette toward the shiny black car parked beyond the procession, whispering into her ear as they went.

My gaze caught on a suit-clad figure off to the side. There Priest stood, hands in his pockets and his gaze on me. I hadn't seen him since Wynter's wedding where he'd turned me down hard and fast. Embarrassment racked my body as I thought back to that day. It was barely a year ago, yet it felt like decades had gone by.

I waited with bated breath for the slow ticking to explode into a full-blown war. And through the whole tense ordeal, my gaze tracked Priest.

He'd been keeping to himself since this reception started, usually in the company of his cousins and brother. Spotting him alone now, I slowly made my way over to him, silently whispering encouragement to myself with each step.

"Hey," I greeted him nervously. The man looked incredible in a tux, and I couldn't help picturing him on his knees, my leg thrown casually over his broad shoulder, my fingers slipping through his golden hair.

When he flicked a brief glance my way, my anxiety grew. Maybe he didn't even remember Philly? After all, months had gone by.

I shifted uncomfortably, then continued, "Umm, not sure if you remem—"

"I remember," he cut me off, his jaw clenching.

Surprise washed over me, but before I could relish in the fact, realization sunk in. He was pissed.

"I'm Ivy, by the way," I said, the catch in my voice betraying my confidence.

Priest shrugged. "I know."

Tension sent a nervous tremor through me. These mafia men usually left me unaffected, yet something about him and his size—or was it the darkness that surrounded him?—turned me into a puddle.

"Aren't you going to tell me yours?"

I wanted his hands on me, his head between my legs again, and even more... I wanted him inside me.

"No." I froze, and before I could conjure a thought or a word, he continued in a cold voice. "You confused our last encounter with something it will never be."

I blinked. "Excuse me?"

"That day in the hallway... It'll never happen again." Conflict and something else waged in his eyes, but before I could identify it, his gaze coasted above me, his jaw pulsing in thought. "You need to forget about it."

My chest went cold and humiliation planted seeds inside of me.

What was I thinking?

Just because I was a virgin didn't mean I had to fall

for the first man who'd made me orgasm. God, I was a walking cliché.

I swallowed. "You're right. You're nothing I'd ever want for myself. I'm glad we're both on the same page so we can move past it."

"Agreed," he snapped.

Hurt and confused, I turned around and left, the weight of his gaze burning the back of my neck the whole way to the car.

The cutting ache of his rejection still stung to this day. If I was smart, I'd turn my back on him and find my brothers.

But I didn't feel like being smart today.

"Did someone blackmail you?" I asked, raising a brow in fake amusement. I'd be damned if I showed him how much his rejection burned. "Or are you here out of some misplaced duty to mourn his loss?"

His jaw clenched and he shook his head, his gaze dropping to the ground. When it came back up to me, it was so haunted it pinned me to the spot.

"I'm not a heartless monster, angel." Shock rocked me at my center, stealing my breath. He hadn't called me that since the day at his club when he'd put his mouth on me. "I'm sorry for your loss."

"Thank you." I swallowed, familiar pain throbbing in my chest. "I'm going to find who killed him."

My words shook with emotion. I didn't know why I said them. I hadn't even dared to think them until now.

The vengeance would be the only thing that could cool the fire in my blood.

"Trust me, it's better this way." He looked around the cemetery, landing where my athair's casket full of flowers lay. "For you."

My lungs felt tight. "That's not for you to decide."

His gaze was steady, and I knew his next words would be harsh, so I cut in. "Do you want my thanks for rejecting me and making me feel like…" I trailed off, my throat burning, but I steadied myself. "It no longer matters, because I've moved on."

It was a lie, and he must have known it. We stared at each other as that awareness settled between us.

"That's good," he gritted. "It's not like there's any love lost."

"Definitely not. It's not like it matters anyhow," I retorted, my heart beating hard against my rib cage.

He shook his head, hissing through his teeth. His eyes lifted to mine, and they flashed with possession. With his handsome face, he looked ready to dole out some punishment. The question was on whom.

"It matters, angel." I couldn't think. Couldn't breathe. Suddenly I was terrified of the look in this man's eyes—dark, violent. "The next time I touch you," he bit out, "I'm going to break both of us."

I swallowed, the insinuation of his words sounding more like a promise than a threat.

Something about them warned me that I should keep

my distance. Nothing good could come from this untapped chemistry.

He took my silence as rejection and shook his head.

"Go back to your family, Ivy."

He turned to leave and I knew, deep in my gut, that I wouldn't see him again for the foreseeable future.

Chapter Two

PRIEST

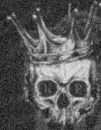

Secrets had a tendency to fester inside your body and soul. It was inevitable that sometimes those secrets destroyed the people around you too.

I'd seen the impact on my brother, Dante. I'd felt an impact firsthand. Over a decade of abuse was hard to forgive and forget. Unlike me, Dante wasn't a bastard son, so he was spared some of it. We shared a father, and although we grew up believing we shared a mother, we've since learned that wasn't true. My blond hair and blue eyes were finally explained. My biological mother was Aisling Brennan Flemming, who recently became DiLustro. Wynter, my newfound half sister had a better life than Dante and me, but there were invisible scars etched in her soul too. Courtesy of the secrets Aisling kept buried. My cousins Basilio and Emory suffered too, and it all boiled down to the things our parents kept from us and the cruelty we endured either by their hands or as a result of their fuckups.

But it was the deeds that were best left unspoken that had the power to ruin everything. They were like nuclear weapons we kept close to our chest while everyone else stood at arm's length.

Until *her.*

The redheaded angel that made me too fucking weak. Some days I thought she was it, the only one who would ever penetrate my pathetic excuse for a heart. I'd had one taste over a year ago now, and it was enough to consume me. I often thought about her when I lay in bed at night, her face as she came pinned to the backs of my eyelids.

And then there were the days I truly believed she was my trigger, the pulled pin to my grenade, and if I didn't stay away from her, everyone I cared about would perish. Not that it was a particularly long list, but I'd miss my brother and my cousin.

After my sister-in-law's involvement in Ivy's athair's death, I decided it was best to distance myself from the entire Murphy clan. Her brothers, the infamous Irish pricks, had a tendency to kill first and ask questions later.

I wasn't a good man, not by a long shot. I'd learned from a young age to be jaded, that some people were just plain bad. And while I believed in delivering justice to those who existed in the dark shades of gray, I didn't want the innocents to pay just because I couldn't have the Irish mafia princess with a soft tongue and even softer touch.

Ivy Murphy had buried herself in a far-reaching corner in my mind. Even now, in the middle of an important meeting, I couldn't shake her.

As I sat back in my chair in my club's conference room, restlessness ghosted under my skin. I was surrounded by five men from the Corsican mafia who wouldn't hesitate to kill me if I made a singular wrong move. Especially after they'd been forced to turn over their half of the city and go back to France with their tails tucked between their legs. That shit show was courtesy of Dante's negotiation with Alessio Russo—he'd needed to get his woman out of Afghanistan, and Russo just so happened to owe him a favor.

Needless to say, they weren't exactly our friends, and in recent months, the Corsican mafia had been trying to make a move back on my territory, making plays for the ground they'd lost. Nightclubs. Development sites. Docks overlooking the river.

But money talks, and I was able to make a deal with them to keep them appeased. Let them do their shit in France, not here. Things got a bit tense when we'd first sat down, the greedy fuckers wanting more than they could chew, but we came to an agreement that benefited all parties.

The only downfall? My brother, cousins, and my papà were here too. And they were far too opinionated. I preferred to run my city alone—the way I'd always done it—so having them descend on me like some overbearing nonnas and zias had my eye twitching.

"I don't see this as a token of goodwill," said Jean-Baptiste, the head of the Corsican mafia, his voice penetrating my thoughts.

"You're getting a ten percent stake of our drug trade in Europe. It is more than you have now," I pointed out.

"Here's an idea, why don't we—" I wasn't surprised he tried to push for more.

"Why don't you spare me your ideas and fuck off," I cut him off, my voice remaining impassive. "Take it or leave it."

A tension crept through the room, but I refused to sit here for another round of dick measuring. Jean-Baptiste was reckless and arrogant. How he'd survived this long was beyond me. If the Corsicans valued their standing in this world, they'd have to look to his brother for a better leader.

"I was only trying to help us both," he seethed, standing.

"If I wanted help, I would have asked for it. But rest assured, it wouldn't be from you. I'll give you twenty-four hours to make your decision. You can see yourselves out."

Jean-Baptiste and his men stomped through the room like bratty children and slammed the door on their way out. Good fucking riddance.

Silence followed, and I narrowed my eyes on my family. "Are we done here?"

With some shifting gazes, my cousin Emory spoke from where she sat next to me. "Someone needs to get laid, and it isn't me." She cocked a loaded brow and added, "And I'm guessing all the young, married couples"—my papà cleared his throat and she quickly corrected herself—"and not so young, are getting plenty, so it isn't them either."

An understatement if I'd ever heard one. But there was one thing nobody knew. Sex wasn't my first or last choice when I needed some relief. It was dishing out revenge on those who wronged me. Even though I knew I became a jackass when I abstained from getting my hands dirty—*okay*, maybe the correct term was torture.

Except, it had been close to six months now since my last encounter with the redheaded angel at her father's funeral and not even that seemed to give me any respite. Maybe I needed to see her more frequently, touch her… I didn't know, but the urge was beginning to burn, to bubble over until it became an absolute necessity.

"Not good business, son, pissing off our business associates," my papà said, lighting a cigar and leaning back in his chair. He shook his head, disappointment etched between his wrinkles.

"I would hardly call them our business associates," I pointed out.

I glanced down the table to see three pairs of eyes on

me. Dante tapped his Italian leather–clad loafers, looking at me like he knew exactly what soured my mood, while Emory and her brother, Basilio, sat beside him, their keen attention on me as well.

At that moment, Aisling breezed into the conference room. My already foul mood dampened, and it didn't take a genius to work out why. Even now, a year and some months after learning she was my biological mother, I still felt betrayed by her.

She'd left me in hell.

Fucking. Left. Me.

Every fucked-up thing that happened from that day forward was because of her, and if I could do to her what had been done to the woman I believed to be my mother and get away with it, I fucking would.

I narrowed my eyes on her in distaste, the itch to snatch her by that slim neck and drag her into one of my dungeons and out of sight clawing at me.

The moment Aisling's eyes fell on me, they softened. I fucking hated that they were the same shade as mine. I resented any similarities, and at this moment, I envied Wynter's eye color. Unlike my blue, my sister's were green, different from Aisling's.

"Christian," she greeted me, but when I remained quiet, she turned to the others. "Hello, everyone."

Her face shone with affection and love as she looked at Papà. It would seem Aisling and Frank DiLustro would be a forever thing. *Fuck.* How could he forgive her? Her love for my papà was tangible, and yet she'd left him too. Handed him their newborn son before leaving us all behind.

I should give her a taste of the medicine we all endured under the late Mrs. DiLustro and see how she liked it.

"Don't think about it, brother," Dante hissed under his breath, sticking to Italian, probably because he read my murderous thoughts.

My eyes narrowed on him and my jaw tightened. "What's the occasion for your visit during our business meeting, Aisling?" I asked, ignoring Dante and instead addressing the woman who was desperately trying to be my mother, two decades too late.

She stopped next to my father, her shoulders tensing.

"Son, that's not how you talk to your mother," he warned.

"Giving birth to me doesn't make her my mother," I deadpanned, a clear warning lacing my voice. They both fucked up, but it was my brother and me who'd paid the price. While he was out there running his empire and Aisling was off coaching Wynter, Dante and I were left to be tortured by a madwoman.

A frustrated noise escaped Aisling and she turned on her heel, marching out of the room.

She'd barely stepped out of the room when my papà jumped on my ass. "You will apologize."

"I will not."

My brother and cousins groaned audibly, knowing full well when I decided on something, there was no changing my mind. And Aisling was one of those decisions. I'd rather let myself be dragged through gravel than talk to the woman who gave birth to me.

"Can I talk to my son in private?" Papà demanded, shooting the others a look that brooked no argument.

Basilio was first to stand up, probably eager to get back to his wife—my half sister. Wynter was raised by Aisling, but from what I gathered she was more interested in securing Olympic gold than loving her daughter. Emory followed, shooting me a worried look, and I gave her a terse nod, letting her know all was good.

My brother was the last to stand up but not before stopping by our papà. "Aisling needs to work out her problems with Priest on her own. You can't keep playing mediator."

"She's fragile." Dante and I scoffed. It was the way he chose to see her, but there was nothing fragile about Aisling Brennan—or was it Flemming? Whatever the fuck she wanted to call herself was not my problem, but I sure as shit wouldn't think of her as a DiLustro. I didn't need yet another thing binding us together. "I won't tolerate you two ganging up on her."

I shrugged. "I'd prefer it if we never saw her again."

"We don't gang up on her, Papà," Dante chimed in. "We barely ever see her."

Thank fuck.

28

Dante was a replica of our father. In a way, so was I, except for the blond hair and blue eyes. The three of us shared the proud DiLustro nose and we were all about the same height. Papà's face had gained a lethal edge over the years, giving him a harsh look, and the same could be said about Dante.

"Give us a moment, Dante, will you? Let Papà berate me in peace."

My brother exhaled but left without another word. If I asked him to stay, he would, but I knew with his recent reconciliation with Juliette, he hated being away from her. Besides, I didn't need a sidekick.

I held my papà's gaze as my brother excused himself, never faltering or flinching. After all, I was a pro at keeping my demons under lock. So was my brother, although there was one thing he was spared. I wasn't so lucky.

"You need to work out your problems with your mother." He jumped straight to the point. "It's not just about you anymore; you need to think about your sister and what's best for the future of this family. It breaks Aisling's heart every time you push her away."

My expression remained the same. "That's easily remedied. Tell her to stay away."

"How about you stop beating around the bush and tell me what your problem with her is, son."

"I don't have a problem?" That wasn't supposed to come out as a question.

"No objections about your mother, then?"

Aisling's presence triggered something I didn't like to think about. The period when Dante and I were left to our own devices—when there was no safety.

"None whatsoever," I answered. *As long as she stays the fuck away from me*, were the words I chose to keep to myself. For now.

"Good, good." Papà rubbed his hands, taking my words at face value. His mistake, not mine. "Now, I want to talk to you about something else." I raised a brow, waiting for him to continue. "I know you're young and marriage is the furthest thing from your mind"—Jesus fucking Christ, could this day get any worse?—"but with the Corsicans constantly testing the strength of the Syndicate in Philly, it's important we forge an alliance."

Despite my desire to never settle down and be forced to endure the bullshit that came with marriage, I knew that I'd eventually have to. I just thought I'd have another decade... or three. As the men of the DiLustro family, the goal was always to rule New York, Chicago, and Philadelphia.

Basilio's marriage to Wynter had been a surprise, but it wasn't until Dante married Juliette that whispers of arranged marriages for Emory and me started. Killian already had his sights on Emory, or maybe it was the other way around—I couldn't tell, and I didn't care enough to ask.

As for my future wife... I wouldn't be going there.

I gritted my teeth as I tried to picture a woman on my arm, but only red hair and full lips flashed through my mind. There was just one problem… If I married her, she was bound to learn my darkest secrets. And when she did, she'd look at me and see the truth. She'd be disgusted.

It was something I couldn't allow.

"I'll handle my own marriage," I snapped, then pushed away from the table and left without another word.

Chapter Three

IVY

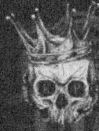

I loved a rainy day as much as the next girl. Something about seeing lush green fields glisten and the sky slowly turn dark and spooky gave me thrills. Today though, I loved it more than usual because it offered time away from my overbearing brothers.

"I should have studied something more useful than photography and arts," I muttered under my breath. Truthfully, I barely passed because I wasn't good at it all. But scheming and stealing with my girlfriends... Yeah, I was pretty good at that one. After all, it was a team effort with my best friends.

Sitting outside, huddled in a raincoat and boots, I watched the pasture become a muddy mess. When I was a little girl, I loved chasing the sheep, combing my fingers through their wool and assigning them names.

Fluffy. Snowball. Whitey. Mr. Beady Eyes. They were my companions until I learned they were only raised to be slaughtered.

The door opened and closed, the sound of heavy boots approaching behind me.

I recognized Bren's voice. "Where's Ivy?"

"In her bedroom," Aemon answered. "What did you find out?"

I stiffened, debating whether I should announce my presence, but before I made up my mind, Caelan started. "Nothing good. Athair really fucked up."

"Explain," Aemon demanded, his voice curt.

"He was involved with Sofia Volkov." I stiffened, pulling the raincoat tighter while curling into myself. "It must have been going on for a while because he had kids... twin girls. With her."

"*What?*" Aemon bellowed.

"Shut up," Bren scolded. "I don't want Ivy hearing this."

"Who all knows?" my eldest brother asked.

"Not many." Caelan dipped his chin. "Everything points to Sofia taking him out, but something's not adding up."

"What is it?"

"A few things," Caelan commented. "But mainly... why would she kill him now? Decades of working together and then *bang*? It doesn't make sense."

"Who knows why that psycho bitch does anything," Bren spat.

The phone in my pocket buzzed and I fumbled for it, silencing it. I held my breath, waiting for one of my brothers to show up in front of me, but they continued their conversation.

"We have to find Sofia Volkov and end her," Aemon barked. "Her twins too. We cannot have any connections to the Volkov family."

Shock slammed through me at his words. We had half-siblings? And he was willing to end their lives without even looking into them? Killing Sofia Volkov I could understand; she'd caused so much pain and destruction. But her daughters...?

My phone buzzed again and I clicked the side button as I glanced at the screen.

> Juliette: I want you all to know something.
>
> Wynter: What is it?

I watched the text bubbles appear and then vanish.

> Davina: Come on, Jules. Don't keep us in suspense.
>
> Wynter: Did you set another house on fire?
>
> Me: Good ol' times.

Oddly enough, Juliette's reply still hadn't come through.

> Me: Maybe Jules got sidetracked with her husband.

Juliette: I didn't.

> Me: So what did you want us to know?

My brothers' voices were muffled by the rain, but they were still oblivious to my presence. I stared at the screen, pondering whether I should tell my best friends what I just learned.

> Me: I just learned something too.

Not waiting for a reply, I continued typing.

> This has to stay between us.

Promise emojis all followed and I sent the next message.

> Athair had an affair with Sofia Volkov and she killed him.

Incoming call on silent

Juliette: Ivy, pick up the damn phone.

Me: No. I can't talk.

Wynter: Answer the call so we
can have a group FaceTime.

Me: No. I have to go.

I powered off my phone and put it back into my
pocket just as hushed voices and footsteps faded into the
house.

I jumped to my feet and then started running. Soon, I
broke into a sprint, darting into the woods that stretched
around the Murphy castle. Before long, I was at the lake,
staring out over the misty water, the memories I thought
long buried closing in on me.

The sky darkened and thunder rumbled, rattling the
earth and pushing the memories forward.

Everything felt the same, except for one thing.

Me.

Chapter Four

IVY

Then

"Don't cry, princess." Athair's voice was soft but his grip was firm as he led me through Dublin's narrow streets. "You're with your old man. You're not scared, are you?"

I shook my head, long curls sticking to my tear-streaked cheeks, and followed along for what felt like hours, trying not to trip over my feet. When we stopped in front of a big metal container, I was scared and didn't understand why we were here.

"Mama won't be happy," I murmured, my eyes locked on the women huddled together in a corner.

"We won't tell her."

"But—"

Athair came to a stop, grabbing my other hand and pressing it to his chest. "No, Ivy. This has to remain our secret."

My eyes darted around, Athair's bodyguards standing discreetly behind us. "They're crying... What if they're hurt."

"I know, my heart," he urged. "But this is to keep *them* safe."

"Who?" I whispered.

"Your sisters." A cold voice came behind me and I whirled around, fear taking hold of my lungs.

"Ivy only has brothers," Athair stated, his voice like a whip. "As you well know, Sofia."

The woman smiled, but there was a hint of sadness in it. Something about it pulled on my chest, and I took her slim, elegant hand in mine. "But I've always wanted a sister."

The woman's gaze grew wet and she lowered to one knee, pressing a kiss to my forehead.

"I'll count on that, little Ivy. When the time comes, be good to them."

My fluttering heart warmed and I nodded, trying to seem older than my five years. "Who are you?"

Sofia smiled sadly. "I'm the villainess, ruling in the darkness because of the men."

"I'm scared of the dark," I admitted. Athair's grip on me tightened, the gesture silently comforting. It said *you are safe*. My gaze darted to the little boys and girls around us. "They might be scared of the dark too. Can we help them?"

Her beautiful face turned harsh. "Someone has to pay for their parents' sins."

She rose to her full height and met Athair's tall frame, their eyes locking. "I can't keep doing this, Sofia. My wife suspects something."

"Then bring Ivy along."

His grip on my hand tightened and I whimpered. "Athair, you're hurting me."

He rubbed my little hand affectionately. "I'm sorry, princess." His eyes returned to the strange woman. "I'm taking my daughter out of here."

Sofia blocked his way out. "First, I need you to do something."

"If you think I'm getting you more... merchandise, you're out of your mind. The Cullens are already onto me."

"I'll put you in touch with someone, and the Cullens will be dealt with."

Athair stiffened. "Fuck you will. They're young parents. Aiden Cullen is just sticking to the code—you know how everyone feels about human trafficking."

"He's weak and this stupid code is making *me* weak." My brow furrowed. Nothing they said was making any sense. "The only way to protect the twins is for me to take the power that is rightfully mine," Sofia said. "You know that as well as I do."

"But trafficking these kids—"

"I was sold like cattle and survived."

Athair snorted. "If you call this survival, you've lost your fucking mind, Sofia."

"I couldn't protect my firstborn and her daughter; I will protect my twins. You should want to do the same. They're yours as much as little Ivy is, after all." Shocked, I tipped my head back to look at Athair, but he kept his eyes on the woman. "So you will help me with this. We'll rule the world at any and all costs."

"You mean *you* will rule the world," he spat.

My gaze bounced between them, following their exchange, but I only had more questions. Who were these twins? Why would Athair have more daughters? He said I was his only princess.

"Athair, will you and Mama be di—vo—r—ced?" I asked. I heard the word spoken by our cook who left her husband. I didn't quite understand it, but Mama said it means two people no longer loved each other. Surely, if he was here with this mean woman, he didn't love Mama anymore.

"Absolutely not. We shall go back home to Mama and your brothers. The six of us together, forever."

His assurance made me feel better, but still left me confused.

Chapter Five

The best way to prevent betrayal was to never let anyone get too close.

In my twenty-seven years, I'd been betrayed enough by the people closest to me to last me a lifetime. And despite my papà's betrayal being unintentional, he'd failed in keeping his wife and her wrath away from Dante and me. I'd forgiven him for the most part, but I didn't think I could ever forget.

So now I lived my life refusing to give anyone a chance to fuck me over—family or not.

I'd seen what caring too much did to people. First with Basilio, then with Dante. Even Emory was teetering on the edge, playing with fire when it came to Killian Brennan.

I vowed to never fall victim to those circumstances.

Yet there was one person who kept getting under my skin, determined to see the filth beneath my carefully curated facade.

I'd be willing to bet everything I owned that she'd change her mind real quick if she saw me now, standing in a pool of blood. I wondered if this would be enough to prove that I was beyond redemption.

The frail arms I had tied to a chair in the basement of this abandoned warehouse, knuckles stained red, belonged to the only witness of my deprived bloodthirst.

"Should have really cleaned yourself up," I sneered, looking at the one person I despised beyond all else.

"You can't keep me in this filth forever."

The face that still came to me in my nightmares was almost unrecognizable. A monster, no less.

"It's the only thing suitable for someone like you," I drawled, reaching for a cigarette. I shoved it between my lips and lit it. I only smoked when surrounded by the ghosts of my past, and I worried this half-empty pack wouldn't get me through the night.

"How much longer do you plan on keeping me here?"

"You know the answer to that stupid question."

"*Tell me.*" The scream echoed, bouncing against the sharp stone walls. *Do it. Shout until your lungs give out; there isn't a soul around for a hundred miles.*

"Until your dying breath," I said simply. "So you better get used to it."

My prisoner stared at me with bulging eyes while silence enveloped us. How many times had the roles been reversed? How many times had I stared this monster in the eye and prayed that I'd be saved?

Years. My entire childhood. Dante's, too.

It was destroyed—stolen—thanks to the evil in front of me. The evil that nobody knew was still alive. It was the one secret I had kept from everyone.

There was one other person who deserved a similar punishment, but the church was hiding them. Untouchable. No matter. I was a patient man, and I would get my revenge before I left this earth.

"Please, Christian."

A soft murmur, but it was all I needed. My legal name from her mouth was my trigger. In a flash, I reached for my knife, cigarette still dangling between my lips, and sliced a finger, the sound of crunching bones lost between the buzzing in my ears.

"May the Holy Spirit free you from this miserable life and your sins swallow you whole." I added the severed finger to a rope where it joined a number of other body parts. "Amen."

Chapter Six

IVY

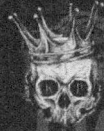

The Dublin club owned by my brothers, aptly named Irish Pricks, sparkled under dim lights while confetti rained from the ceiling. I stood in the center of the room, the bar right behind me, when shouts filled the crowded space.

"Happy Birthday!"

Balloons floated to the ceiling. "Birthday" by Selena Gomez flooded the room as my best friends ran up to me wearing stilettos and looking like a million bucks while I felt like I'd been run over by a freight train. I'd been trying to dig up everything I could about Sofia Volkov and her twin daughters so I could avenge Athair's death, but all I'd managed to do was run into roadblock after roadblock. It was clear I was no match for the psycho villain.

"Are you surprised?" Juliette asked, smothering me in a hug.

"Don't you think it's a bit much?"

She frowned, stepping aside so I could see my other friends' disappointed expressions.

"But it's your twenty-fourth birthday." Davina kissed my cheek. "You're almost a quarter of a century old."

"Almost doesn't count." Smiling, I kissed her back, then embraced Wynter and Juliette. "But it's perfect because you're all here."

"The entire DiLustro clan came," Wynter beamed. "Even Aisling."

I winced. "And Priest is okay with that?"

I didn't even know why I cared. His issues with his biological mother should be none of my concern, but despite his rejection, I couldn't help but feel sorry for him.

"He's ignoring her," Juliette answered. "Nothing's changed there."

"He can't hold a grudge forever," Wynter muttered. "Nobody holds a grudge forever."

Davina and I shared a glance but said nothing. Christian "Priest" DiLustro was known as an unforgiving mafia prince in the underworld. After all, it was the reason he was able to climb to power at such a young age and run Philly with an iron fist. He even chased the Corsican mafia out of Philadelphia.

My world tilted as someone picked me up by the

waist and spun me around. The spinning stopped and Bren's face came into focus as my feet still dangled a foot off the floor.

"Happy birthday, baby sister."

Aemon was right behind him, looking impeccable with his hand tucked into the pocket of his suit. "I remember the day you were born like it was yesterday."

"Mama would be proud of the woman you've become," Caelan drawled.

I smiled, hiding all my doubts and insecurities behind it. My brothers still didn't know I'd overheard their discussion, nor did they know I'd been snooping around Aemon's office.

Sofia Volkov would pay for Athair's death. He and my brothers might have shielded me from this life, but it was part of me. I was born into this world, tainted by its deeds and sins, and no, it didn't bother me. It was just the way things had to be.

"I'm glad you recognize that I'm no longer a little girl." I brushed a piece of nonexistent lint off his shoulder. "You should let me go back to the States."

A dry grunt of amusement escaped him as Bren set me back on my feet. "It's safer this way."

"Like I was ever in any danger over there," I said, stepping between them, knowing it was my oldest brother who called the shots. "I would even be willing to accept a bodyguard."

I fluttered my eyelashes innocently while Aemon

gave me a half smile, bringing a glass of whiskey to his lips.

"You mean you'll accept a bodyguard only to lose him the second you touch down in New York."

"She'd never do that," Juliette chimed in.

"Besides, Ivy's always been the responsible one," Wynter added, lying shamelessly. We all knew Davina took the cake on that one.

My brothers let out a collective sardonic breath. "I'm sure she is."

"Come on," I whined, pouting. I'd learned how to work my brothers over the years. It was a necessity for surviving life in this family; otherwise, they'd smother you with their overbearing ways. "That's all I want for my birthday. I won't stay as long as I did last time."

My brothers gazed behind me at the same time, and I turned to see a man I didn't recognize—gray suit, short hair, a glint of ruthlessness in his eyes.

"Who's he?" I asked.

"None of your business," Aemon responded, his eyes locked on the man as he approached. He pulled me against his chest in a hug. "Happy birthday. Stay at the party."

"Sure." He palmed my face playfully, then he and Bren disappeared.

Juliette bumped shoulders with me as she followed their winding path through the sea of people—most of whom I'd only ever met once. "Isn't that Aiden Callahan?"

Aiden Callahan was brother-in-law to Luca King DiMauro, often assisting with the Omertà. He also ran the Callahan Irish mafia.

"He looks like a walking red flag," Wynter muttered and she wasn't wrong. The man had a reputation and was a walking red flag if I'd ever seen one.

I shrugged. "Not my kind of red flag," I answered, uninterested. My heart jolted for one man and one man only lately, and I hadn't seen him in six months. "Speaking of, where are your husbands?"

I couldn't outright ask where the arrogant mafia prince was. He wasn't interested; fine. Neither was I.

Wynter flicked a glance over her shoulder, and I followed her gaze to the VIP section where Liam Brennan, Davina's husband, sat alongside all three DiLustro men. My heart hitched, stopping my breath, and I couldn't keep my gaze away from him.

He looked up and I gasped, holding his gaze as he sat like a king waiting to be serviced.

"Whenever I see a man"—one blond man with blue eyes, to be specific—"who might as well be a bold red danger sign, I just paint my nails to match."

In truth, I'd thought about him too many times late at night—the rough glide of his palm against my cheek, the press of his lips against mine, the heat of his body.

"You know there's a term for that," Juliette deadpanned as strobe lights flashed red, purple, and yellow across her stunning face.

"Yeah, a 'fix-a-ho,'" Davina chimed in. "Meaning, you find a bad boy and try to fix him."

"A fix-a... what?" I repeated softly, wondering if there was a way to fix him. I didn't think so, which left only one other alternative: accept him as he was. But then we were back at the beginning—at the fucker not *wanting* me. A thorny, painful feeling ripped through me. The one I pushed somewhere deep down every time I thought of him: rejection.

"Let's dance," I announced. "It *is* my birthday, isn't it?"

Not long after, I was lost in the bottom of shot glasses, bathroom trips, and a heady, uninhibited rush in my blood. The club was crowded with pulsing bodies moving together, sweat dripping down our backs. My friends laughed as their husbands joined them, and I threw my head back, luxuriating in the bizarre energy that came with turning another year older. I danced like my life depended on it, Priest's burning gaze watching my every move. The lights cast a glow against my bare arms and sage-green dress.

I lifted my heavy red strands off my shoulders and looked up. Priest's gaze was still on me, dark and vehement.

Holding it, I rolled my hips slowly. Seductive.

A few men started dancing around me, taking advantage that I was the only one dancing alone in our group. Holding his stare, I pressed up to one of them, hands on his chest. Rotating my hips, I thrust my chest out and raised my arms. The blood in my veins heated, my nipples tightening.

His eyes darkened and I smiled, lifted a hand, and blew him a sweet kiss.

Take that, I thought smugly. *You're not the only fish in the sea.*

Turning my back to him, I continued dancing with a handsome stranger whose smile was admittedly beautiful.

He leaned over. "What's your name?"

His voice was rich and deep, the kind that made you feel like you were the only girl in the world as it caressed your skin.

I blushed. "Ivy. You?"

A hot sensation trailed down my spine before I heard another voice. "Do you value your limbs?"

I turned slightly and my heartbeat incinerated in my chest. Priest's eyes flicked to my dance partner and narrowed.

To my surprise, he didn't miss a beat. "I actually do like my limbs. Very much. And so do the ladies."

"You'd be wise to stop touching her."

The guy took my hand in his and kissed it like a gallant gentleman, ignoring Priest's cold presence.

"I'm Tyran Callahan and, my dear Ivy... it's been a pleasure."

He turned around with the grace of a panther and strode away, and suddenly, I was fighting off the urge to kill the man next to me.

"What is your problem?" I hissed, my body still moving to the beat, careful not to attract attention—especially from my brothers. The last thing I needed was a brawl resulting in an attack on a member of the DiLustro gang. I had no interest in starting a war.

Priest slid his hand into his pocket, the heat of his gaze burning right through me. How was a girl supposed to forget him when all he did was demand attention?

"No problem. It's a nice evening." He was toying with me—he had to be—but I refused to play this game. "Happy birthday."

I rolled my eyes, then did what any sane person would do: I turned my back on him and carried on like he didn't exist. It must have worked because he disappeared, leaving me to dance alone.

It wasn't long before I stumbled off the dance floor on shaky legs, disappointed that the stubborn mafia prince hadn't plowed through the sea of dancers and insisted that I dance for him. None of these feelings made any sense, and all it left me was frustration.

I drifted upstairs in search of a restroom to quiet the thumping pulse of music in my head. Thanks to soundproof walls, it felt like a completely different world up here. Eerily quiet.

Five minutes later, I exited the restroom and paused, my hand still on the knob. A familiar blond stood with his back to me. He had a phone to his ear, although I couldn't hear what he was saying.

I took a step back when his back tensed. He hung up and slowly turned, the stark blue of his eyes hitting me square in the chest. We stared at each other and a thick, almost suffocating tension filled the air. The scent of his cologne made me feel warmer and more intoxicated than any of the alcohol I'd consumed.

His hair was slightly longer on the top, just enough to run my fingers through it and hold on.

The thought reminded me of another hallway in another club, his mouth devouring my pussy like it was the most delicious fruit he'd ever tasted.

I shoved the memory aside.

"Happy birthday, angel."

I narrowed my eyes on him. "Don't call me that."

Something dark moved through his eyes, but as soon as he leaned back against the wall, it disappeared. "Why?"

"Because I said so. Besides, if you wanted me to have a happy birthday, you'd make yourself scarce and stop scaring off my dance partners."

His lips lifted. "I sincerely doubt Tyran was scared."

I eyed him suspiciously. "You know him?"

"I know of him. Trust me, he's not for you." My mouth dropped open, and he let out a deep chuckle. "If you keep your mouth open like that, angel, I'll find something to fill it with," he said softly.

His words set fire to my blood and my legs wobbled, threatening to give out under the desire to fall to my knees and taste him.

As if he could read my thoughts, he took a step toward me and I took one back, hitting the wall behind me. His hand appeared above my head and the pressure of his chest against mine sent a tremor through me. He had me pinned in more ways than one.

The walls felt as if they were closing in, like there wasn't enough oxygen for the two of us.

I couldn't think with him so close to me, the idea that he might touch me sending every nerve ending in my back tingling with brutal desire.

One I intended to resist at all costs.

Chapter Seven

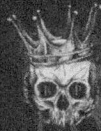

The Murphy mafia might not operate in the States, but their name carried weight in the underworld. Anyone with an agenda knew to turn up at Ivy Murphy's birthday tonight—from the Callahans and the Brennans to the Corsican mafia. However, I was here to get to the bottom of the Murphys' negotiations with the Callahan mafia.

At least, that was what I kept telling myself.

I *should* have been out there collecting intel at this very moment, not stalking this redheaded angel.

"Why are you here?" she asked, fighting the spark igniting her eyes. "To ruin my birthday?"

"I'm here for business."

The confusion on her face flickered, but she swiftly

masked it. "My brothers would never do business with you."

The scent of strawberries filled my nostrils and I took a step back, needing some space for my own sanity. I watched her inhale slowly and then release it.

"Never say never, angel."

"Don't," she snapped, fixing her best scowl on me.

"Why? Don't you like your name, angel?"

She held my stare and crossed her arms over her chest, eyes narrowing as her body trembled from either fury or arousal; she was impossible to read.

"I do, very much. But you seem to constantly forget it. It's Ivy. Get a tattoo or something."

My cock stirred in my suit pants and the beast within me stretched awake. This impact she had on me floored me every time. These last few hours in her proximity were the most I'd felt alive since I last saw her. Hell, since the first time I'd dropped to my knees before her.

"Maybe I will. I know someone who'd happily brand it on me. Maybe I'll even have them carve it into my skin with a rusty blade—make it so when I take you, you'll see exactly who you belong to."

I shook my head once the words had left my mouth. What was wrong with me? Years of therapy, of learning how to control my impulses, down the drain. I blamed her for that. She looked like a fucking goddess, wearing a dress that fell down her body in silky lines, accentuating her curves. A slit up one side to mid-thigh giving me a glimpse of her long, toned legs.

"What—" She couldn't get her words out, her cheeks flushing deep crimson to match that wild mane of hers. "Something's wrong with you."

I leaned forward, a merciless smile curving my lips. "You have no idea, angel. If you only knew the thoughts I've been having…"

Maybe if I gave her a glimpse of my darkness, she'd keep her distance.

"I hate you, Priest."

"And I hate you." *For making me feel.* "But I still want to press your face against the wall and fuck your pussy until you can't take it anymore."

The delicate veins in her neck thrummed and her mouth gaped, no doubt shell-shocked at my bluntness. I scraped my hand over the stubble on my chin, fighting to rein in my desire.

But then, to my surprise, she took a step closer, her eyes narrowing to slits.

"It's you who wouldn't be able to handle it, Christian *Priest* DiLustro." The way she hissed my real name had my cock twitching. I quite liked her when she was angry. "You had your chance and you blew it. Now get out of my fucking way and stop cockblocking me."

She sidestepped me, leaving me staring after her.

"You like her."

My brother appeared behind me, catching me completely off guard.

"Who?" I feigned ignorance. It would be a cold day in hell before I admitted my feelings to anyone.

"The Irish princess," he clarified, as if there were any other woman who could possibly catch my interest. "For the record, I think she'd be good for you."

"Because she's stolen from us, is difficult, and doesn't know when to keep her mouth shut?" I muttered. "Not to mention how awkward family gatherings would be knowing Juliette's secret."

Dante cleared his throat, not disagreeing, as he turned to me. "Tyran announced to anyone who would listen that you've staked your claim on Ivy Murphy."

Of course the prick would. *God save me from the fucking Irish.*

Yet, even as I silently uttered that prayer, I knew deep down there was no saving me from this self-destructive path.

I was on my way out of Irish Pricks when someone caught my eye in one of the side rooms: Aiden Callahan. He was seated at the private bar, nursing a glass half-filled with amber liquid. Danil Popov was seated next to him, his back stiff and the two in a heated discussion.

I should leave—I knew not to start shit—but even as I told myself that, my feet headed in his direction.

I stopped in front of Aiden, my dark mood on display, and he raised his head, arching a brow.

"Priest," he greeted me, smiling smugly. "I hear you *almost* danced with the birthday girl." The challenge in those blue eyes was unmistakable. "You should snatch her while you still have the chance."

While I contemplated whether to punch the smirk off his face or just beat him to a pulp, Danil cleared his throat.

"I'm getting the fuck out of here."

Neither one of us looked his way as he stood and left.

"What? Cat got your tongue?" Aiden grinned wanly at me. "Ivy Murphy has that effect, doesn't she?"

I got the distinct feeling he was fishing for information. Rather than play into his hand, I tilted my head and rolled up my sleeves. I might have bared my teeth too, one couldn't be sure.

"Don't ever say her name again," I growled.

Aiden stood abruptly and stumbled off the barstool, clearly unwilling to appear as though he was cowering. He came toe to toe with me, watching me savagely.

"What's the matter, old man?" I taunted against my better judgment. "Can't handle your liquor?"

He scoffed, his eyes darkening on me, and glanced down at my fisted hands.

Aemon, Ivy's brother, must have been alerted to the commotion because he was at Aiden's side in a heartbeat. "I don't recall inviting you, Italian," he spat, glaring at me.

This was about to go down.

"What the fuck is going on here?" came out of thin air.

I glanced over my shoulder, finding my brother and cousin there, ready to square off, matching snarls on their faces.

I shrugged. "This Irishman can't handle his liquor."

Basilio snickered. "If he had a lick of Italian blood in him, he'd have no problem. I daresay there are probably *many* things he can't handle."

A look passed between the men that I couldn't decipher, and it set me further on edge.

"Mr. Callahan is my guest tonight. We don't want any trouble," Aemon hissed, eyeing us all coldly. The unspoken words—*this is a Murphy party*—hung in the air.

"Let him be," Aiden muttered. "Maybe he'll finally realize what we can all clearly see."

My eyes darkened and I stepped forward, reaching to wrap my hand around his throat, my other fist pulled back. Suddenly, Dante grabbed my arm.

"Not in front of the women," he warned.

"Yeah, fucker," Aiden said with a smirk, shoving my hand away.

My eyes darted to the door, where Ivy stood staring at us, an indecipherable expression on her face. Davina, Wynter, and Juliette were there too, wide eyes darting between us.

"Just one night of peace," Aemon hissed, pinching the bridge of his nose. "Is that too much to ask?"

"Maybe you should attract better clientele."

"I agree." Aemon glared past me, at my cousin and brother, a note of warning in his voice. "I suggest you Italians find another club in Dublin to stir up trouble in."

Basilio shook his head. "Nah, we like it here too much. Right, cuz?"

"Right."

"Besides, one Callahan for the day was quite enough. We shouldn't fuck around with another one," Dante chimed in, smiling smugly. "Fuck, hopefully we didn't hurt Tyran's feelings."

My brows furrowed. Dante had to be messing with Aiden. He wouldn't be so foolish to start a war with the Callahans. Nobody was that stupid.

"If you laid a finger on Tyran, I'll skin you alive, DiLustro," Aiden growled, his warning increasing the tension in the room.

Basilio chuckled. "The manwhore that he and his twin are, I didn't have to."

Aemon sighed heavily. "Why in the fuck do all the crazies come here?"

"This isn't over," I warned, locking eyes with Aiden before turning to leave.

"Oh, I'm fucking counting on it, Priest."

Aiden's chuckle followed me out of the room.

Chapter Eight

IVY

I let my vision blur as that familiar grief returned and sadness dominated the room. Whenever I thought of him, my chest squeezed painfully and fire ignited in my veins, hungry for revenge. Sofia Volkov was on a lot of radars, but she was a very difficult woman to find.

The business of Athair's will had lingered over us for months, and the day had finally come. Why it took so long, nobody seemed to know. A part of me was also terrified that Athair's secrets would be revealed today.

My brothers sat around me, but I didn't look over. I couldn't. Ever since Athair's passing, they'd been smothering me, so I could only imagine how they'd act if I told them my chest felt tighter than it ever had and that I also might be sick in the potted plant to my left.

Thanks to my eavesdropping, I knew they feared retribution for his involvement with Sofia. Hence, I was practically a prisoner in my own home. Everywhere I went, bodyguards tailed me or I had one or both my brothers breathing down my neck. Even my birthday was a disaster—one that still gave me goose bumps whenever I thought of it.

So, most of the time, I kept to the walls of this fourteenth-century castle like some medieval maiden waiting for a knight to swoop in and save me.

Aemon sat on my right, while Bren and Caelan boxed me in on my other side. It was the time to read the will. My guess was Aemon would get most of it, and Bren and Caelan the rest. I doubted I'd even be listed— as was customary in these old families. My brothers would inherit the Murphy fortune, our enemies, and the responsibility of caring for me.

Our family lawyer sat uncomfortably at our athair's desk, rifling through his briefcase to locate the paperwork. I just wanted to get this over with.

It'd been six months already. My brothers were busy handling the Murphy operation and cleaning up the mess left behind while I twiddled my thumbs, calling my girlfriends and living vicariously through them from dreary Ireland. My friends hadn't been out to visit since my birthday, which left me bored out of my mind and lonely. Not to mention, I had way too much time on my hands to think about Sofia Volkov and the mysterious twins, wondering what it was that Athair even saw in her.

Although, this lonely spell was about to end.

My brothers promised I could visit the States after this business with the will was behind us.

The lawyer glanced at his watch, then at the door, and unease slithered through me. What was he waiting for?

"Can we get this started?" Aemon snapped, just as impatient. Ever since his meeting with the Callahans, he'd been on edge. Sometimes he'd look at me, and I swore there'd be pity in his eyes. But then he'd mask his expression and be the same old big brother I'd always known.

"We have one more person joining us," the lawyer said, trying to placate us all with a feeble smile.

My brother stiffened, his gaze darting to me. Just as he opened his mouth to speak, the door of Athair's office flung open and a man strode into the room like he'd been here a million times. Like he *belonged* here.

My jaw dropped as I watched a man dressed in jeans and a white dress shirt, piercing blue eyes, and a square jaw take the seat next to Aemon.

Aiden Callahan.

"*Fuck*," all three of my brothers muttered at the same time, their gazes locked on me.

A deep frown marred my brow and my hackles rose.

This better not be another fucking revelation. There were only so many mystery siblings I could handle.

I jumped to my feet, confusion and uncertainty surging through my veins.

"Aemon?" I hated the way my voice trembled. "What the fuck is going on?"

My words made Aiden's shoulders tense, and his eyes found mine. It took every ounce of willpower not to take a step back. It had to be his size and the dark aura about him. Definitely nothing to do with the beast I sensed lurking beneath the second most attractive male I'd ever laid my eyes on... No. Certainly not.

"Apologies for my tardiness," he started, his deep, rumbling voice filling the air around me and commanding the attention of everyone in the room.

"No fucking way," Bren hissed. "We agreed to wait."

Aiden's perfectly shaped brow lifted before he shifted to face me, his eyes dropping down my body.

"No, you asked that we wait. I said I'd consider it," he reasoned, shrugging. "I considered it."

My youngest brother's eyes lit up, his jaw rolling ominously, when Aemon's hand came to rest on his shoulder.

"There isn't much we can do," he pacified him. "It was Athair's call."

"What was?" I asked curiously. Why did it always feel like I was invisible when I stood among the men in my family?

"Let's get started," the lawyer announced, cutting through the tension in the room and clapping his hands.

Aemon's shoulders slumped. "Ivy, I'm sorry. I was trying to buy you more time."

"You'll find out soon enough," Aiden stated matter-of-factly, and the self-important way he carried himself irritated the hell out of me. I couldn't stand that he knew something about *my* life, *my* father, that I didn't. He made himself comfortable in a chair, spreading his legs wide, making the fabric of his pants stretch across his muscled thighs. "Sit down."

"Don't fucking tell her what to do," Bren, always my protector, barked.

Nonetheless, I took a seat and signaled to the lawyer I was ready. Page after page of instructions and wealth—legitimate and illegitimate—were read aloud before my name was brought up, and I straightened up in my spot.

"Ivy, my princess, you are to marry Aiden Callahan and the Murphy empire will finally have backing to—"

My world tilted on its axis, the room spinning.

"No," I hissed, cutting off whatever else was coming. "There is no fucking way Athair would demand I marry a stranger." I shook my head back and forth, unwilling to believe what was happening. "There's no way I'm marrying that... that—"

"I'd think twice before you finish that statement," Aiden stated, clearly unfazed by what was going on.

"Or what?" I shouted, my blue eyes met his defiantly.

His eyes are the wrong shade of blue, my mind whispered. There was a sinking, dreadful feeling that filled my chest despite the knowledge that there'd never be anything between Priest and myself. "What kind of man agrees to marry someone he's never met?"

I shouldn't have been surprised. After all, this sort of thing happened in our world. Arranged marriages. Bargaining for power. Using daughters to obtain more power.

My blood froze at the thought of my life becoming a bargaining chip, marrying this stranger with a smug smile. What made him—or my father—think that they could do this to me? Without a warning! I wasn't a puppet to be played with.

Ripping my eyes from the wrong shade of blue, I turned to my oldest brother. "You knew!"

Two words. A heavy accusation.

"Ivy, I know this comes as a shock—"

"We'll find a way out of this," Caelan said fiercely, surging toward me and wrapping me in his arms. "I promise you."

But I knew better than to believe it. Agreements like this could only be broken by starting wars, and I didn't want that for my brothers. I couldn't live with myself if something happened to them.

"Just so we're clear," Aiden interrupted. "Whatever it is you're planning, you must consider what it will mean for your business relationship with the Callahan mafia."

I sighed, bringing my hand to my forehead as I prayed for strength. There was a movement and all the hairs on the back of my neck lifted. Before I had time to move, I caught a movement in my peripheral vision as Caelan stepped up to Aiden, coming chest to chest. I barely had time to blink when I realized what my brother was about to do. He clenched his fist and pulled his arm back, throwing a punch into Aiden's face.

"I told you at the fucking club to find a way out," Caelan said, his chest rising and falling. I knew what would follow. I jumped to my feet and moved in front of the window just as my brother lunged for him, but Aiden effortlessly restrained him. "You touch even a hair on my sister's head, I will end you."

Aiden glared at my brother while Aemon and Bren ripped him from the other man, keeping him at bay. The air crackled loudly while my heart pounded in my ears. "I assure you, you little Irish prick, every woman wants me to touch a lot more than the hair on their head." Caelan kicked against our brothers, rage clear on his face, a promise of retribution. "And I promise you, women love it. Your sister will too."

It was the wrong thing to say because now all my brothers lost their shit and lunged for Aiden, tables and chairs tumbling and cracking. My eyes darted to the window, miles of lush green grass and mist stretching for miles as I mentally checked out from the chaos inside this room.

We all knew we were only delaying the inevitable.

Eight hours later, I stared out the window of the private jet, the Statue of Liberty in all her copper glory greeting me back. The only problem was the man in the plush leather seat next to me.

I glanced at Aiden, who hadn't said a single word since we took off from the Dublin Airport. Neither had I, but you wouldn't see me cracking first. *I* wasn't the one who arranged this stupid marriage.

"If you have something to say, do so. Don't just stare."

My eyes narrowed on my fiancé. "Why would I have something to say?"

He shrugged, never lifting his eyes. "Are you saying you agree with our impending union?"

"What gave me away?" I scoffed, my voice dripping with sarcasm.

He kept clacking away on his sleek laptop, oblivious to my rising blood pressure. "You haven't stopped glaring at me."

"And how would you know if you're staring at your computer screen like your life depends on it," I mused.

He knew I was baiting him. I'd been bursting to discuss how this would play out. I wanted to know the expectations—while also hoping there were none—so I could mentally prepare. I sure as fuck hoped the man didn't think I'd fall into bed with him.

He finally lifted his head from his laptop, his gaze finding mine. Asshole tendencies aside, Aiden Callahan was a gorgeous man—if you were into tattoos, dark hair peppered with gray, and icy blue eyes. Unfortunately for everyone involved, they were the wrong shade.

"Tell me, Ivy," he started, his voice still holding that note of indifference. "What would you like to talk about?" When I huffed and directed my glare back out the window, he chuckled and added, "I'll give you this. You're cute when you're pouting."

I raised a brow. "What are you? My brother?"

It was what they used to say to me. Of course I'd hoped I'd outgrown it, but apparently not.

He gave me a heavy look. "No, but maybe we can be friends."

I stifled a laugh. "That would be great, if only we weren't arranged to be married."

"Can two people not be friends if they're to be married?"

"Not if we would rather not get married." I might be significantly younger than Aiden, but it didn't take a rocket scientist to recognize the signs. The man didn't want to get married either. "Why did you agree to it? Do you even *want* this?"

His lip curled in distaste. "The decision was made without my knowledge."

"Oh." We remained quiet for a moment, both of us lost in our own thoughts, before I found his gaze again. "And there's nothing that can be done about it?"

"We have a duty to respect our families' wishes."

"It's primitive," I muttered begrudgingly. "Especially if neither one of us wants it. My brothers wouldn't enforce it if you broke it off."

"Yeah, I got that when they attacked me." His lips tipped up as if amused at the memory.

"You held yourself well against the three of them," I remarked.

"I've done my share of fighting."

I let my eyes travel over his muscular form. Aiden was tall and objectively handsome; in another life, he probably could've been a boxer or model. Still not my type.

"So who wants this to happen?" I questioned. "Not you. Not me. Not my brothers. My father, obviously, but he's dead." That old pang pierced my chest while flames of vengeance flickered. I still hadn't given up on my quest to find Sofia. "Who's left to enforce it?"

"My uncle."

"Well, let's get rid of him."

He threw his head back and laughed, the sound ringing through the jet's luxurious cabin, and I shot him a surprised look. He didn't look like someone who laughed a lot.

"That's what you think it'll take, huh?" he repeated, mirth still lacing his voice.

With an uneasy sensation filling me, I nodded. "Why not? We could make it look like an accident."

He shook his head. "I guess I can see what he sees in you."

My brow furrowed. "Who?"

"Don't worry, Ivy. I have a feeling everything will work out just fine." He leaned forward, putting his big palm over mine and patting it. Like I was a kid, and the gesture kind of pissed me off. "But we won't be killing my uncle. I happen to like him."

I didn't share his conviction, but as the plane started its descent, he returned to his work, refusing to elaborate further.

Chapter Nine

PRIEST

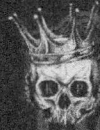

I sat in the principal's office with my orange pop, my feet swinging beneath me on the too-big chair, when he came in. He was wearing a floor-length, ruby-red robe that reminded me of a Halloween costume. I wanted to tell him he looked like an idiot, but I opted to keep my mouth shut. I couldn't get into more trouble or my mother would beat me black and blue until not even Dante could save me.

He approached and sat in the empty chair next to me rather than taking a seat behind the desk as usual—I was no stranger to getting called into his office.

When he spoke, he slurred his words. "In trouble again, Christian?"

I puffed out my chest. "I didn't start the fight. He broke the keyboard and I taught him a lesson."

"Tough boy."

He smiled at me, but it didn't reach his eyes. Even at that age, I knew there was something wrong with that smile.

He extended his hand and I took it hesitantly. His cold, wet skin made my face scrunch up. He patted his lap and I froze, but that didn't keep him from insisting.

"Don't you want to make your mamma and papà proud?"

I puffed up my chest. "Only Papà."

He shook his head, the wiry white strands swaying with the movement. "This would make him extremely proud."

I swallowed and took one more step. He pulled me the final inch, closing the distance, and soon enough, he was hugging me, setting me on his lap. I didn't know how it happened, but suddenly my pants were half-open and the principal was trying to get inside my underwear.

"What are you doing?"

Papà said nobody should ever touch or see my privates but me.

"Your mamma gave me permission," he whispered, his breath in my ear sour and hot. It was wrong. I wanted to push him away, but I felt like my arms and legs were stuck in quicksand. "It will make her happy, but it has to be our secret. If you tell anyone, your big brother and papà will die."

I sat stiff while he fumbled around, holding my breath the entire time and wishing he would stop.

"Please... just let me go. I won't get into any more fights. Please."

"The Holy Spirit frees us to do what we need to keep our sins from swallowing us whole. With the grace of the Holy Spirit, this will be for us. Amen."

When I finally found my voice and shouted for help, his free hand wrapped around my mouth. "Keep your fucking mouth shut."

I snapped and bit down hard on his hand. His hold on me loosened enough that I jumped off his lap, bolting out of his office. I ran fast and hard down the hallway, then I tripped and fell, realizing that my pants were at my ankles. I let out a sob and pulled them up, then took off running again.

Tears streamed down my face, making it hard to see. I ran through the empty hallways until I slammed into Dante. My brother didn't hesitate to wrap his arms around me protectively.

"What happened?" he hissed, pulling us into a corner. "I'll fucking kill those kids. Tell me what they did."

I shook my head. "I want to go home."

I couldn't tell him what happened, and the longer he studied me, the more I was filled with shame. I hated myself. I hated my mother. I didn't want my papà and brother to know; it'd destroy them. They'd blame themselves.

The next time Father Gabriel cornered me, I wasn't so lucky. My mother ensured that.

And so, the cycle repeated, over and over again, trapping me in a vicious, inescapable nightmare.

I awoke with a start, that old, familiar feeling of self-disgust flaring. It was always present, never buried too deep.

Fuck. I scrubbed a hand down my face as I attempted to gain control of my breathing. I needed control.

I hadn't dreamed of those days in months, but it never got any easier. I swung my legs off the bed and dropped my head into my hands. *Deep breath in, deeper breath out.*

When the helplessness finally subsided, I headed to the bathroom where my reflection stared back at me. I looked like shit.

That's what months of tracking a certain redheaded Irish mafia princess as she traipsed all over Ireland did to a man apparently. This fascination with her had reduced me to some kind of creep who lurked in the shadows.

I'd been back from Ireland for five days, managing all aspects of the new club opening in Philadelphia and already itching to see what the woman I rejected was doing.

It was pointless. Ivy Murphy stirred in me everything

I wanted to forget; it was for the best that she was a whole continent away.

Running the Kingpins of the Syndicate and Philly should—keyword *should*— be my only concern.

I stepped into the shower and turned it to the coldest setting. Once I'd scrubbed my body hard enough, I stepped out and quickly dried off, then dressed in suit pants and a white shirt.

I rolled up the sleeves, displaying the tattoos that encircled my arms. My Patek Philippe read eight fifty in the evening—I slept the whole day away. I took the private lift from my penthouse, catching up on emails on my phone until the doors slid open to the main foyer.

"Good evening, Mr. DiLustro," the concierge greeted me. "Your vehicle is waiting for you, as requested."

My black Range Rover Sport was parked in front of the building, looking as unassuming as a quarter of a million dollars of protective detailing could afford. Performance tires, explosive protection, full armored exterior with bomb and bullet-proof glass, complete with high-powered weapons stashed in various compartments. She was a thing of beauty.

"Thank you," I told the valet, accepting my keys and slipping him a generous tip.

I ducked into the driver seat and buckled in, relishing the quiet. My father hated that Dante and I never employed drivers or armed guards. Driving myself was one of the few things I enjoyed, so there was no fucking way I'd give up the luxury. And as for bodyguards, they were worthless. They certainly hadn't protected us when we were children at our most vulnerable.

I was halfway to my club when I made a last-minute decision and stopped at the tattoo parlor. They knew me there and wordlessly led me to the back where the artist waited for me.

Three hours later, with a sore groin and a grimace on my face, I was pulling up to the back entrance of my new club, The Angel. My head doorman greeted me the moment my handmade Italian oxfords touched the pavement.

"Good evening, your guests are here."

I stilled. "Guests?"

"Yes, your brother and cousins."

I ran my tongue across my teeth, a sardonic breath escaping me. "You let them in already?"

He hesitated. "Yes, sir. You said to always allow your family in."

He was right; I did say that, but I wasn't in the goddamn mood for them today.

"Where did you send them?" I asked, my gaze coasting down the hallway that led to my office. I fucking hated how every fucking hallway reminded me of Ivy. I was almost tempted to tear them down and enforce open-concept clubs, but I suspected that would be damn difficult to explain.

"The conference room."

I nodded and headed inside, weaving through the packed club, lights flashing across the ceiling and illuminating the sea of bodies grinding on the dance floor, the thunder of music vibrating the walls. I took a detour down a dark hall and up to an imposing iron door. A breath of cool air hit my skin as I traveled down the hallway, doing a decent enough job of shaking my thoughts of Ivy free.

I took in a steadying breath before entering the conference room and finding the whole entourage here— Dante, Basilio, and Emory. *Fuck.*

"To what do I owe the pleasure of your *unexpected* visit?" I asked as I took a seat at the head of the table.

They knew I fucking hated surprises.

"We need to talk," Emory said, chewing on her bottom lip. This nervous tic was further warning—she'd learned to don a hell of a mask while running Las Vegas. This couldn't be good.

"What about?"

"We want to know what's going on between you and Ivy Murphy," Dante said, casually rocking on his chair's fragile legs. It was something he'd done since we were kids, unable to sit still. He'd been a lot less tense since he got married, and despite initial challenges, my brother and Juliette found whatever it was that kept people happy and in love.

"What makes you think there's anything going on?' I challenged, my face impassive.

"It could be the way you've pulled men from their posts and assigned them to her tail?" my cousin Basilio chimed in wryly, standing and pacing the room.

"Maybe I don't trust her. Maybe I want to make sure the Murphys are keeping their baby sister in line. Ever consider that?"

They weren't buying it, and I was only making myself look more unhinged.

"Cousin, don't bury your head in the sand," Emory stated. "It will land you *and* the woman you love in a dangerous situation."

I snorted. "Love drowns people." Then, because I knew they had me, I said, "I wouldn't call whatever I'm feeling toward her love."

"But you're admitting to feeling something," Dante pointed out as Emory stood up and slowly made her way past Basilio over to the window, her slim body pressed against the wall and her attention clearly elsewhere. She and I were the most damaged in our little group, her wounds courtesy of her father, and mine... well, I never went there.

The four of us had been raised as siblings, and we'd stayed close all our lives. It was only natural that we became kingpins, surpassing our fathers' power and wealth, as well as taking over their seats at the table. Basilio ran the New York Syndicate, Dante ran Chicago, and I ruled Philadelphia, but it was Emory who was unique among us. She was the only female at the Syndicate table, ruling over Las Vegas and pulling the strings, and nobody even knew it aside from us and our fathers.

"Well, you'll have to work on your covert techniques," Basilio drawled. "Especially now that she's about to marry." Alert shot through me, but I remained still. Impassive.

"We all know Aiden Callahan is a possessive asshole," Dante muttered. "If he notices you even glancing her way, he'll start a war."

For a moment, I was too stunned to speak. Furious, even, as something green burned through my veins like a lit wick.

"If war is what Aiden wants," I finally said, running my hand across my jaw, "then war is what he'll get."

Chapter Ten

IVY

I lifted a double shot of whiskey to my lips and downed it in one go, thanking my Irish blood for the tolerance that'd been passed down to me. The bitter taste coated my mouth as fire burned down my throat, but I ignored it. Anything to relieve the pressure in my chest.

After the events of the last few days—reading Athair's will, a round of fists between my brothers and Aiden Callahan who, it turned out, was my *fiancé*—I was glad to be back in the States and closer to my friends.

Although, I had to wonder why Aiden had brought me to Philadelphia and not New York, considering his family was mainly based out of there. Furthermore, he insisted this club was the only suitable club for me to visit. It was odd, considering it belonged to the Italians,

Priest DiLustro specifically. And then, to make matters even weirder, he let me come alone with a bodyguard he assigned me the minute we touched down in the States.

But I knew better than to complain.

When I told my best friends, they got all excited and insisted I needed a night out. So here I was on the dance floor, getting down and dirty with some thumping club music, tolerating the foul mixture of liquor and sweat.

My gaze landed on my bodyguard, the intimidating man with a permanent scowl who lingered in the shadows, and I gave my head a subtle shake.

"As long as he stays well enough away," I muttered to myself, letting euphoria fly through me as I swayed to the beat. Here and now, I was okay, the pain of the last week dulled to the point where I no longer felt it.

"What?" Juliette yelled, her worried gaze on me. Wynter and Juliette had been doing their best to keep my spirits high, which included rescuing me from the penthouse I'd been holed up in—one of many the Callahans seemed to own.

I waved my hand to signal it was nothing. Distraction was key to suppressing worries, and I was determined to drink all that I could handle.

"I can't believe you're here." Wynter beamed, her hips rolling slowly, her husband (surprisingly) nowhere in sight.

"I guess there are some benefits to arranged marriages," I said, flashing her a dry smile. Aiden had been invisible since we parted ways at the tarmac, deepening my suspicions that he wanted as little to do with me as I did with him. *Suits me*, I thought with a sly grin. "Speaking of, where are *your* husbands?"

Basilio and Dante hated being separated from their wives, usually lurking close by.

Juliette shrugged. "They have a meeting in the back somewhere."

I smiled, fighting the temptation to ask if Priest was with them. I knew he traveled just as much as my brothers, but the DiLustros usually moved as one unit. So, my plan was to keep myself good and tipsy in case he *was* in the city. The last thing I needed was to be blindsided by another run-in—my birthday party was still too fresh.

"We won't let them ruin our night, will we?" I said, grimacing like an idiot as my gaze darted to the side where my bodyguard lounged against the bar, his expression one of boredom.

"How are you doing?" Wynter asked.

I shrugged. "Fine."

"You're not fine." She knew me too well. "I thought you… and Priest would—" She struggled to find the right word. "We could be sisters. I know I'm biased because he's my brother—"

"And my brother-in-law," Juliette chimed in.

Wynter continued, "But you are perfect for him, and he'd be good to you. Just imagine, all four of us would be best friends and actual family. Our children would grow up as cousins."

I flashed her an uncomfortable smile. I never told my friends about Priest's rejections—which still stung—and I had no intention of reopening that wound.

"It just wasn't meant to be," I told her. I certainly wouldn't chase after the arrogant prince. As the saying went, he could kiss my Irish ass, because I sure as hell wouldn't kiss his. "Besides, I'm engaged."

I lifted my ring finger as if to prove it, but I completely forgot it was still ringless.

"Don't tell me you're into Aiden?" Wynter challenged. "He's not even your type." She took my hands into hers. "Priest is just complicated. Just get into his space and demand his attention. He stares at you like it's his full-time job."

I rolled my eyes, but I'd be lying if I said that Wynter's words didn't make my stomach flutter in all the ways it shouldn't considering I was marrying someone else.

"I'm engaged to Aiden," I reasoned, stating the obvious.

"You're not really going through with it, are you?" Juliette questioned, scrunching her nose. "Aiden Callahan is old enough to be your father."

It was an exaggeration, though not completely outside the realm of possibility. At forty-one, Aiden Callahan had no business being unmarried—at least not in our world—and I had half a mind to put an ad in the paper and pray that a woman would snatch him up.

Saving me from responding to Juliette's question and nearly bursting my eardrums in the process, a shriek sounded in my ear, followed by a set of hands wrapping around me. I turned and found a couple smiling down at me, flanked by two guards the size of mountains. I didn't need to peek inside their suit jackets to know they were carrying.

My face lit up. "Davina!"

She grinned. "Surprise."

We all collided in a messy, laughing group hug that would've ended with us on the floor had Davina's husband—older than Aiden Callahan, I might add—not steadied us.

"I thought you couldn't make it!"

She rubbed her growing stomach, her eyes glowing with mischief. "There will be no baby coming anytime soon, so I demanded these two get my butt over here." She hiked a thumb over her shoulder in the guards' general direction.

She gave me an extra hug after we untangled from the other girls. "How are you doing?"

"Excellent now." I squeezed her tight. "I can't believe you're here even at eight months pregnant."

Davina let out an exasperated breath. "I'm pregnant, not dying."

"I had to bring her or she would've murdered me,"

Liam added, watching his wife with affection. Beyond his six-foot-something frame, Liam Brennan was one of the best-looking men I knew, aging like a fine wine. He had a heart of gold and treated our girl like the queen she was.

"This brings back so many memories," Wynter said, a glimmer in her eyes as she scanned the club.

"You mean the days when you four went around robbing people?" Liam, who also happened to be Wynter's uncle, added dryly.

"Don't mind him." Davina linked arms with me and we led the gang over to the bar. "Tell me what the deal is with this man you're marrying."

"Oh, he's nobody," I said with a click of my tongue.

"Aiden Callahan is hardly a nobody," Wynter replied.

"He's clearly nobody to *her*," Juliette explained, her voice clear now that we'd stepped away from the dance floor's speakers. I glanced a few feet past her, locking eyes with a man who spoke into his earpiece. My friends followed my gaze and glared at him, unimpressed.

Juliette marched over and I shot my friends a confused look. "What—"

"You need to get lost," Juliette said, shoving him away. "She needs space. Beat it, or I'll have my husband deal with you."

I bit down on a grin when the bodyguard followed her demand, effectively chastised. Why was she being so overprotective? I could handle my own battles.

"Oh my God," Wynter groaned when her cousin returned to stand next to us. "You're going to cause a war."

"If that's what's needed to keep Ivy away from those Callahans, then so be it."

Wynter's face soured. "We have to tread delicately."

"We're too young to become widows," Davina explained, shaking her head. "So, before you act, use that beautiful head to think things through, Juliette."

She rolled her eyes to the back of her head. "But I thought we were planning to—"

Before Juliette could finish her statement, Wynter grabbed her hand and yanked her away.

"What's that about?" I asked Davina, who was already flagging down a bartender and ordering me a drink.

"Drink up, girl," she announced once the bartender appeared with the saltshaker, a lime wedge, and a shot of tequila.

I frowned. "It doesn't feel right drinking alone."

"I would, but you know…" She rubbed her belly and cocked a perfectly shaped brow. "Bottoms up."

Before I could slam my glass on the bar top and focus on keeping the contents of my stomach down, another shot was in front of me. Then another. I winced, choking a little as I bit down on the lime, the room spinning.

"I have to pee," I said, laughing and feeling lighter than I had in a long time.

Davina laughed, glancing behind me. "Perfect."

I turned to see who she was looking at but couldn't make anything out in the amber glow of the nightclub. I slid off the barstool, slightly wobbly, and headed toward the restroom signs at the back of the club.

"There's another bathroom there," explained Davina, steering me to the left. "That one'll be crowded."

I turned down another hallway when my shoulder bumped into a hard body. I started to apologize when I found a familiar gaze sizing me up.

I stole a look at his eyes—these ones the perfect shade of blue—but before I could say anything, I felt a prick in my neck.

"It would seem our last meeting in the dark hallway wasn't enough for you, angel."

My world started to spin, his eyes following me everywhere. Blue. Cold. Destructive.

Chapter Eleven

PRIEST

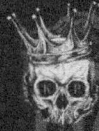

"All clear," I said to the empty corridor, and before long, Basilio, Emory, and Dante appeared. After learning of the marriage contract, I worked faster than I ever had, hacking into the Callahan network—the idiots only had a single firewall up—and digging until I found the contract. I found it suspicious that he had only one copy, but I wasted no time. I changed the names and sent myself the file, then moved on to the second part of my plan.

Stealing my bride-to-be.

After all, it wasn't too long ago that my papà wanted me to consider an alliance to keep the Corsican mafia at bay. I was just going along with his recommendation. The Murphy alliance could prove useful after the Irish pricks get over the initial anger when they learn I kidnapped their sister.

"Well, that went smoothly," Basilio declared, his hands in his pockets and his gaze landing briefly on Ivy before returning to me. "She give you any trouble?"

"No."

"I bet she will when she wakes up," Emory muttered. "Better figure out some way to pacify her."

"And what would you recommend, cousin?" I deadpanned. "Cakes and chocolates?"

Emory narrowed her eyes. "Maybe five centuries ago. You'll have to come up with something good enough to make her forget you just tranq'd her in a grimy club." This club was brand new, but I wasn't sure this was the time to correct her.

"Maybe let her rob you?" Dante suggested.

I shot him a glare. "Maybe let your wife burn down your house?"

"That happened *one* time," he muttered.

The sound of footsteps approached, distracting us from our childish bickering. "Baby, let's just go home and—"

The footsteps came to a stop and Liam Brennan, my uncle, stood there with a storm brewing in his eyes. His gaze traveled over us, lowering only when he arrived at the unconscious body in my arms.

"What the fuck is going on?" he hissed. "Please tell

me that's not Ivy Murphy. What kind of sick game are you all playing at?"

The silence that hovered was thick.

"Honey—" Davina started.

"Is this the reason we *had* to come to this club?" Liam cut her off.

Her shoulders slumped and her hands came up to cradle her protruding stomach. "She can't marry Aiden Callahan. He's too old for her."

My uncle shot her a dry look. "He's younger than me, céile."

Davina flashed him a sweet smile. "Yeah, but I love you, so it's different."

Liam locked eyes with his wife, his expression softening. He was silent for a moment, then he turned his attention to us.

"I'm going to pretend I didn't see this, but you better call Ivy's brothers and assure them nothing—and I mean *nothing*—will happen to their sister." When I didn't acknowledge him, Liam's tone turned dark. "Priest, tell me nothing will happen to Ivy."

"Of course," I lied, looking my uncle straight in the eyes and hoping he wouldn't detect it. Nothing *bad* would happen to her, so I didn't feel any guilt about lying.

He grumbled. "And you're calling her brothers."

My brother and Basilio rolled their eyes. "There's no

reasoning with those Irish pricks. You know how they get with their tempers."

Emory mimed a bomb exploding.

"Just fucking call them," he barked, then turned on his heel and disappeared with his wife, who threw a look over her shoulder and winked.

The moment they were out of sight, I let out a grunted, "Fuck."

"You don't have to call them," Basilio reasoned. "Just take her and disappear for a while."

I shook my head.

"No." My morals might be skewed, but my uncle was right. Ivy's brothers deserved to know she'd be safe with me. "If this were Emory, you know we'd raze the continent trying to find her."

I bent my head to find Ivy knocked out in my arms, her lips slightly parted and looking so peaceful my chest tightened.

"Here, I'll dial them," my brother offered.

Despite the late—or I should say early morning—hour in Ireland, the call was answered on the second ring.

"Dante DiLustro. Do you have any idea what time it is?" Clearly Aemon Murphy wasn't thrilled to be woken up.

"This is Priest," I answered instead, getting straight to business. "I'm taking your sister with me for a while."

The sound of a loud crash came through the line, so loud Dante had to reduce the volume on his phone.

"What?" he snarled. "What is my sister doing with you?"

"Don't worry. She's fine."

"Then why isn't *she* speaking to me?" His voice was venomous.

"She's asleep." It was the truth at least.

"First Aiden fucking Callahan, and now *you*, a goddamned Italian," he hissed. "If you touch a single hair on her head—"

"Now that would be impossible," I said flatly. "And technically, I have some Russian and Irish blood in me."

"I'll destroy you and every fucking member of your family, you son of a bitch. And there'll be nothing technical about it!"

I smirked. "Good luck with that. Our family's complicated—you might need a flow chart."

"Motherfucker!" There was shuffling on the other line, then the unmistakable sound of a gun being loaded. "You are a dead man!" he yelled, followed by a deafening bang.

"I guess he's done talking." I shrugged, holding out my brother's phone and confirming he hung up.

"Told you," Emory murmured. "All those Irishmen are fucking crazy."

"Did the lunatic really think that bullet was going to make it across the pond?" Dante muttered. "Jesus Christ,

Priest. Better hope Ivy doesn't have that temper or you'll need more doses of whatever you just injected her with."

Gripping the sleeping woman in my arms, I stared blankly at him. Had he forgotten the things she and her band of friends had done?

"Where is Ivy's bodyguard?" Emory interjected.

"I don't know, but keep him and Aiden Callahan off my trail."

Then I walked away with the only thing that mattered tucked securely in my arms.

Chapter Twelve

IVY

I sighed and stretched out my toes, basking in the feel of the sun warming my face and the soft bird-song trickling through the window. There was a strange ringing in my head, and I reached up to rub at it.

"Shit, how much did I drink last night?" I mumbled into the pillow.

A low chuckle. "I'd imagine it was probably too much."

I shot up and swung my legs out of the bed, my bare feet hitting the cold marble floor. Dizzy from the sudden movement, I squinted my eyes open as my vision adjusted. Someone had removed my heels, but I was still in last night's dress.

I darted around madly, trying to clock the unfamiliar surroundings. The area was cool and sophisticated, all sleek tan furniture, white-and-blue decals, and custom artwork that looked like it was plucked off the showroom floor. A white wooden bookshelf filled with dozens of leather-bound tomes occupied the space between two sets of bifold doors where sheer curtains danced in the breeze.

Then my eyes landed on *him*.

"You," I hissed. "Why am I here?" I questioned in a raspy, slightly shaky voice.

"I'm keeping my promise."

I blinked in confusion. "What promise?"

"Making sure we both receive salvation." My jaw dropped. "Besides, it was about time I took a wife, and you fit the bill."

I choked on my fury.

"Where's my bodyguard?" I'd demand he take me out of here.

Priest shrugged. "No clue."

"I hate you."

Anger scratched at my throat and the backs of my eyes. Ever since Wynter's wedding, he had ignored me, and now that Aiden came into the picture, he waltzed into my life, kidnapping me.

Bitterness stung, and it had everything to do with his rejection.

"I can work with that." Frustration chafed beneath my skin and I opened my mouth to curse him out, when his next words left me speechless. "I hear it's a thin line between love and hate."

His gaze met mine: blue darkening under a stormy sky. A flicker of something bright passed his expression, out of place in the current context. And then it clicked.

It was madness.

There was no other explanation for it.

"What do you think my brothers are going to say about this, huh?" Shit, what about my *fiancé*? Who knew what he might do if he thought I ran off? "I'm afraid you missed your window"—I forced some confidence in my tone—"because I'm about to get married."

He scoffed. "Yes, to me."

My eyes widened. "Have you lost your mind?" I screeched. "After your whole spiel about drowning and smothering? I still have no fucking clue what you meant, and now you think I'll marry you? Are you fucking crazy?"

He flashed me a grin, one that was half sexy, half crazy and would probably have most women falling to their knees. "Quite possibly."

Swallowing hard, I took a step back. "Have you been here the whole night?"

He shrugged. "More or less."

I fisted my hands and marched across the room until I was standing right in front of this slightly deranged god of a man. "When my brothers find out, they won't hesitate to start a war with your family and level you with—"

"They know." Priest's lips widened into a lopsided smile. *Red flag*, my mind warned. "Get cleaned up and changed. Breakfast will be waiting for you downstairs." I gaped at him as he turned to leave, but just as he reached for the handle, he said, "Everything you might need is on the right side of the walk-in closet. Any toiletries should be in the bathroom."

Then he left the room, shutting the wide mahogany door behind him.

The moment Priest's footsteps faded away, I ran to the bathroom to use the toilet, my bladder ready to burst.

When I moved to the sink to wash my hands, I made the mistake of checking my reflection in the mirror. Jesus, I looked like I'd been to hell and back. My hair was a mess, my white skater dress wasn't looking so pristine anymore, and there was dirt—or was that drool? —smeared on my cheek. In summary, I looked ragged.

But that didn't compare to the turmoil going on inside me. I stood there, trying to unpack his every word and meaning. If this man was serious about marrying me —why in the hell did the thought send my heart galloping?—then maybe he could be my ticket to getting close to Sofia Volkov and her twin daughters. My *sisters*.

Good plan.

But first things first. I eyed the shower and decided I'd get cleaned up before making any rash decisions. After all, I couldn't have the mafia prince, Christian "Priest" DiLustro, looking better than me.

Shedding my clothes, I stepped under the warm spray, letting it wash away the cobwebs. My head was still pounding and I scolded myself for not drinking enough water between drinks last night. I reached for the shower gel and froze. Chloé, my favorite scented shower gel, and a bottle of Amika shampoo and conditioner stood next to a distinctly manly shower gel.

How did Priest know what products I used?

I glanced over my shoulder, almost expecting to see him standing there, lurking and taking notes. When I found nothing but empty space, I squeezed a hefty amount of shampoo into my hair before doing the same with the body wash.

Once I was sparkling, I tiptoed out of the bathroom directly into the walk-in closet. The doors opened soundlessly and lights flicked on automatically, revealing the grand interior and its contents. Suits. Dozens of them lining the rack on my left—black. Blue. Gray. His button-down shirts were even nicer.

And then there was a shelf with… holy mother of God… gray sweatpants.

My cheeks heated and I pictured Priest wearing them low on his hips, the outline of his—

"Wipe that image out of your mind," I muttered to myself, tracing my fingers lightly over the expensive fabrics before letting go and turning to the right, finding stacks of clothes in exactly my size. Just as Priest promised.

I picked one of his white dress shirts and a pair of loose-fitting jeans, then headed out of the room only to come to a screeching halt, my hand flying to my mouth.

A Belgian Malinois, a beautiful shepherd, sat in front of the bedroom door, watching me like I was his next meal.

Chapter Thirteen

PRIEST

Tension had been building inside me to the point of near madness, and I knew the very thing that would put me at ease.

I descended the stone steps one at a time, stopping in front of the musty dungeon where I peered through the metal bars, searching for the familiar glowering look.

"Back so soon, Christian?"

An ugly smile with a gaping hole stared back at me and my lips twitched slightly as I unsheathed my knife. It was stupid to taunt me, but some people never learn.

"You sure you want to taunt me today, Mother?"

She spat at my feet. "Pure evil. You are no son of mine."

"Tough words for a dead woman," I said lightly, stepping closer. "Let's see how tough you really are."

I slammed my fist into her side, right over her left kidney. She coughed, blood dripping down onto her shirt as she gasped for air.

"Wow, you must have kept a diary of every beating you've ever gotten," she said, laughing maniacally. "That was my favorite move. I still remember the way your ribs cracked."

I wrenched her off the chair, her muffled cry replacing her laugh as the metal crashed against the backs of her legs from where she was still bound.

"Fuck you," I growled. This woman wasn't fit to care for a fucking snake, never mind children. Yet, my father was so fucking blind, he'd left us in the hands of a monster to be forever damaged.

"Should I expect that next?" The buzzing in my ears got louder and louder until the only thing I could focus on was the rush of blood in my ears. "But then I bet you can't even get it up, can you, boy?"

I shoved her away and she slumped back into her rusty seat, her eyes rolling back briefly before they met mine. She'd lost a lot of blood over the past few weeks, but I always administered a transfusion before it became a real issue. I needed her to endure the same amount of torture that I had. That my brother had.

She wouldn't leave this torture pit alive.

My blinding rage dominated every fiber of my being, rolling like an unstoppable wave. My chest throbbed with pain from the memories dating two decades.

Knowing she'd gotten under my skin, a nasty laugh burst from her, cutting through me like an acid-coated knife. "I know you well, Christian."

My hands balled into fists, the static in my ears growing louder.

Until a soft crunch came from behind me and I whirled around.

Time stopped as I was faced with Ivy's horrified expression, her eyes roaming the scene around me. Cobra, the guard dog I had trained to protect Ivy using the scent from the clothes I'd instructed my men to lift from her Irish estate, stood next to her, hackles up and growling, perceiving *me* as a danger.

I'd rest easy knowing my trainers were successful, though now it might cost me my life.

An ear-splitting sound escaped her lips, her eyes wide and her pupils dilated, when she took in the sight of the woman behind me, her face bloody and her wrists bound.

When her voice turned raspy and she stopped screaming, her pale expression made the hairs on my neck rise.

I reached for her in an attempt to steady her and explain, but she fought me off, shoving me away with more strength than I thought her small frame was capable of and beelining for the stairs.

"You don't understand," I growled, trying to catch her legs but only managing to get kicked in the chin. I stumbled back, the sound of my adoptive mother's mocking laugh from where she followed me into the corridor filling my ears.

It was the final straw for Cobra, who lunged at me, eyes black as he foamed at the mouth. I jumped to the side and she narrowly missed me, biting my prisoner in the leg instead.

Chapter Fourteen

IVY

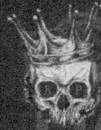

I followed the dog who seemed loyal to me and eager to guide me through the halls from my bedroom, thinking she'd take me to her owner in the living room. Maybe lead me outside, where she'd do her business and then beg for a treat.

What I found in that dank basement cell made my heart stop.

I was greeted by bloody fingers dangling off a rope. A woman sat in a metal chair, her hands and ankles tied. Her face a collage of black and blue, her clothes soaked with blood and filth. The dungeon had a chill of terror curling in my stomach.

A fucking *woman*.

My stomach roiled, but the confusion and horror trumped the dizziness that tried to pull me under. Any decent man—whether he was attached to a criminal organization or not—did *not* touch women and children.

I only needed to stand there for thirty seconds, listening to the darkness tainting his voice.

My blood drummed in my ears and my mind screamed. All the signs were there all along, but I was blinded by his beautiful angel-like face. Except there was no more hiding. I could see it clearly now; he was thriving on pain and control.

My vision dimmed, terror inflating in my throat, and my gasp of horror must have not escaped my host.

Priest's blue gaze, full of cruelty and something psychotic, came my way. For a moment, I couldn't breathe, paralyzed by what I was seeing and the brutal savagery in his eyes. But then adrenaline jolted through my veins and I ran.

The horror of what I just saw played on repeat in my head as I made my way to the top of the basement staircase. I just had to make it through the foyer. The front door was closed… too far away, but maybe I could hide somewhere.

Tears ran down my cheeks as soft footsteps registered behind me.

A wretched, painful scream pierced the air—from the woman? from me?—and I flinched.

I had my hand around the door handle when blood-stained arms caught me from behind.

I opened my mouth but his hand covered it, muffling

my screams, while I fought against his iron grip. Dread tightened my lungs, smothering each breath before I could inhale.

"Angel," he rasped, the soft endearment putrid against my ear. He shifted me around and I froze, the fight leaving me all at once. "Let me explain."

Priest's eyes swallowed the shadows in the room, something in them freezing my blood at the source.

"What's there to explain?" I breathed, suddenly exhausted.

Maybe he intended to imprison me as well, the sick, demented creep. The sound of my ragged breathing filled the space between us as my thoughts strayed to the horrendous possibilities. It was enough to drive any sane person to madness.

"Who is she?" I blurted, shaking with fear. "Are you going to do that to me?"

"You're nothing like her," he gritted through clenched teeth. "I'd *never* harm you."

I stared at him, my pulse racing. What did it say about me that I heard the truth in his voice? "Then who is she?"

"Vittoria DiLustro." *What. The. Fuck.*

"Your stepmom?" I exhaled incredulously. Okay, maybe my intuition was failing me and the safety I felt around him was all bogus. "Release me," I demanded.

He held my gaze. "You're staying with me."

My eyes darted around, the sound of barking

breaking through the fog of uncertainty. "Where is the dog?"

"Cobra," he said hoarsely, and I gave him a blank look. "The dog's name. It's Cobra. She's been trained to protect you."

Protect me? Why was *he*, of all people, concerned about my safety? Confusion entwined with the hot buzz beneath my skin, the strain settling thick in my lungs while I tried to catch my breath. The barking intensified, thump… thump… against the basement door.

Just then, the latch came undone, giving Cobra just enough space to squeeze through and place herself between Priest and me, baring her teeth and barking at Priest with menace. Or maybe she was after me, I couldn't be sure.

Priest spoke to her softly, but Cobra kept barking, tail flapping and fur standing on end. "Angel, you have to tell her you're safe. That everything's okay."

"Everything is not okay," I breathed. I should have minded all his red flags and stayed far away from him. "There's a bloodied woman in your basement, and I'm stuck here between your psycho ass, a growling dog, and a locked front door."

He sighed. "I swear to you that you are safe. I'd rather cut my own throat than harm you."

I stared at him while my mind screamed to run, but the wisps of words echoed through my heart. *I'm fine. I'm safe.* If he wanted to hurt me, he would have already.

"Does *my* dog have a trigger word?" I asked, not ready to blindly trust this man.

"*Ionsaí.*"

I shot him a surprised look. It meant *attack* in Gaelic. Priest must have known I'd never forget a word in a language I was fluent in.

"Cobra, stop. We're safe."

And she did, looking up at me proudly as she sat next to me.

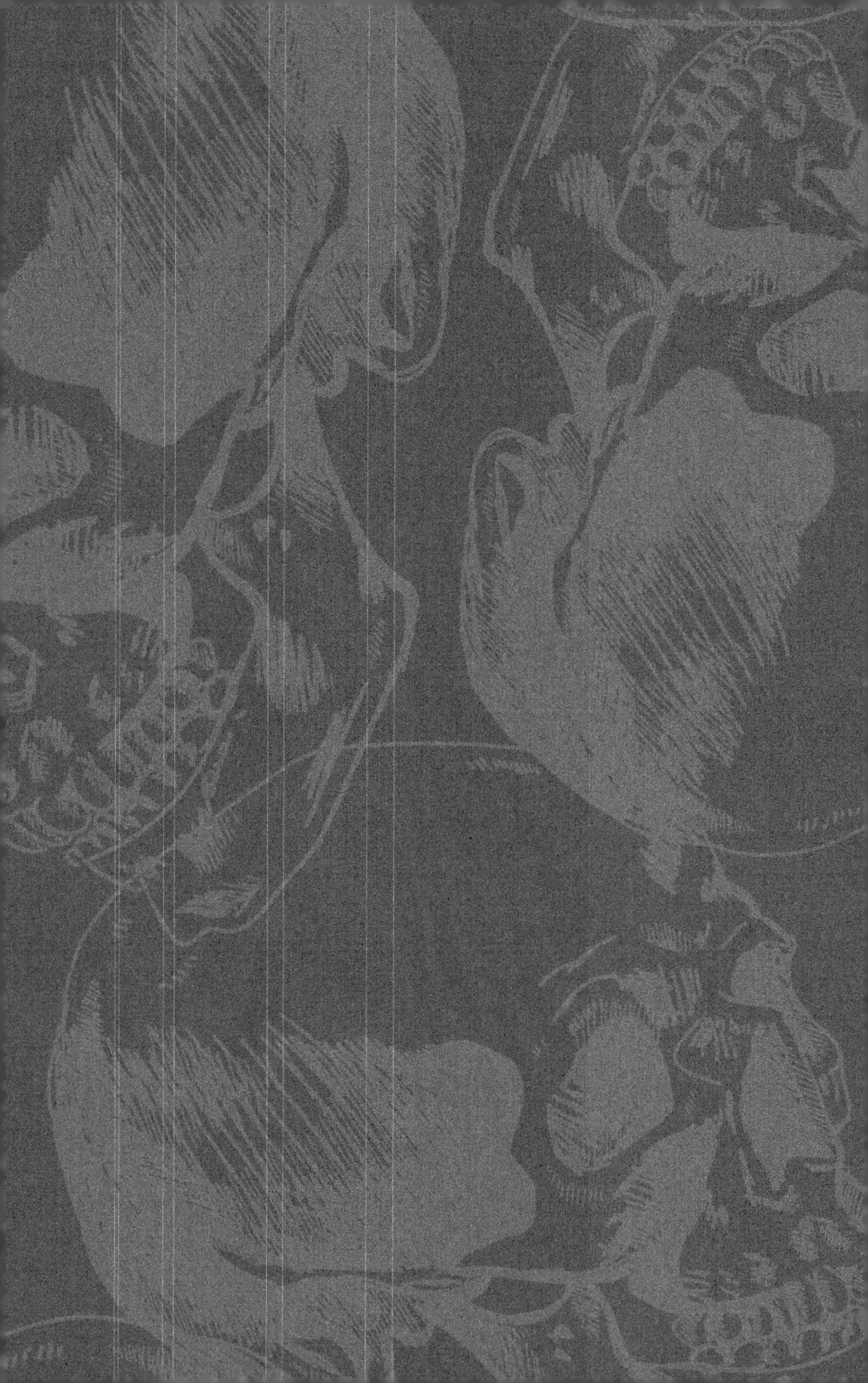

Chapter Fifteen

PRIEST

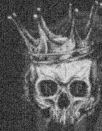

"How is it that the late Mrs. DiLustro *still lives*, when your papà remarried and the whole world thinks she's dead?" Ivy demanded.

I rolled my shoulders and gestured toward the settee in the foyer, choosing to pace along the marble floor as I prepared to share the parts of my life that I wished I could forget. I wouldn't give her the entire morbid story, but I knew I needed to offer her something after what she'd witnessed. I needed her to know that I was a good man, that there was a reason I did what I did, why I was who I was.

And so, I blew past the beginning and middle and landed right at the end, willing the memory not to drain me completely.

Dante and I stepped out of St. Gabriel's Catholic School, our four guards walking ahead of us. We watched them check the area, then nod and usher us to Pa's waiting car.

"Who's ready to see the Yankees lose?" was Pa's greeting as we slid into the back seat of his black Rolls-Royce. "That will teach your cousin Basilio a lesson. The Sox dominate the league. Show me any other team that's won twenty-four consecutive series. They lead the majors in runs scored year after year, they're unstoppable!"

"For sure," Dante grumbled, probably mentally preparing for the game. It wasn't uncommon for Dante and Basilio to get competitive, even if neither of them played the sport—which was the case with baseball. Emory and I just sat back and rolled our eyes, letting them bicker.

"How was school today, boys?"

"Boring," Dante muttered.

"I got in trouble with Father Gabriel," I said stiffly, lowering my eyes. I couldn't bear to meet their gazes. The fear and disgust festered inside me, growing like a fungus, and I no longer knew how to deal with it. "I got the ruler over my knuckles."

Among other things.

Once I was older and stronger, I'd be free of Father Gabriel and my mother. It was the only thing keeping me sane.

Pa scrubbed a hand over my hair, his gaze falling to my bruised knuckles. "What for?"

"I told him one day computers would rule the world." I shifted in my seat and made sure not to let my voice crack. "And he called it"—and me, but I left that part out—"the devil's work."

I didn't tell Pa that Father Gabriel and Mother were forcing me to join the priesthood, whipping me until I memorized every prayer. Making me recite them while Father Gabriel put his hands on me. But soon I'd be strong enough to fight.

My eyes burned, but I knew no tears would fall. They were all dried up.

I couldn't say anything to Pa and Dante. I hated myself and my "pretty-boy face" that Father Gabriel loved so much.

"They will, and then we'll hack into the Vatican's mainframe." Dante supported my theory about computers, but I couldn't find it in my heart to be happy about it today.

Pa's lips quirked as he reached to scrub his palms over our heads again. "That's right, boys. Always have each other's backs."

"Pa, my hair," Dante muttered. He was into girls now and had started to care about the way he looked. My lips curled in disgust at the idea of anyone fucking touching me. I'd sooner cut their fingers off and make a necklace out of them.

"I hope it exposes all the fuckers." I realized my slip too late, but thankfully Pa took it in good humor and snorted.

"Destructive little fuckers," Pa grouched as he put the car in drive. He sped down the streets of the third-largest city in the U.S., and I watched as famed restaurants and bars along the river passed us by for miles until we got on the highway.

But it was once we got moving and the world outside the windows became blurry that the knot in my stomach tightened. It signified each mile closer to the building that should be home but was anything but.

It didn't matter that going with Pa to the baseball game would delay our alone time with Mother. When he dropped us back at home, we knew she would be there, waiting and ready to torture us.

I flicked a glance at Dante, his knuckles white and folded in his lap. His dark eyes met mine and he pulled me closer to him protectively.

"I know," he whispered. "One of these days, I'm going to…"

The unspoken words were loud between us, charring both of our souls.

"What was that, son?" Pa asked from the front seat, but before Dante or I could say anything, his phone rang and his question remained unanswered as he flipped it open. "What is it?" he barked.

Several heartbeats passed and the sound of

screeching tires followed as Pa took the first exit off the highway.

Dante and I shared a glance, then I shot a look over my shoulder. I could clearly see the three black cars tailing us—Pa's and our bodyguards—swerving to stay in our eyesight.

"Fucking Irish and their leprechauns," Pa cursed, then hung up the phone and flicked us a glance. "Just know this, boys. Our world is cruel, but we can never—" Then, as if he wanted to ensure his message got through to us, he added, "fucking ever hurt women and children. A real man never hurts a woman."

"What happened, Pa?" Dante asked while my confused mind whirled over what he said. I had so many questions. What if a woman was evil and hurt everyone? Was it okay to fight back then?

I never got the chance to ask.

"I'm sorry, boys," Pa gritted through clenched teeth. Whatever happened, it must have been bad. "Business calls. We'll watch the Yankees lose some other time."

My stomach lurched and I had to swallow the bile rising in my throat. I didn't want to be home with Mother. Anything but that.

It wasn't long before he pulled down our driveway and Dante and I jumped out of the car. He left the engine running—we never shut our cars off unless we were in his private garage. Pa instilled this rule in us in case there was a bomb set to explode upon triggering the ignition.

"Vittoria, we're home." No answer, but Pa didn't seem to notice. "Work's come up. I'm leaving the boys."

Still no answer.

Pa just shrugged and hugged us before turning around and leaving us in hell.

Dante made his way into the kitchen while I tiptoed to my room. Once in there, I'd lock the door and keep out of sight. My bedroom was the first one on the second floor, and the moment I reached the top of the stairs, my heart started to thunder with hope. There it was, within sight, and I held my breath, scared she'd hear it.

Maybe today I'd manage to escape her.

Five steps away… four… three…

The stench of alcohol and heavy perfume registered too late. A hand yanked me around and I met my mother's dark eyes, scowling down at me.

My eyes darted around her, worried Dante would appear. If he did, she'd berate him too, and I didn't want him to get in trouble. Yes, he just turned eighteen and could leave now or when he finishes high school, but he stayed because of me. I was only sixteen.

"There he is," she slurred. She grabbed my hair with one hand and slapped me upside the head with the other, then sneered, "My son."

I flinched, but before I could pull away, another slap sent my head jerking to the right, and I stumbled back.

My hands fisted, the need to fight back burning through me. I wanted to punch her back, but Papà said a real man never hit a woman. A real man didn't hurt a woman. Ever.

She pulled me back by the hair and another slap followed, stinging my face. Slaps turned into punches. Again. And again. And again.

I clenched my teeth, careful not to make a sound. I wouldn't let Dante hear.

A woman her size shouldn't be so strong, but my mother spent as much time exercising as she did drinking. I always wondered if she stayed fit to be able to do this to me and my brother.

She grabbed me by my hair again, fisting it tightly, and threw me into the solid handrail.

"Stop it," I choked out.

Anger twisted her face, distorting it into an ugly mask. A belt appeared—or maybe it was there all along —and came down with a whoosh. The second strike followed close behind. Then the third.

I fell to my knees, my head in my hands. I wanted to strike her back. To end this. To end her. *The strap landed again and again, harder each time, while my mind drifted somewhere else.*

Somewhere safe.

Where nobody touched me. Where nobody hit me.

On my knees, I tuned it all out, swearing to myself that one day I would destroy them all. All the evil mothers and filthy priests.

The belt hit the ground and hands wound around my neck as she fell on top of me, flattening us both on the carpeted floor.

"Get off of me." My muffled voice was full of anguish and disgust. I couldn't handle her beating after everything that had happened today.

My control snapped. Pa said never to hurt a woman, but this wasn't a woman. She was... I didn't know what, but she wasn't someone who needed protection. She was twisted, and she deserved to be hurt.

I headbutted her with the back of my head, but it wasn't enough.

"Son of a slut," she breathed against my ear. My stomach turned, acid rising in my throat. Was she calling herself a slut? Had she lost her mind for good?

"What are you doing, Mother?" Dante's voice was like a whip, but it didn't make her stop. She mumbled incoherent words into my ear, her foul breath against my skin.

Dante grabbed her hair, yanking her away from me.

"What the fuck is wrong with you?" Dante shouted at her.

Mother started laughing hysterically, rolling around like she was possessed, and I fucking snapped. I was done being a victim. I was done being touched.

I. Was. Fucking. Done.

I kicked her body with all my might and she rolled

down the wooden steps. Thud... thud... thud... until she hit the bottom step.

Dante and I stared as the scene unfolded, wide-eyed, then locked gazes. We raced down the stairs, finding our mother's body limp but still breathing.

"She's alive," I muttered, wishing with all my heart it wasn't so. I kicked her again, the tightness in my chest loosening for the first time. It was the first whisper of the psychopath I would become—reveling in the pain of others in order to experience release.

Dante disappeared for a moment, returning with a can of gasoline he must've gotten from the garage.

"We should burn the house down," he whispered, shaking a box of matches. "It's our chance to end this."

Staring up at him, seeing the years of pain lurking in his eyes, I nodded.

So, he began pouring gasoline all over the furniture, the walls, the woven rug at our feet... over our mother. Then, just as he was ready to light it all up to hell, I stopped him.

"I want to do it," I said, an idea blooming in my mind. So dark. So vicious. So fucking righteous.

"It shouldn't be your sin to—"

"I want to do it," I repeated, refusing to let this stain my big brother any further. Dante flicked me a look packed with uncertainty, but he eventually caved in and handed me the box. "Wait outside."

"No fucking way, Christian. I'm responsible for you."

"I'll be right behind you," I reasoned. "I just need this... for me."

"Fine," he caved, then threw a final hate-filled glance at the unconscious woman. "May you rot in hell, Mother."

Once he was gone, I dragged my mother's gasoline-soaked body out of the foyer and through the back door to the bunker on the edge of our property—ironically the same one I'd stumbled upon years ago when I was looking for a place to lick my wounds. Wounds she inflicted. It took all the strength I had left to get her all the way inside, lock her in, and run back into the house.

Where I lit a match and let it all burn.

I didn't know then that the years spent under her thumb would shape the rest of my life, and that my legacy would include hunting down evil and ridding the earth of it.

The shadows from the chandelier faded, leaving me exposed. There was nowhere left to hide.

Ivy's face was pale, her hand covering her mouth.

A bitter laugh escaped me, followed by an almost deafening silence.

A moment passed. And another.

Would she scream? Demand I send her back to Ireland? Demand I take her back to Aiden Callahan? Would she pity me?

I couldn't handle any of it; the thought made my throat tight, and I wished there'd been another way. I needed her to look at me like the man I was *now*, not the boy I'd been.

I took a deep breath and found her eyes.

For a second, I was taken aback by her expression as she examined every line and mark on my face. Was she trying to understand my scars? The possibility sent shivers ghosting down my spine.

"Why do you go by Priest rather than your birth name?" she questioned softly.

I froze momentarily, then shrugged, hoping she didn't pick up on it. "I excelled at prayers when Vittoria and Father Gabriel attempted to force me to join the priesthood. I did it to spite them, I think, but it worked out for the best. First man I killed, I recited final rites. Basilio jokingly called me *priest*, and the nickname stuck. The fact I continued reciting rites probably didn't help."

I didn't tell her that I hated my first name because Vittoria liked to use it when she beat me. And when I learned that Aisling was the one who'd named me, I hated it even more. I wanted to punish my birth mother for abandoning us and creating hell for Dante and me. It was clear that Vittoria hated and tortured us to get back at our papà and Aisling.

"It feels wrong to call you Priest now," she muttered.

"I like hearing my first name on your lips." Surprise

flickered in those hazel orbs as she studied me. "I wouldn't mind you calling me Christian."

"It's set, then," she murmured. "I'm going to call you Christian from now on."

My cock twitched in response. "I'm going to hold you to it."

Silence stretched as we stared at each other, until her next words shattered it.

"You have to let her go." I narrowed my eyes at her, wondering if she was reading my thoughts. Could she tell I wanted to torture Aisling too? "Or better yet, kill her and end it."

Ah, she was talking about Vittoria. Of course she wouldn't know that I wanted to punish Aisling, too.

"That's it?"

"What?"

"Your reaction. You're not going to…" I searched for the right word and came up short. "You're not going to view me as damaged goods? Less than, because of how I treated her? A *woman*?"

She took a step forward, Cobra close at her heel. "A woman who should have protected you but failed. As did this Father Gabriel. None of that makes you 'damaged goods,' Christian."

A corner of my lips lifted.

"I wish you were right." She didn't know this darkness inside me, something so dangerous and volatile that only eased when I tortured those who'd wronged me.

"I'll never be right up here." I tapped my fingers against my temple while acute pain sliced through my chest.

"You're not responsible for your mother's choices. You're the victim, she's the perpetrator." I breathed harshly, my chest rising and falling. "And an eternity of torture isn't enough to pay for her sins, but while you're keeping her alive, you're also suffering."

She took my hand in her softer one, and a strange warmth expanded in my chest as she took a step toward me.

"There is *nothing* wrong with you," she repeated. "Sometimes healing takes time. But, Christian, you have to cut the cord."

It had been a decade, and still, I had yet to move on. Could she be right?

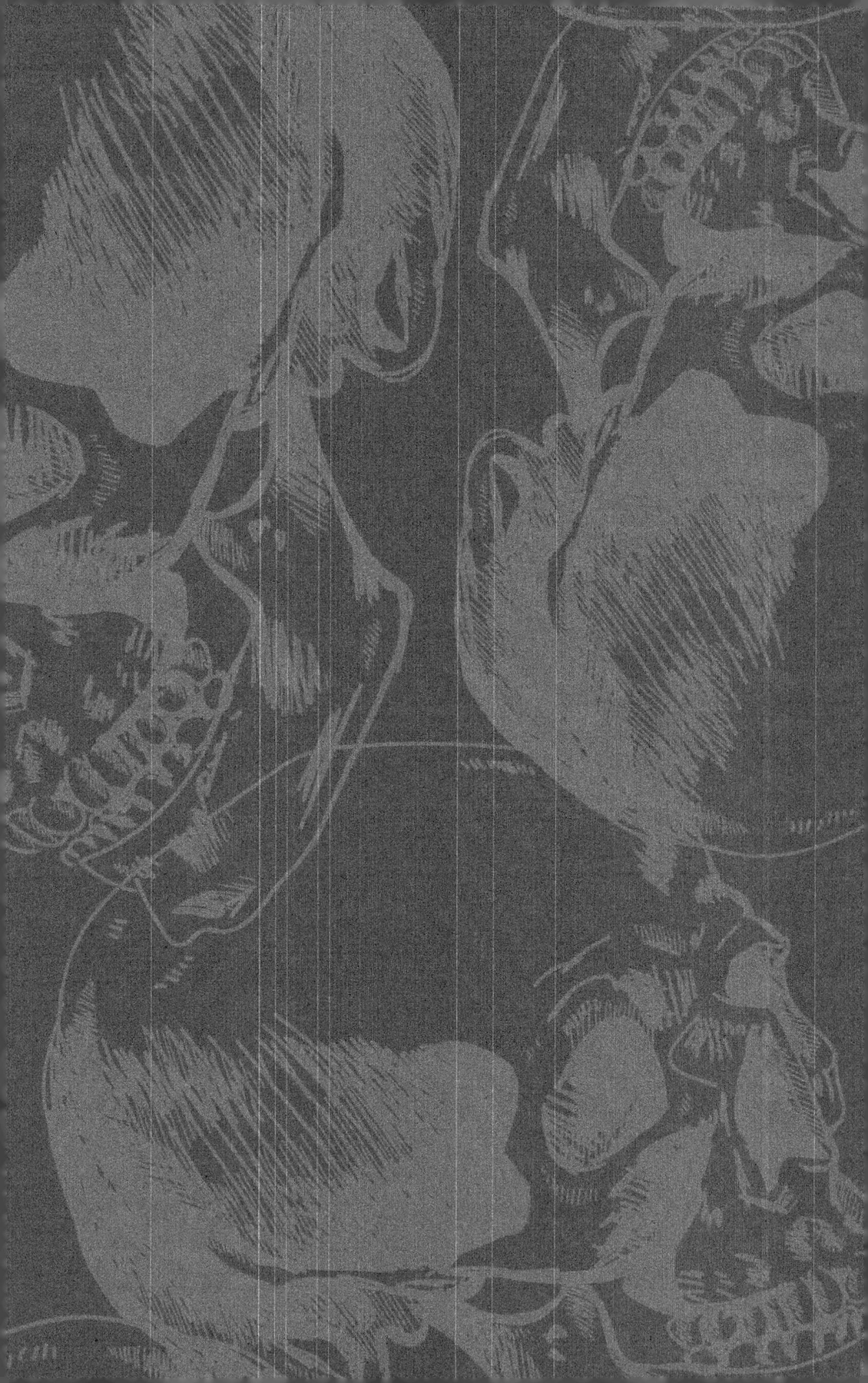

Chapter Sixteen

IVY

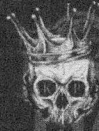

My heart beat loud and fast as I held his hand, the first "normal" gesture to occur between us since we crossed paths. Our first touch in a darkened nightclub was a moment of mindless lust. The subsequent times, he barely looked at me. Until Athair's funeral on a cold winter's day when he came to offer his condolences. Until my birthday party when he came to give birthday wishes and stir trouble.

I suspected what he told me wasn't the entire story, and that thought alone made me ache for him. I'd been tempted to run into his arms, bury my wet face in his shirt, but I didn't think he'd appreciate it.

The woman I was before starting Yale and meeting my best friends was sheltered and would be at a loss for what to do. But after the shenanigans we'd gotten ourselves out of—burning down a house, robbing Juliette's father, breaking the house during Wynter's poker game, even robbing an armored truck that belonged to this man—I was no longer sheltered, hardly innocent. And I certainly understood the "eye for an eye" rule in the underworld.

I curled my fingers into fists, my knuckles whitening. On one hand, Christian kidnapped me, but on the other, he'd been honest to the point of being blunt. It made it easy to trust him, and truthfully, his story affected me.

My spine steeled and my mind made up, I asked in a trembling voice, "Can you kill her?" He shot me a surprised look. "If it's too hard for you, I... I can organize it. I'll get my brothers to help me if I have to." I closed my eyes for a second before prying them open, trying to stay strong. "For you. She doesn't deserve to have this effect on you."

Christian's jaw clenched. "I need to make her suffer for as long as she made us suffer."

I swallowed. "And how long is that?"

"Twelve years." His jaw clenched, molars grinding. "I was sixteen and Dante eighteen when we burned down the house."

There were so many layers to this man, I wasn't quite sure what I'd find at the core of him. "Even at the cost of your own happiness?"

His face remained immobile. "Torturing her, and others like her, brings me joy."

I just stared at him as his words sunk in and some pieces of the puzzle fell together. It was his coping mechanism. We all handled trauma differently; who was I to judge? After all, my encounter with Sofia as a little girl hardly compared, yet I'd made myself forget.

This man in front of me re-lived it every time he tortured this woman.

I swallowed, his words not lost on me. "How many others have you tortured?"

"I've lost count. But none of them mattered."

My skin prickled with emotions I didn't know what to do with. "Who counts the most?"

He let out a mocking noise. "The fucker who hides behind the church and his red robes."

"Father Gabriel."

That set Christian off. His features contorted, and it looked as if he was now transforming into a monster. Or rather, an avenging angel.

I suspected his story was more gut-wrenching than he let on, and I squared my shoulders, squeezing his big hand.

"I'll help you," I said with resolve. Christian growled, clearly thinking me a fragile, delicate flower, but I was far from it. I wasn't scared. I rolled my eyes. "If you're worried about me, don't be. Just remember how I took a big part in stealing from you and getting rid of your armored truck." His eyes darkened. I'd only been messing with him, but the blood in my veins heated as his gaze fell to my lips. My heart beat in the base of my throat, tripping up on itself. "And you'll help me." He didn't look convinced, so I added, "Unless you want me to get Aiden Callahan's help."

It was a bluff, but judging by Christian's look, it worked a bit too well. He appeared ready to hunt down my should-be fiancé and make him regret the contract between his uncle and my father.

"I'll ruin him and his whole family before I'll allow him anywhere near you."

"You didn't ask what I need help with," I pointed out, trying to keep the smugness off my face.

"Tell me, then."

A heartbeat passed and I dropped the bomb on him. "I want you to locate Sofia Volkov for me."

He didn't miss a beat. "Okay."

"Aren't you going to ask me why?" I challenged, tipping my chin up.

"Why?"

I narrowed my eyes. "Because she killed my father."

Surprise flickered in his blue eyes. "And you're sure of this how?"

"It's of no concern to you," I stated calmly, keeping the knowledge of her children with Athair to myself. "All I can tell you is that I'm sure."

"Then we have a deal," he stated matter-of-factly.

"We'll help each other," I agreed. We'd been playing this game of cat and mouse for years, and anticipation buzzed in my veins. My eyes fell to his strong, veiny hands, and memories of his rough touch filtered into my mind. I wanted those hands on me, his head between my legs and him inside me, but I knew it could never be.

After all, he told me so himself.

"On one condition." His voice startled me and I met his darkened gaze, trying to keep my thoughts out of my expression.

Tilting my head, I asked, "What?"

"You'll marry me."

His words hit me like a blow to the chest, and I sucked in a breath.

"Marry… you?"

Tension rolled through him, his presence becoming larger than life.

"Yes."

"But you said—"

"Nobody is allowed to touch you—fuck you." His voice drifted to a dark rasp. "You and I both know it was over the moment I touched you. There's no going back."

My stomach dropped and I gulped. "If I marry you, the Callahans will start a war with my brothers."

His smile was wicked. "And I'll finish it. For you."

The sun was high in the sky when we made our way back down the stairs.

The woman who'd spent years tormenting her sons sat, still tied to the chair, the flesh on her leg hanging loose and weeping from the open wound.

Vittoria DiLustro kept her gaze fixed on the ground.

"Not again," she sputtered, shaking in her filthy rags. "You can't torture me again, Christian."

I refused to feel sorry for her, not after hearing his story. Maybe being born into this world had tainted me from the start, or maybe I believed in an eye for an eye.

Christian pulled out a gun from the waistband of his blood-smattered jeans.

"You want to know what I hate more than cruel bitches?" He stepped closer, the gun lax in his hand. "Cowards."

My eyes slid between the two of them, my breath held in anticipation.

"Angel, you shouldn't have to see this."

"I'm not leaving you."

His gaze flicked to me in surprise and I gave him an encouraging nod. I might not fully understand what made this beautiful man the way he was, but I knew that permanently eliminating this woman from his life would bring him peace.

But also, there was a part of me that wanted to ensure he followed through. The darkness inside him tempted him with revenge, and although I understood it, it made me distrust his choices when it came to Vittoria DiLustro.

"*What?*" Vittoria had the audacity to act shocked. She turned to me, her bottom lip quivering like the greatest actress who ever lived. "I don't know how I got wrapped up in this, but you have to help me. Christian is crazy. You should know he needs to be committed—"

A dark chuckle escaped Christian and he tsked. "Still refusing to take responsibility. I'm the product of your actions, *Mother*."

"You're no child of mine," she spat, ignoring his words. She tried to scurry back, the chair rocking from the force of her movements. "You're not my son. You are *not* my son!" she screamed.

"Thank fuck," I interjected. "You don't deserve to have any children, let alone be around other human beings."

Something in my eyes must have made her realize I'd be of no help because her face blanched.

"Time to say your last prayer," Christian said as he walked toward the woman, kicking her knee so hard a sickening crack sounded.

As her chair tipped over, his boot slammed into her face. She groaned, blood spurting from her nose as her lips moved in a prayer uttered in Latin. But she was no longer the focus of my attention. It was Christian and the expression of euphoria on his face.

Every second around this woman he was growing

increasingly intoxicated. It must derive from the control he exerted over the person who'd taken it from him when he was a child.

Vittoria watched him with cruel eyes.

"I'll always h-haunt you," she snarled, her teeth chattering. "Even in death. And so will Father Gabriel."

"End it, Christian," I told him softly. His eyes lifted to mine. After a second of staring at me, he turned to Vittoria.

"May the Holy Spirit free you from this miserable life and your sins swallow you whole with the grace of the Holy Spirit. Amen."

A chill passed through me and I stared wide-eyed as he aimed his gun at her head. That was a bit... scandalous. I'd heard rumors of his famous last rites in the underworld, but hearing them stated was a bit too much.

"Wait—" Vittoria uttered, but she never got to finish whatever pathetic plea she'd been about to spew.

It was so quiet I could hear my own heartbeat when Christian's gaze suddenly came to me. And just like that, our marriage agreement was set and sealed.

In sin. In blood. In stone.

Chapter Seventeen

IVY

C obra's soft snores echoed all around me as I read—correction, *tried* to read.

It had been twenty-four hours since Vittoria DiLustro was shot, her body buried in an unmarked grave. Soon after, Christian brought me and Cobra to his penthouse in the heart of Philadelphia.

The moment we passed the threshold of the luxury penthouse, he'd said, "There's food in the fridge. Stay here. Cobra will protect you."

"But—"

"We'll get married in forty-eight hours. I'll handle everything."

Then he turned around and disappeared, leaving me alone in his home. I thought he'd be back, but as the hours passed, it was clear that he wasn't returning until the wedding.

"Maybe he's old-fashioned and doesn't want to see the bride before the wedding day," I muttered to Cobra, who lifted her head from where she was curled up next to me. I sighed. "Yeah, the theory is far-fetched, but that's all I got."

Cobra laid her head back down, nuzzling her nose against me, and I sighed, going back to *not* thinking about the fact that I'd be marrying Priest DiLustro in less than two days.

Throwing the book to the side, I reached for my phone and opened my Pinterest page, studying it sadly. The wedding board held all the hopes for my dream wedding. Down to the type of flowers and brand of scented candles. But it was the wedding dress and jewelry—my mother's—that was the centerpiece.

Being born into the mafia world, I knew finding love with a man and creating a family with him was unlikely. My future was written the day I was born. But still, I dreamed and hoped that one day I'd fall in love and have a wedding fit for a princess.

Just like Athair used to call me.

A knock on the door stopped my train of thought. Cobra barked and I startled.

I jumped to my feet, Cobra right at my heel. My room was wrapped in darkness aside from the low light of the reading lamp. I flicked the rest on and padded out of the bedroom and through the empty penthouse.

I checked the peephole on the door, then let out a little squeal when I saw my girlfriends standing outside holding a bottle of wine and a plastic bag with Chinese.

"Cobra, our friends are here," I said, beaming. And as if she understood me, she instantly sat down obediently and watched the door as I opened it.

I welcomed my friends into my arms, not caring that I was jostling the containers and probably sending sweet and sour sauce leaking onto the floor.

Juliette, Davina, and Wynter laughed, all of us a tangle of limbs as everyone spoke at the same time.

"Holy shit, you have a dog," Davina remarked.

"Cobra is our newest gang member." I glanced at my faithful companion and grinned, seeing her tail waggle excitedly. "Cobra, give kisses to our friends."

Woof. Woof. In the next second, she was all over us, giving us unconditional love. The kind only dogs were capable of.

I pulled back to smile at my girls. "How did you know where I'd be?"

"Christian phoned me," Wynter said, gently pushing me back into the penthouse behind the other two and kicking the door shut.

"He told you?" I asked, taking the bag of Chinese as Juliette took the bottle of wine, Davina rubbing a kink out of her back as she wobbled behind us.

Cobra's attention zeroed in on the Chinese in my hand, running circles around me. The little rascal probably wanted to trip me so food would spill all over the floor and she'd have her second dinner.

Juliette and Wynter led us toward the kitchen and it occurred to me they'd been here before, which would make sense—Priest was Juliette's brother-in-law and Wynter's half brother after all.

Wynter winced slightly but recovered just as quickly. "Yeah, he told us about the wedding." She took my hand in hers, giving it a squeeze. "Now we're all family."

"Who would've thought when we started our studies that we'd not only be best friends but also family?" Davina remarked.

"Life works in mysterious ways," I mumbled, glancing at my companion. "Right, Cobra?"

She barked once, twice. I took it as her confirmation, but it was probably just her asking for some Chinese.

"We're family, through thick and thin, and nothing will change that," Juliette said, eyeing me meaningfully as she uncorked a bottle. "Okay?"

"Okay," I confirmed, images of Christian torturing Vittoria flashing through my mind. Would Wynter be freaked out by his actions? She had been trying to rekindle the relationship between her mother and her brother, but I couldn't help but wonder if she'd stop that if she knew what he had endured because her—their—mother abandoned him.

"What's that?" Davina asked as we started pulling glasses and plates out for dinner.

"What?"

"That look on your face," she said with a jerk of her chin.

I waved my hand, dismissing her concerns.

"*Oh*," Juliette teased, waggling her brows at me as she uncorked the bottle. "It's definitely something. Spill it or we're about to have a pillow fight in this immaculate penthouse."

This was one of the reasons I loved Juliette. She had a sixth sense when something troubled me and knew how to defuse the tension. But this bit of information about Christian wasn't something I would share with anyone. It was his secret… our secret.

And I'd never betray his trust.

"I guess pillow fight it is," I said as I snatched a full glass from her, drank it down, and then gave her a feral look.

She threw her head back and laughed, and God, it felt good to have my friends here with me. I hadn't realized how lonely I was without them over the past few months.

I blinked and was transported back to the old days in our dorm rooms. The girls abandoned the fragrant boxes of food and took off running in different directions, their sock-clad feet making them clumsily bump into furniture. Or it could have been Cobra nipping at their toes too. The two of us chased them around Priest's home, all

143

of us squealing like wild teenagers. We stopped every so often to take a bite of Chinese or down more wine, our cheeks aching from smiling.

"Best bachelorette party ever," Davina sighed, rubbing her belly and sipping on her sparkling mineral water. "I think the little guy agrees, Cobra too."

"He should be a girl." Juliette laughed. "Little traitor."

"But I bet your dad is thrilled it's a boy," I pointed out. Liam Brennan adopted Juliette and her brother when they were children, and he considered them his own, but Grandpa Brennan insisted it be Liam's blood relative who eventually took over the Brennan mafia empire.

"He is," Juliette agreed. "Killian, as well."

"Where is he anyhow?" Davina asked. "I haven't seen him around much."

Something passed Juliette's expression but she quickly masked it. "I don't know."

My brows rose nearly into my hairline. "You don't know where your brother is?"

"Nope."

I knew her tells well enough to know when she was lying. *Interesting.*

It looked like we were all keeping some secrets from each other.

"So how does it feel marrying one of the sexiest men to ever breathe air?" Juliette expertly changed the subject.

"Are you talking about your own husband?" Davina surmised. "Or Ivy's soon-to-be one?"

I shook my head at them, but my lips twitched despite myself. "He's okay."

Wynter turned me to face her, keeping both hands on my shoulders, her face serious. "Ivy, do you not want to marry him?"

"I said yes, didn't I?"

"He didn't force you, did he?" Juliette asked. "After all, these DiLustro men have an affinity for acting first and asking for our acceptance later." She rolled her eyes.

I burst out laughing and nodded toward the living room. "Well, Christian must be an exception, then. He asked, and we've come to an agreement."

"Now isn't he a gentleman," Juliette said, refilling our glasses as we collapsed onto overstuffed linen cushions scattered tastefully on the polished hardwood. Davina chose the loveseat and immediately propped her swollen feet up on the coffee table, looking like she was in heaven.

"Well, he is my brother," Wynter said with a laugh, teasing. "It's to be expected. I'm so glad he fell in love with you, Ivy."

A twinge of hurt accompanied her words, but I didn't let anyone see it, not wanting to ruin the mood. Christian hadn't exactly spoken about love. And me... could I be in love? With a man I hardly knew?

I didn't have a straight answer.

I just knew it was dangerous how often I thought of him. How little it bothered me to learn of Christian's dark tendencies.

Did I really care that he tortured Vittoria for years? Or that he'd finally killed her?

No, I didn't. We'd already established that. What bothered me was the force of what I felt. All my life, I promised myself I would never fall in love with a man from our world. It was my only protection against having my heart shatter into a thousand tiny pieces.

And here I was, about to marry one. Having... *feelings* for one.

Except, my friends found love in their marriages, didn't they? They made it look... well, not *easy*, but definitely exciting. I wanted that.

As if sensing the direction my thoughts had taken, Davina shuffled over and rubbed my arm affectionately. I shook away my worries and smiled warmly at her, hoping it wasn't wobbly.

Juliette gestured to the food with her chopsticks. "Are you going to have the last bite?"

"You go ahead." I glanced over to Wynter. "Do you know where Christian went?"

She flashed me a smile, not batting an eyelash. "I do, but I've been sworn to secrecy."

Chapter Eighteen

PRIEST

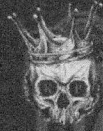

"Priest, I've been expecting your call," Aiden greeted me over the line.

"Have you now?" Phone to my ear, my gaze drifted over the estate where Ivy grew up. Lush green grass. Centuries-old castle towers rising up to touch the clouds. It almost looked like a scene from a fairy tale. It made me wonder whether her life so far had indeed been a fairy tale, which would make me… what? The villain? The anti-hero to her white knight? I let out a sigh and continued. "Forgive me if you hoped to hear from me sooner, but I don't take kindly to demands. Even less when you send not one but four messages in the span of twenty-four hours."

"I want your assurances that you'll treat Ivy Murphy well," Aiden commented tightly.

"Don't concern yourself with Ivy," I growled. "In fact, I'd prefer if you never uttered her name again."

His chuckle grated on my nerves. "Possessive much?"

Two could play this game.

"I don't believe it would take me long to find a certain raven-haired woman with whom you share a past," I drawled.

"You go anywhere near her and I swear to God, I'll murder you," he rasped, the harshness of his tone vibrating through the phone. It was my turn to laugh.

"Maybe you should consider kidnapping her," I recommended. "Caging her. But then, you'd know all about that, wouldn't you?"

"You're a fucking asshole."

"Ditto," I deadpanned. "Now, what do you want? I'm busy preparing."

"I want to make sure this wedding is going ahead," he spat out. "And soon."

I huffed. "Why? So you can blame us for not following through with a binding agreement set by two different assholes?"

"You and I both know she doesn't want me," he pointed out, and something about his words flickered a light in my darkness. "I want to make sure you won't pull some boyfriend-girlfriend bullshit. It needs to be official."

Just like that, the heaviness that had been pooling in

my chest for weeks—fuck, months—snuffed out some of the anger and bitterness.

Was it really that simple?

"I'm marrying her tomorrow," I answered, intent on wrapping up this call. I hadn't flown all the way back to Ireland so I could shoot the shit with the man who'd almost taken Ivy from me.

I hung up on Aiden without waiting for a reply, then went back to studying the Murphy castle's ancient-looking blueprints before folding it carefully and tucking it into my back pocket.

Ivy believed Sofia killed her athair and it was the only reason she agreed to this marriage arrangement. She needed my help to get to her. I used that to my advantage, although I knew it was incorrect. But scruples were for better men and I wasn't one of them. Although I would ensure Ivy got exactly the wedding she always imagined.

Hence the reason I was here, on the Murphy property.

I made my way along the forest edge, my only companion the eerie shadow following right behind me over the soft grass. As I approached the imposing fortress, the image of a mischievous red-haired girl flashed through my mind.

I entered the castle through a small cellar at the base of the east-facing tower, the door probably long forgotten if its rusty hinges and fixtures were any indication.

Keeping my feet light against the stone floor, I crept up the steps, using my phone's flashlight to guide my way.

I finally found my way into Ivy's bedroom after encountering a few dead ends. Considering the modern wings I'd been forced to navigate around, I imagined parts of the castle had been restored over the years. A trail of silvery moonlight leaked through the open blinds and the corners of my mouth curved up as I soaked in her space. The decor seemed to be stuck in teenage fashion —pink lace pillows and a plush white duvet covering the canopy bed, posters of Justin Timberlake and Justin Bieber decorating the walls. I chuckled imagining a young Ivy twirling around her room, blasting pop music and pissing off her brothers.

I'd just made my way into the walk-in closet when the bedroom door flew open with a thud and three men with the same shade of red hair as Ivy's appeared, furious as hell.

Somehow I knew they wouldn't bother with questions, and when the first punch came, my suspicions were confirmed.

"May the best man win," I muttered, charging into them.

Chapter Nineteen

IVY

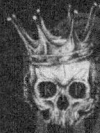

I'm getting married today.

That was my first thought as I opened my eyes. But it was when I saw the white gown hanging against the door that my breath caught in my lungs. I blinked several times, my brows knitted in confusion, convinced I was seeing things.

And still, the sophisticated, romantic dress of my dreams stayed put as I stared in utter shock at the replica of my mother's gown. The same semi-sheer bodice making up the A-line shape, the delicate Chantilly lace appliqué, and glittery misty tulle train that pooled onto the floor of my room from where it hung.

I sat up in the bed, my heart pounding, and spotted a figure sitting on the upholstered chaise lounge to my right: my soon-to-be husband, a shadow of stubble on his beautiful face, watching me with an unreadable expression. I gasped as I took in the bags under his eyes, his split lip, and the purple bruise running the length of his jaw.

"Good morning," I murmured. When he said nothing, my eyes darted back to the dress. My dream dress. "What happened to you?"

He shrugged. "Wild bachelor party."

"Oh."

He nodded to the door. "You like it?"

"I—yes, I do. Very much." I adjusted the blanket, pulling it around my body. "It looks just like my mother's."

The corner of his mouth quirked. "That's because it is."

My hand flew to my mouth, where it tried and failed to muffle a squeal. My head whipped to Christian.

"How? When?" He didn't answer. "But my mother's dress is stored away on our family's estate. In *Ireland*." His stare crept under my skin, flustering me. "Was your bachelor party in Ireland?"

He stood up, his tall frame dominating the room and his bruised jaw hinting at an answer. "Maybe."

"Please tell me you didn't."

If my brothers found him anywhere near our home, they wouldn't have hesitated to shoot at him.

His non-answer had my stomach fluttering with butterflies. That he would go to such lengths... Oh my

God. I just couldn't believe it. My heart was one more kindness away from melting into a puddle at his feet. Aemon told me one time years ago that if someone did something for you without expecting anything in return, they were a keeper.

"And what do you want from me?" I breathed.

"Nothing." My gaze coasted down his body and his eyes darkened. "Today, I want you to have the wedding you dreamed about." *Fuck*.

"How did you know?"

He smirked, and the confident, borderline cocky man I knew was back. I relished it. "Your Pinterest page."

Three words, and I was speechless.

This man was hot for me and the proof was piling up.

Our gazes locked, and he must have read the startling realization in my eyes because his eyes darkened and he ran his tongue across his teeth.

After he'd dismissed me at Wynter's wedding reception, his rejection stung, and I worried I was alone—not to mention delusional—in feeling this chemistry. Yet, it seemed the man was a tad obsessed with me. Maybe it was my vanity or just the woman in me, but I reveled in the power I suddenly felt.

"That was incredibly dumb." I slid off the bed, wearing nothing but my pink boyshorts and a white tank top, and went to stand in front of the dress. I traced my finger over the layers and layers of silk and tulle and lace and fought back tears. Still facing the back of the door, I whispered, "Thank you."

His warm, masculine woodsy scent came behind me and my pulse drifted between my legs. I tried to ignore the way Christian invaded my senses and made every one of them fuzzy. It was like a hit of the most powerful drug that you couldn't resist.

I could hear my heartbeat as I held my breath, the heat of his body at my back. Too close. Too far away.

"I can't wait to see you in it." I glanced over my shoulder, at his boyish grin, and almost climbed him right then and there. "I'll be the one in the best-looking tux, waiting at the altar."

The sun glimmered between 18th Street and Benjamin Franklin Parkway as the car pulled up to where I'd become Mrs. Christian DiLustro. The Cathedral Basilica of Saints Peter and Paul, with its massive stone columns and a great dome, gave the illusion that we'd been transported to Rome.

I exited the car, gripping the bouquet in one hand. When my eyes lifted to the church, I almost stumbled over the hem of my dress. At the foot of the steps leading to the church stood my brothers, looking dashing in their tuxedos, their hands tucked into their pockets.

"Aemon, Bren, Caelan…?" I whispered, bewildered.

"Hello, princess," Bren greeted me.

"You didn't think we'd miss our only sister's wedding, did ya?" Caelan drawled, smiling widely.

I let out a squeal and picked up my skirts with my free hand, then ran toward them where they stood in a row, looking dashing in their tuxedos. Aemon lifted me up, my feet dangling in the air as I laughed, tears burning in my eyes.

"I can't believe you're here," I sobbed out. "How?"

My brother put me down, sliding his hands back into his pockets and swinging on his heel.

"Your idiot fiancé broke into the house." It was then I noticed the bruise on Aemon's cheek. "I figured if he's willing to risk his life like that, he has to be a better option than Aiden Callahan who has a woman stashed away in his penthouse." My jaw dropped. "Plus, your soon-to-be husband said you're doing this willingly. Is that true?"

I nodded. Like my brother said, he's a better option than Aiden who apparently couldn't be faithful during the short period.

"Really?" Bren questioned, studying me with hawkeyed attention.

"Yes, really," I uttered. "Does Christian know you're here?"

Caelan grinned. "Of course. After we brawled and—"

"And he fucked up Aemon's pretty face," Bren interrupted, flashing me a wink.

"I was going to say Aemon's *ugly* face," Caelan chimed in, humor lacing his words.

"Are you done?" Aemon said to our other brothers, who just shrugged. "Your fiancé invited us, sister."

"Ignore them," Bren grumbled. "Now, let's get you inside before your betrothed loses his shit. Fucker's unhinged."

I rolled my eyes. "He's not that bad." *Most of the time.*

Aemon and Bren took my arms, each at one side, as Caelan procured a basket from somewhere.

"I'm your flower girl… flower boy… man… *Fuck*!" He seemed to give up and simply bowed, twirling his arm like some eighteenth-century duke. "Anyhow, I'm at your service."

"Get in front of us, douchebag," Aemon muttered. "You got it right the first time, flower girl."

Caelan flipped him off, then made his way toward the church, launching flowers like they were grenades. My brothers and I shared an amused look as we followed him inside, the scents of sage, frankincense, and myrrh—rich, smoky, and slightly bitter—filling my nostrils. The combination of scents—citrus and pine— brought me back to when Athair used to drag us to Sunday service when we were young. I smiled and took it as a sign that he was here with me, happy, even though he'd envisioned someone else waiting at the end of this aisle.

As I moved farther along the pews, the man with the piercing blue eyes came into view, his towering frame like a target for my thumping heart. I found myself drawn to his darkness—to him.

My steps grew in sync with the soft piano notes and my heartbeats. My clammy hands gripped my wedding flowers, white roses wrapped in green ivy, while our families and friends stood on either side of the church, their eyes boring into me.

But I was aware of only one set.

The sun's rays shone through the stained-glass windows and stopped before his feet, leaving him swathed in shadows that he alone seemed to rule.

I struggled to breathe as he watched me walk toward him, pure bliss flowing through my veins. This—us— hadn't started in a conventional way, but I couldn't help feeling like it was everything I wanted and needed. We had all the time in the world to learn about each other, and I was choosing to see the promise in today.

I reached him and he rasped, "All mine, angel."

We stood face-to-face, the priest reciting our vows. I tried to give the white-haired man with kind eyes my full attention, feeling myself flush under Priest's gaze.

The rest of the ceremony went by in a blur: Christian making minor corrections to our vows, rolling his hand to gesture for the priest to wrap up the proclamations of good versus evil, and then repeating our lines and uttering our *I do*s. Finally, it was time to exchange rings.

A rumble of satisfaction traveled up his throat as he slid a ring on my finger, marking me as his. "You like it?" he asked, brushing a thumb across my cheek.

I blushed again under the intensity of his gaze, the tenderness of his touch. Swallowing the lump in my throat, I whispered, "It's perfect."

It was a white gold Claddagh ring with an emerald crown that marked my heritage and some of his, although I suspected he only picked it because it was front and center on my Pinterest page.

"You may kiss the bride," came a raspy voice.

My heart stilled.

We had yet to share a kiss. The only time we'd been intimate, Christian's lips were nowhere near my face as he savagely devoured me in a dark hallway.

I held my breath as his strong, rough palms cupped my face. A violent, stormy blue swirled among the clouds as he leaned closer.

One breath... two... three... and his lips brushed against the corner of my lips. The touch was light as a feather, the disappointment heavy.

The crowd stood in unison, clapping and cheering, while I tried to understand what just happened.

Did I just make the biggest mistake of my life?

Chapter Twenty

PRIEST

When the ordeal was over, I took Ivy's hand in mine and we moved outside to the garden where a long banquet table was set up, its centerpiece a large fountain adorned with angels.

"Why did you two decide to have your reception in the church garden?" Juliette, my sister-in-law, asked.

Ivy just shrugged and I almost groaned. I didn't have to wonder why she stood stiffly next to me, not even looking my way, pretending I wasn't here.

I. Fucked. Up.

I should have pushed past my reflex and sealed my mouth to hers.

She was the first woman I ever willingly touched. Sure, I'd had women, but the idea of intimacy always stirred nightmares and a cold sweat beneath my skin. So, until my encounter with Ivy, I'd usually let women get down on their knees and suck me off and then be on their merry way. After all, I was a sinner, never a saint.

Ivy had been the first to make me forget my aversion and bring me to my literal knees.

The moment I'd spotted her in my club, I recognized her from the little heist she and her friends performed in Chicago. The girls royally fucked up when they decided to dump medical-grade essential oil all over my brother's Royally Lucky casino, their diversion tactics doing little else than cause a shit storm that would take weeks to set right and make it so that I could never smell lavender without seeing red again. I'd studied the surveillance footage enough to have memorized Ivy Murphy's every feature.

So, I decided to teach her a lesson. I didn't expect to enjoy touching her or to become fucking obsessed at the tender age of twenty-five. For almost two years, I'd been stalking and fantasizing about this woman, unable to move on. One taste of her and I got addicted.

"You two are acting weird," Juliette muttered as we all sat down, her eyes on Ivy and myself.

My sister-in-law hadn't been the same since Ivy's father's death. Dante mentioned she'd been experiencing depression episodes after each visit with her friends. He recommended avoiding them, which would be a feat in itself, considering how close the girls were. Obviously,

Juliette refused, claiming she deserved any and all punishment. She wanted to stand by her friends, no matter what.

It was a commendable decision, but probably unwise.

"Let them be," Dante scolded softly. "It's their day, and if they demand we stand on our heads, we will do that."

"Don't worry, we won't ask that of you," Ivy assured them, while I was certainly tempted. It didn't escape me that my wife threw curious glances Juliette's way. "You've been kind of anxious lately, Jules. Are you okay?"

I watched my sister-in-law grab her glass of wine and gulp it down in one go. "Of course, I'm always great."

Ivy raised her brow. "You always say that. Even as you set the house on fire, you tried to convince us all you're great."

Juliette grimaced. "Fake it till you make it. Isn't that our motto?"

I'd have to have a talk with Dante about her. If we were to keep her secret, she'd have to stop acting so suspicious.

My brother took a large sip of wine before he leaned over to me. "Are you okay?"

"Perfect."

"Don't tell me you're nervous about your wedding night?" he teased.

Fuck, maybe I should admit to my big brother I'd never

kissed a woman. Or maybe better not. He might die from laughter. Goddammit, I should have stopped at a brothel and practiced some kissing with a random woman before my wedding day, but the thought had me breaking out in hives.

I decided to change subjects, speaking in an Italian dialect that was usually difficult to understand for anyone who wasn't native to it. "You'll have to calm Juliette down. She's acting suspicious."

He nodded, understanding where I was going with this. "It's almost worse that they're best friends."

My eyes found Ivy, who was listening to something Wynter whispered in her ear, and the two chuckled. Basilio stared at his wife, as if willing her to look at him. He just couldn't live without her, and considering what Wynter and Basilio had gone through, it wasn't exactly a surprise. My cousin only had eyes for Wynter.

Kind of like you with your wife, my mind mocked.

My wife. Fuck. Ivy was all fucking mine now, and I'd be damned if I let anyone hurt her. Except, how in the fuck was I supposed to explain that I hadn't kissed a woman and I was almost twenty-seven?

"You got a strange look on your face, Christian." Dante tilted his head toward Ivy. "Just follow your intuition. Or maybe her lead."

I narrowed my eyes at him. "What are you insinuating?"

"The girls are... were... a bit wild." He grinned.

"Best if you stop talking right now," I remarked coldly. I had no intention of having this conversation with him. Some things were sacred.

"All I'm saying is don't overthink it."

I raised a skeptical brow. "Really?"

He nodded, then was jostled in his seat as Basilio appeared out of nowhere, smirking like the jerk he could sometimes be.

"Apparently all the girls are singing your praises," he drawled, clapping a palm on the back of Dante's head. "Because Ivy told them you actually *asked* her to marry you."

"Unlike the rest of y'all," Emory chimed in. "Oh wait, my bad. Christian did drug her and then kidnap her, so... more or less like you, Basilio." My cousin's dark eyes met mine. "The question is... how in the fuck did you manage to keep her after that?"

"It's a secret," I answered, then chose to skirt as close as possible to the truth. "And sort of an alliance."

"Alliance?" Emory questioned. "What kind?"

I shrugged. "The kind involving Sofia Volkov."

My cousins shared a glance, before Basilio asked, "You know anything involving Sofia turns into disaster. Nothing but death and heartbreak follows that woman."

"I know, but this kind of alliance with my wife will end Sofia's life," I said. "I'll update you via the Syndicate."

They all nodded, understanding my unspoken meaning. We couldn't discuss this in the open.

"Either way, Ivy and I are on the same page about Sofia."

Basilio shrugged. "Good for her, because sometimes love is a battlefield."

Emory shot him a look of disbelief. "Are you quoting some cheesy song?"

Basilio gave an exaggerated bow in her direction. "In another life, I'd be a songwriter and help my sister find her lover."

Emory shot him her best glare. "Someone already wrote that song and your sister can have as many lovers as she wishes. She doesn't need anyone's help. How about you stick to being a kingpin and serenade your own wife."

Dante must have seen where this was headed because he rose from his chair and clinked his knife against the champagne glass to silence the small group.

I sent him a warning look, which only made him grin. "Ladies and gentlemen, today we celebrate the wedding of my brother and Ivy, no longer Murphy, but DiLustro." Ivy smiled tensely. "Welcome to the family."

I flinched when I saw her hand curl into a fist, clutching her wedding dress. For some reason, I wanted to reach out and unfurl her fingers, link them with my own. But I knew after my fuckup, she'd probably pull it back and punch me.

It was time to send everyone away and make things right with my wife.

If she'd have me.

———————

I was enjoying the sound of Ivy's chiming laugh as she beamed at her brothers. The pricks were protective, doting over her since they arrived. It was risky having them here, too close to Juliette and the shit that happened with Ivy's father, but I couldn't find it in me to regret the decision.

My wife looked happy. For the most part.

"Hello, son." My papà's voice pulled my gaze from my favorite view.

"Hello, Christian. Thank you for inviting Frank and me," was Aisling's greeting. I just nodded slowly, staring past her and onto the makeshift dance floor surrounded by flowers. "I have a gift for you."

I didn't turn to look at her. I couldn't, not without thinking about my dark history. The sort of history that shaped me, destroyed my childhood, and molded me into this twisted, dark person.

She might have not participated in my torture like Vittoria, but Aisling had a hand in turning me into the fucked-up person that I was today.

"I have property in Ireland, and I'm giving it to you and Ivy."

When I said nothing, my papà decided to chime in. "Christian, I believe a thank-you is in order."

"I don't have any need for property in Ireland," I deadpanned. The truth was, I wanted nothing to do with her, but I didn't think my father would take that information well.

"Nonetheless, it's yours," Aisling interrupted, tipping her chin stubbornly. I'd seen the same mannerism in Wynter, and while it didn't bother me with my sister, it agitated me to see it on my birth mother. "I've already transferred it to your and your wife's names." I remained silent, my jaw grinding painfully. "I hope this gives us all a chance to start anew."

I barked out a cold laugh. "Start anew? You want me to be cordial?" This woman, who left her child behind with a *stranger*, had the audacity to show up here today bearing gifts? My papà opened his mouth but I didn't give him a chance to get a word in. "Do you think Vittoria enjoyed raising your bastard child?"

Surprise flickered in his gaze, his expression grim.

"What is he talking about, Frank?" Aisling questioned.

"I have no idea, love."

Tension crept through the space between us, seconds ticking by in silence while wheels turned in my papà's brain.

"Unbelievable," I finally said quietly as my eyes flashed with rage and my lips curled. "Please understand this, Aisling. Whatever you want from me, you're never going to get it." I let my words sink in before I continued. "So why don't you do us all a favor and stop trying?"

I turned to leave, my pulse hammering, when Aisling's words had my step faltering.

"I'll never stop trying," she shot back, her voice too soft for anyone else to hear her but Papà and me. "Not until my dying breath."

My hands curled to fists and I kept walking, not sparing her another glance. She didn't deserve it.

Chapter Twenty-One

IVY

"He makes you cry, say the word," Aemon warned in a hushed tone before slipping into the back seat of the town car they arrived in.

"We'll kill him," Bren added, and I laughed. If they'd made this offer a few hours ago, fresh off yet another rejection (this time at the altar, in front of my friends and family), I might've taken them up on it. But I could already feel myself softening to him, and my resolve weakened each time I rubbed the ring on my finger or felt my dress sway around me. I reminded myself that the man I married had many layers.

"We'll bury him six feet under, princess," Caelan chimed in, his eyes shining darkly. Then he hugged me and slipped a piece of paper into my palm. "The information you asked for."

I stiffened, my eyes widening. "Already?"

After Christian shared some of his story with me, I did a bit of sleuthing and ran into a name. Father Gabriel Metto. A little more and I discovered he was the principal of the school the DiLustro brothers attended. Knowing the kind of sickness that lived inside Father Gabriel, it wasn't hard to draw conclusions. If I was wrong, Christian could correct me.

"I have contacts in the Vatican." He winked. "I took the liberty of booking you and my shiny new brother-in-law a private flight and hotel suite in Rome."

Game. Set. Match.

The priest who dared hurt my husband would never see us coming.

I took my brother's hand and squeezed it gratefully. "Thank you so much."

"Of course. Anything for my baby sister." He kissed one cheek, then the other. "And if you need anything else, you'll call. Yeah?"

"Yeah."

He climbed into the back seat and I watched my brothers—our last guests—drive away, leaving me alone with my new husband.

I let my gaze roam, but Christian was nowhere to be found. With everyone gone, the church and its gardens felt deserted, despite that only minutes ago it brimmed with energy. The chirping birds outside and hum of the organs inside swirled as I made my way toward the rectory.

The doors of the cathedral creaked as I opened them and stepped inside the cool, dark space.

They closed behind me with a loud thud, making me jump and whirl around. All the candles had been extinguished, leaving it almost pitch black, the faded daylight barely making its way through the windows.

My skin tingled with anticipation.

"Christian?" My voice bounced off the centuries-old stone, the stillness somewhat eerie. "Hello?"

Did he disappear again?

I heard some shuffling behind me and whirled around, my anxiety climbing tenfold.

I scanned the darkness, trying to distinguish shapes, but there was nothing.

My heels clicked as I walked deeper into the church until I reached the altar. A distant howl that could have been the result of my wild imagination sent my pulse into overdrive. My breaths became ragged as I backed against a pew, my thigh jamming against an iron coat hook, but I didn't even register the pain.

My mouth went dry as I whipped around and around, my head spinning.

"Christian, I swear to God—"

His hand reached over my shoulder and covered my mouth as he pulled me back against his muscled body.

"There she is," he rasped into my ear. "Don't scream."

"What are you doing?" I asked in a muffled voice.

"I've been fantasizing about tasting you again for far too long."

I gasped against his palm, darting my tongue out and licking his hand. A rumble vibrated in his throat and he pushed his free hand through my scalp, sending tingles of pain shooting through me.

"Someone will see us."

"Then I'll end them right after I fuck you."

My thighs quivered at that thought and my nipples tightened, this reaction confusing me. This wasn't me. I didn't have kinks.

You don't know, my mind mocked. *You're just a virgin.*

Maybe I should have told him. It seemed wrong to lose my virginity like this. Yet, I couldn't push words from my lips. Deep down, I knew I wanted this. I wanted him to take me. Roughly. Without mercy.

I was desperate for him to take all of me.

As if he sensed my surrender, he spun me around and tugged me closer. One moment I was pressed against him, and the next I was laid out on the cold marble altar, golden candle holders and cups flying around, clanking against the ground.

"You're mad at me." I shook my head. "Don't deny

it." His voice was low and deep, growling. "You're upset because I didn't kiss you."

He was too damn perceptive. I'd have to keep that in mind.

"Yes," I admitted. "You should have kissed me properly in the church."

"Except, I don't kiss."

His words sent shock through me but before I could dwell on it, he gathered up my dress and shoved it up above my hips, exposing my bare pussy and thighs, both slick with my arousal.

"You're liking this." He laughed roughly. "Maybe you're as sick as I am."

I shook my head frantically. "Not if we both enjoy it," I protested breathlessly. "You should kiss me."

A fleeting brush of his lips against mine. It could hardly be called a kiss but pure lust erupted inside me so violently I grew dizzy.

"Whose fucking pussy is this?" He cupped my pussy, slapping it. *Hard.*

I cried out as he smacked me again and then started to rub me savagely, the friction making pain and pleasure build within me.

His fist tightened in my hair right before he rammed two fingers into my soaking wet pussy, wrenching a cry from my throat as my back arched off the altar.

"I asked you a question, wife," he rasped. "Whose fucking pussy is this?"

"*Yours!*" I sobbed. "Please, Christian... I have to tell you something."

He stilled, his eyes finding mine.

"You—" I watched his Adam's apple work as he swallowed. "You don't like this."

His fingers still inside me, my breathing turned ragged.

"I do, but—" I swallowed and held his eyes as I whispered, "I'm a virgin."

Surprise flashed in his eyes and his expression softened before his admittance came in a rough voice.

"I'll make sure it's good for you. Always good." He chuckled, bitter amusement passing through his gaze as he added, "I remembered you from that night in Chicago. I meant to teach you a lesson for what you and your band of amateur criminals did, but I fell under your spell, didn't I." The tip of his nose came to nuzzle mine. "You're the first woman I have ever truly wanted. And once I tasted you... touched you... I couldn't stop."

A strange kind of possessiveness shot through my veins and I lifted to my elbows, my wedding dress still bunched around my waist.

"You're the first man to ever go down on me," I whispered. "I've fooled around with other men, kissed some, but never that." I inhaled a deep breath before exhaling. "Although, I've used plenty of toys by myself." My cheeks burned with embarrassment.

"I want their names." It was a harsh demand, but his

voice was so full of lust and need it drove me crazy. He ran a rough hand down my bare legs. "And I want to see those toys."

I had to bite down on a laugh. "Christian, I don't even remember them, and anyway, forget the toys. You're the only one I want."

"No matter," he murmured, pulling out his fingers. "I'm going to find them."

I rolled my hips, rubbing myself against his thick erection. The friction drew a moan from my lips and his gaze darkened into stormy blues.

He dropped lower between my legs, dipping his head and licking me from entrance to clit.

"Fuck, I missed the way you taste." His growl vibrated against me, and I was already fighting the imminent orgasm, wanting to hold on, not wanting it to end. He ran a rough hand down my leg, pulling my thigh over his shoulder, then pushed his tongue inside me. My eyes rolled back in my head as he worked me over. In and out. In and out.

It was like he knew just how much to give before pulling back. I grabbed a handful of his hair and moved my hips at the same time, trying to keep his attention where I needed it.

In my mindless haze, I ground my hips into his mouth. Sparks burned hotter, and then, suddenly, the pressure exploded. I came so hard my ears rang, immediately followed by a languid sensation pulling on my muscles.

The sound of a belt buckle registered through the fog. My eyes fluttered open to find his head still between my thighs but his gaze on me.

His hands traveled up my body, sending a tremble through me, making their way up my stomach, until his gentle yet unyielding grasp latched on to my throat, my body melting against his.

He titled my head with his thumb, and for a moment, I thought he'd kiss me. Instead, he nipped a line down my neck, pulling the skin between his teeth and lightly sucking. My heartbeat dropped like a weight between my legs.

He traced my lips next, his eyes dark pools and full of lust. I leaned up to kiss him, but before our lips could meet, he pushed the straps off my shoulders and tugged my wedding dress down my waist, exposing my bare breasts to him. He captured a nipple with his mouth and a blinding light shot behind my eyes. He switched to my other breast and nipped at it—*hard*—only to ease the sting with his tongue.

The intensity of his touch licked at my skin, making me burn hotter than I'd ever thought possible. I was so far gone, this maddening lust swirling inside me, that I was ready to beg him to fuck me—kiss all but forgotten.

He grabbed on to my hips and lined his hardness to my soaked entrance, his thickness sliding in. He cursed in Italian, tightening his grip as he seemed to go completely still. In a far corner of my mind, I heard his hiss, then he thrust all the way in, his head thrown back and the tendons in his throat visible in the dim light.

He groaned.

I gasped.

Then, as if a beast had been unleashed, he started to fuck me, violently. Punishingly.

"Look at you taking my cock so good," he purred, one hand leaving my hip and traveling back to my chest, my neck. "This is *my* fucking pussy."

His words filled my chest with heat, feeding the hot buzz in my veins. I screamed, my toes curling and my thighs quivering as I hooked them around his waist.

"You're mine," he snarled.

"All yours," I cried.

He wrapped his fingers around my throat as he thrust into me, over and over again, every taut muscle sheathed under the material of his tux. Our heartbeats raced together as he fucked me, the sloppy wet sounds filling the church.

My body trembled as his pelvis ground against my clit, every fiber inside of me shuddering with the intensity. His hands were everywhere now—the back of my neck, sliding down to my breasts, twisting my nipples, brutalizing them, gripping my hips to ram into me harder.

He shoved his fingers into my mouth as he rutted into

me like a wild animal, watching me suck them greedily, gagging on them. He thrusted them to match the tempo of his frantic movements, and I was almost overwhelmed with how it felt. It was everything he'd promised; he wasn't treating me like some fragile, virginal princess in her tower, he was making me feel *good*.

I felt his hard cock everywhere. Then he cupped my jaw, his pace quickening, becoming rougher while our eyes locked. Always checking in on me, constantly making sure I was on the same page, and *fuck* was I ever.

My vision blurred and I gasped, coming so hard I felt my mind drift from my body. The fire inside me burst, spreading a warm, tingling sensation throughout my body.

With a wrenching cry, I screamed, "Oh, God… Oh, God… Fuckkk."

He drove into me one last time, spilling his hot cum deep inside me while my core spasmed around him, milking him for everything he was willing to give me.

I finally let go, my body melting onto the hard cold marble, sighing out a ragged *"My husband"* as Christian collapsed over my chest.

He ran a hand across my cheek, and kissed the corner of my lips as shock and warmth erupted in my chest.

Chapter Twenty-Two

PRIEST

I could think of nothing but how good she felt, how smooth her skin was, how she'd tasted.

It would appear that this woman wrapped in my arms, her breath tickling across my chest, was what I'd been waiting for my entire life.

She was breaking down the walls I'd built and rules I'd set to protect myself.

But there was also a sense of shock that vibrated through me. I'd always hated the intimacy that came along with sex. It was the reason I never got attached, never had women stay the night, and was always careful to keep from touching them and forming that deeper connection.

Until now. Until her.

The fact that I couldn't get enough of her should be

alarming, but it wasn't. It felt strangely right. I was starved for more—so much more.

Her soft lips curled into a dreamy smile as I reached down and brushed a lock of her silky red hair back from her face. I had my driver take us across town, back to my penthouse, and held her hand the whole way as she dozed in and out. Her cheek was hot against my chest and her small hand splayed across my thigh felt sinful. Almost as if she were claiming me.

I knew I was gone for her, that I'd never look at another woman again, and to know she might feel the same way, feel a sense of ownership over me...? Well, that had my blood sizzling for her all over again.

Once my driver parked us in the underground garage, I scooped up my wife, bridal-style, and carried her to the elevator, which took us to the top floor.

"You know I can walk," she protested, her wedding dress crumpled up around her soft curves.

"I want to carry you over the threshold."

She chuckled softly but didn't complain again. Once the doors slid open to the foyer, Cobra greeted us, waggling her tail excitedly. Ivy smiled softly at her, whispered praises, then leaned over to scratch her behind the ear, and jealousy shot through me.

"Cobra, go to your bed," I grumbled begrudgingly. "Ivy's mine now."

My wife laughed, and repeated the order, then with Cobra gone, I walked us straight to the master bathroom where I set my wife down and started a bath. Her eyes followed my every move as I dumped her favorite salts into the tub, then tested the temperature of the water.

"You don't have to do this," she protested, her eyes locked on mine through the mirror. I tilted my head and took in the scene around us from her perspective. Ivy, standing a foot and a half shorter than me now that she'd taken off her shoes. Her hair was disheveled and her eyes half-lidded, wearing a thoroughly fucked expression that matched the state of her dress.

Fuck, had we ruined it? "I'll get it cleaned, I promise," I murmured, pinching the material between my fingers and letting it fall gently.

Her breath caught and she gave me a shy smile. "I'm not worried, but thank you. It'd be nice to pass the dress on to my daughter one day."

Daughter.

We'd never talked about kids, although now was hardly the time.

I helped her out of her dress and held her hand as she lowered herself into the clawfoot tub, the water quickly submerging her. A soft sigh left her lips and she closed her eyes for a moment.

"Better?"

"Gosh, yes," she moaned. "Thank you."

I removed my jacket, then undid my cufflinks and rolled up my sleeves, noting how my wife watched me through her thick lashes. I crouched beside her and reached for one of the products I had my housekeeper stock for her, pouring it into a washcloth.

Starting with her shoulders, I rubbed circles over her taut muscles. They loosened with every passing second, and her head fell back against the rim.

"For someone who's never done this before, you're doing a perfect job," she said, never opening her eyes, her voice softer than a fresh snowfall.

There were things I never desired or intended to do, but here I was with my beautiful wife, wanting nothing more than to leave her feeling content.

I wanted her to stay here with me forever. Even when all my ghosts came out to play. Even when I was at my darkest and lowest.

Despite the understanding she'd shown me time after time, I was all too aware that she'd spent her life in the care of a family who loved her. Sure, she was fiercely independent and unafraid to take what she wanted, but I couldn't let myself forget that there was a darkness to this world, to *me*, that she'd never been exposed to. How could I expect her to love the ugly, broken parts of me?

The answer came to me as I washed the suds from her locks. It was simple: I would never let her see them.

Chapter Twenty-Three

IVY

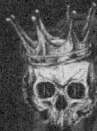

So much for wedded bliss.

After my bath, Christian tucked me into bed and then left. I racked my brain, trying to understand what happened for him to just switch off like that. I tried to stay awake and wait for him, but my eyelids got heavy and sleep pulled me under.

I awoke the following morning with a heavy arm hooked over me, realizing Christian must have slipped in next to me sometime in the night. While I knew there were things we had to work through, the fact he was in the bed—with me—gave me hope.

Careful not to wake him, I padded over to the bathroom where I took a shower and changed into comfortable clothes, then beelined for the kitchen. I brewed myself some coffee and got straight to work.

An hour later, I had a full Irish breakfast prepared: bacon, sausage, baked beans, eggs with (and without) mushrooms, grilled tomatoes, and hash potatoes.

Christian appeared in the kitchen wearing nothing but the sweatpants I now knew lived on a shelf in his closet, looking as hot as the devil himself. He timed it perfectly because I was just plating the toast and marmalade.

He leaned against the doorway and I let my gaze travel over his body, shudders coursing through me. My husband was drop-dead gorgeous, his golden skin looking delicious enough to lick my breakfast off of. This was the first time I was seeing him without a shirt on, and the six-pack he boasted was well worth the wait.

I winced and quietly berated myself.

He might not appreciate my ogling. I was desperate to show him I craved him—perceived imperfections and all—but my intuition warned me to tread lightly.

"Good morning." His eyes darted to the table behind me before they returned to mine, studying me as if he needed assurances that I still wanted to be here. "What's all this?"

"An Irish breakfast." I tucked a strand of hair behind my ear. "Would you like some coffee or tea?"

He closed the distance between us, his bare feet silent against the shiny tiled floor, and cupped my cheeks. He surprised me by pressing a kiss to my forehead. It wasn't exactly what I'd been hoping for in the light of a new day, but we were getting closer. Right?

"Coffee, please."

I nodded. "Sit and I'll get it for you."

"I didn't know you liked to cook," he remarked, his eyes following my every movement.

I glanced over my shoulder at him. "There are many things you don't know about me."

A half smile pulled at his lips. "I wouldn't be so sure, angel."

"Meaning?"

I had a suspicion, but I wanted to hear it from him. "I've had my eye on you." He shrugged and sat down at the table.

"You mean like... a background check?" I batted my lashes innocently.

He rolled his eyes. *This man.* "I guess you could call it that."

"Or we could call it stalking," I said casually, filling his cup with coffee and handing it to him as I took a seat.

He grabbed my hand, pressing it against his chest, right above his strong beating heart. "I mostly wanted to know how to get you settled in our home."

Our home. I thought of the clothes folded neatly in the walk-in closet, all my favorite products lining the shelves in the bathroom, and I blushed. Was it wrong that the gesture made warmth erupt in my chest? It had to be. Could I find it in me to care? Not for a second.

"I'm sure that's what all you mafia men tell yourselves," I teased. "Where did you go last night?" He shrugged, but remained silent. I chewed my lip for a moment but I just couldn't keep it in. "I don't think secrets are a good way to start a marriage."

I held my breath as I waited, ghosts dancing in his eyes. "Sometimes I have nightmares."

His admission shouldn't have surprised me. After all, I'd heard some of his story and I suspected he gave me a lighter version.

"I can handle them," I said with conviction. A small smile pulled on a corner of his lips. "Now eat."

"Yes, wife."

My cheeks warmed, my heart pounding in my ears. I secretly wanted a real marriage and I'd give it my best shot to have it. I felt honesty was a step in the right direction.

I watched him take his first bite. Then another. He ate in silence and I grinned. "Hmm, there might be some Irish in you after all."

I realized my mistake instantly, but it was too late to retract the words.

"I guess you could say that with Aisling being my biological mother."

I worked up the nerve to look at him. His face was passive, and there wasn't any bitterness in his voice. Maybe it was foolish, but I saw it as a sign to broach the topic with him.

"How do you feel about her?"

He was silent for a moment, his eyes stabbing into mine. "Fine."

"I'm sorry," I said quietly. "I'm sorry she wasn't there when you needed her."

He looked at me blankly.

"Nothing to be sorry about." *Nothing?* My brow furrowed. "Aisling is nothing to me. We just share DNA. Unfortunately."

"There's no such thing as a perfect family," I said softly. "Every single one goes through bumps and has issues, and if they tell you otherwise, they're lying."

"I don't imagine many of those people would describe the bumps as being abandoned by their biological mother to be abused by their stepmother." He gave his head a subtle shake. "I mean, what did Aisling expect? That Vittoria would welcome the child of her husband's mistress with open arms?"

He had a point there. On the way home last night, Christian told me about his run-in with his father and Aisling. It had taken a bit of prodding, but he spilled most of the details eventually. My athair might not have been present, and I missed being walked down the aisle by him, but at least there wasn't any drama I had to endure in regards to his relation to Sofia. Christian wasn't so lucky.

"My parents loved each other," I murmured, swallowing a lump in my throat. "Yes, my mother died, and I expect my

187

father had women in his life after her death, but it hurt learning he'd taken up with someone even before she passed away." His eyes snapped to mine. "And it wasn't a brief fling, since he managed to have twins with her." I let out a strangled laugh, the entire situation beyond absurd. "It's actually your great-grandmother, Sofia, who was his lover."

He didn't react, his eyes simmering with emotions I had a hard time identifying. It made me wonder whether he knew already.

"But I take it that wasn't a surprise?" I asked.

"No, but nothing surprises me."

"I met her once… Sofia… when I was a little girl, you know," I said, and something shifted in the air.

"Your father took you to her?" he growled.

I shrugged. "I think I was around five. I didn't understand most of their conversation, but I must have known it was wrong because I never told my mother about it."

"Probably because you wanted to protect her," he pointed out.

"Maybe. The dynamic between the two of them… Sofia and Athair… it was all wrong. He was so protective and dangerous, but around her, he was almost smaller. A completely different person." I thought back to that night and memories of the child that had a hard time comprehending what was going on. "I wish I'd said something to my brothers. Maybe they could have killed her and she would have never had a chance to kill Athair."

"Probably best that you didn't. Your brothers might've ended up dead."

"Maybe." I studied his closed-off expression, hoping to get through to him. "Or I could have saved countless others, my father included." I sighed. "The point is there are no guarantees in life. We could sit here until the end of time pondering our decisions, but I have to believe that Aisling thought she was doing the best thing for you."

I expected him to tell me off, that I needed to mind my own business, anything. Instead, he remained quiet, the silence stretching for many heartbeats. I squinted at him, something about his blank, emotionless face hitting me all wrong.

"Okay," he finally said through his clenched jaw, returning his attention to the plate in front of him. I'd be lying if I said it didn't hurt to be shut down like that, but I couldn't exactly force him to open up. He'd had almost three decades to perfect this obvious strategy of hiding behind his emotions.

"I booked our honeymoon," I blurted, not wanting to dwell.

He paused, turning his head back to look at me. "Honeymoon?"

"Yes, it's when a married couple—"

"I know what it is."

I pursed my mouth, stifling a snarky comment. "We

leave later today. A plane will be waiting for us, taking us to Rome. Are you okay with that?"

A lifted shoulder was my answer.

"Okay, I'll take that as a yes." I stood up from the table and Christian leveled me with a withering gaze. "If that is not a yes, Christian, I'd suggest you speak now or forever hold your peace."

"Yes, I'm okay with that." *This man is going to give me whiplash.*

I shook my head and readied myself to storm away when he grabbed my arm and pulled me onto his lap.

I shivered, feeling his hard-on press against my ass, and watched as his eyes darkened—whether from fury or arousal, I couldn't distinguish anymore.

"Thank you for making me breakfast."

The darkness whose presence I always sensed radiated off him, flexing around us and mixing with something else. Something I couldn't pinpoint.

"You're welcome." I drew in a breath, stood once more, then left him sitting alone in the kitchen.

I scurried up the stairs of the private jet, my heart stumbling with every step. Our honeymoon. I was working up the courage to tell Christian the extent of our plans. We'd go to Rome and find the man who hurt

Christian, and then we'd hunt the woman who killed my father.

Everything seemed surreal. So much had changed overnight and there was no going back. I'd promised him forever, and I intended to keep my vow. I knew he'd do the same.

Christian was already seated in the reclining black leather chair on the left side of the plane.

I plopped into the one closest to him before fumbling with my seat belt. The cabin crew did their checks and offered us champagne, oblivious to my swirling anxiety. I stole glances at my new husband all day as we moved around each other preparing for the last-minute trip, but things were still rocky.

The tension in the cabin as it took to the sky was hard to ignore. Now that we were days, maybe even *hours*, away from confronting the monster who'd hurt him, Christian's haunting past and everything I'd learned had begun to pull emotions I didn't know existed out of me. I was constantly on the verge of breaking down and sobbing.

For him. For me. For us.

Tears formed in my eyes, and deep down, I knew.

I'd fallen in love with my damaged villain.

"Don't tell me you're regretting your decision already?" Christian's voice pulled me out of my thoughts and I met his blue gaze.

"Of course not," I muttered. "We're both getting something out of this arrangement."

He nodded and stared out the window, but the moment we were in the air, he rasped, "I want to fuck you again," so quietly I wasn't sure whether the words were meant to reach me.

I felt each one between my legs, and before I could even come up with a reply, my husband was on his feet, unlatching my seat belt and pulling me into his arms.

"What are you doing?"

"I want a redo," he announced, carrying me toward the back of the plane. The moment we entered the bedroom, the lock clicked into place and he dropped me onto the bed.

Bolts of electricity scattered up my arm when he stooped down to remove my sneakers, dumping them unceremoniously next to the bed.

"Do you want this?" he asked as he toed off his polished dress shoes.

My thighs trembled with desire and my nipples tightened. "*Yes.*"

My pulse rang in my ears when he undid his cufflinks and shrugged off his jacket. He loosened the knot on his tie, his eyes never leaving me as he undid his belt, stripping down to nothing.

I watched him, my eyes at half-mast and my skin buzzing with anticipation. My husband might be damaged, but his body was a work of art.

I lifted a leg, resting my foot on his bare stomach, and he kissed the inner arch of my foot. My body lit up like a Christmas tree. He raked his eyes down languidly before returning them to my face.

My furious pulse dropped from my ears to my clit when he said, "Strip."

The desire in his eyes gave me all the courage I needed. Christian stared at me like I was his salvation and damnation wrapped in one as I unzipped my dress, the sound echoing seductively through the air.

When I shimmied out of it, sending the dress soundlessly to the floor, he drew in a sharp breath.

"Fuck," he muttered, his gaze primal and hungry.

He twisted his tie around his right hand and approached me, his thighs brushing against mine. It was all it took for a low moan to crawl up my throat.

"Are you going to kiss me?" I breathed.

The bundle of nerves between my thighs thumped when a salacious smirk stretched across his face. "Only if you're a good girl."

I rolled my eyes, but the moment his tongue brushed against my lips, all traces of humor were sucked from the room. He ran a rough hand across my cheek and kissed me. Shock erupted in my chest like a volcano, lava spilling through every vein, warming me down to my bones.

He tasted so good, so perfect, and it was at this very moment I knew I was addicted beyond recovery.

I wrapped my arms around his neck as the kiss turned violent, almost like he'd been battling the same pent-up frustrations as I had for months.

Christian groaned into my mouth when I scraped my nails down his abs, my blood thickening with lust. Through a stimulating blur of bites, sucks, and kisses, I became trapped between the bed and my husband. When he curled my legs around his waist, I worked myself along the ridge of his cock, my patience to feel him inside me stretched thin.

He pushed into me, filling me to the hilt. I gasped, arching to take him deeper, and wondered if anything had ever felt this good.

"You were made for me," he murmured into my neck, sighing out a rumble of approval against my throat as he slid into me deep and slow, something soft breaking through.

Not wanting him to retreat or go easy on me, I encouraged him to continue. "More. Please."

The gentle press of his lips against mine, even while he fucked me hard enough I thought I might black out, had me crying out in the dim room.

Somewhere along the way, he'd laid me flat on my stomach, holding my wrists on either side of my head as he fucked me from behind. He stilled, breath heavy, as he brushed his lips against the back of my neck.

"No one touches you but me," he whispered, his hot breath eviscerating me on the spot.

"Ditto," I breathed, losing all sense of reality.

He pressed his face into my neck and growled with satisfaction. He was hitting a spot so deep, so intense, tears were beginning to sting my eyes. His body weight was heavy as he held me down, sending undiluted pleasure coursing through my blood. And then there was this feeling in my chest, a lightness and a heaviness all at once. It was too much. As I tumbled toward the edge of release, I took all sense of reason within me.

I didn't think I'd ever come up for air again. Simple as that, my heart was his.

Signed, sealed, delivered.

Chapter Twenty-Four

PRIEST

It was my first true deep kiss. Ever. And when I tasted the softness of my wife's full lips, I knew I was lost to her. She'd taken hold of my very being, and I welcomed it.

I'd thought I could keep her separate from my mess, in a box of her own, but it was quickly becoming apparent that she'd already burrowed beneath my skin.

As I gathered my wits and began to accept how utterly lost I was for this woman, I understood there was nothing I wouldn't do for her. I'd fight her demons, be her shoulder to cry on, and protect her secrets.

With a single kiss upon her lips, I knew I'd hold on with both hands.

Juliette's face appeared in the periphery of my mind

and I tried to push it away, but I couldn't shake the guilt of protecting her and Dante's secret, one whose consequences I worried would be too great for Ivy to recover from. Slowly but surely, it ate at my black soul.

"I have a surprise for you." I frowned, pulled from my thoughts as my attention slid down to Ivy's face against my chest. We had another few hours before we'd land in Rome.

"Huh?"

"Father Gabriel," she said quietly.

It hit me like a ton of bricks, the memories of that fucker and the things he'd done to me making me want to roar. Break something. Scrub myself clean.

"What about him?" I asked, my voice cold. Detached.

"He was a principal of St. Gabriel's school in Chicago, wasn't he?" That fucking man stole my life. "He's a cardinal now."

I remained silent for a long time while the panic began to take root in my chest. I sucked in slow breaths, trying to will away the sickening images of what I endured.

No.

I wouldn't let him win. I'd come too far, burying the night terrors somewhere deep where only the Grim Reaper ruled.

"I'm sure those red robes match the stains on his soul," I stated matter-of-factly.

The look in her hazel eyes was filled with concern. The telltale signs of sorrow washed over her features— the furrow of her brows or chewing of her bottom lip. If I wasn't mistaken, this woman cared for me. Deeply.

"He hurt you." Her voice softened. "He hurt others too. He should pay so you can get peace."

She... understands.

"And you want to deliver him to me?"

She clutched my elbow harshly, but the pain didn't register.

"Yes." Her voice was a low, furious murmur and it hit me like a freight train. She understood me.

"And it doesn't bother you?" I asked instead.

Her brows furrowed.

"*Bother* me?" Her voice was almost undignified. She released a breath and I allowed a small smile to curve my lips. "I want to murder him for you."

"I hear a woman's wrath is a dangerous thing," I remarked, trying to calm the beast roaring inside of me.

Her arms squeezed around me. "It can be," Ivy whispered. "If you prefer I take care of him, I—"

"No." The thought of that sick bastard anywhere near her made me want to tear the world apart. "You're not to go near him."

Ivy stiffened and I looked away, my eyes stabbing out the airplane window, seeing nothing but clouds. She was innocent and pure. Father Gabriel was an incurable disease, one that needed to be carved out, and I wouldn't be exposing Ivy to him.

"How did you guess?" I questioned. When I told her about the day Dante and I burned our house down, I didn't mention the abuse I'd endured at the principal's hand.

"It was something about the way you mentioned Father Gabriel. Your mind went somewhere dark, lonely, and it set the wheels in motion." She swallowed, meeting my eyes. "I've seen it before."

"Did someone hurt you, angel?" My hold on her tightened.

She shook her head. "No, not me. Someone else. Someone close to me. But that's not my story to tell."

Relief hit me hard, and I loosened my hold on her, the darkness receding a bit.

"I'm going to tell you something I've never told anyone. My whole story."

Ivy looked up at me, and I saw nothing but patience. So, I took a deep breath and began.

"My mother hated my guts. It wasn't until I learned Aisling Brennan was my real mother that I finally understood why." She nodded with compassion. "Not that that explained her hate for Dante."

"Maybe he reminded her of his father," she offered sagely.

"Probably." I rolled my jaw, grateful she was giving me the space to continue.

"Christian, she was an evil person," she whispered softly, her expression sad. "There is no point in trying to understand a person with that much hate inside."

She lowered her mouth, softly kissing my chest, each kiss easing the pain inside me. Maybe she was the cure I'd needed all along.

"I was eight when *it* started." I sighed. She needed— deserved—to know this.

"When your mother's abuse started, or ... what Father Gabriel did?"

"Oh, Vittoria's physical abuse started much earlier." I growled. "This was when it started at school, the only place I felt any kind of peace. He took that from me."

Her face went white as she visibly gulped, then choked on a sob. "Oh, Christian."

My arms tightened around her. "Vittoria gave him permission to do what it took to make me 'behave.' She gave him fucking carte blanche." Hot tears wet my chest. "They told me if I uttered a single word to anyone, they'd kill me. Dante, my father... the only people I still loved," I said quietly. "It went on for years. Until the night Dante and I put a stop to everything."

Ivy's soothing, healing touch made my soul ache less.

"So what you told me was the end." I nodded. "Or maybe it was the beginning for you. Because you took some control back by giving that foul woman what she deserved."

201

"You were right though," I said slowly. "It became an unhealthy way to deal with what had been done to me. And to Dante."

Ivy shook her head, tears streaming down her cheeks. "I'm no expert, but I'm glad she suffered. And I hope Father Gabriel suffers too."

"If there is a God, he must have sent me you," I growled, cupping her face as our eyes locked. "Maybe it's his way of remedying what he let Vittoria and Father Gabriel get away with for so long."

Her eyes searched mine, her graceful fingers stroking my skin, easing the pain. Healing me.

I looked away, fear gripping my chest. "Promise me you'll never leave me," I rasped.

Her soft palm came to my cheek, pulling my gaze back to hers.

"Of course I'll never leave you." Her lips tipped up slightly. "Besides, for better or for worse, we're stuck together. Married, remember?"

"Even though I'm broken?"

"You're not broken," she whispered, pressing her lips softly to mine. It was hard to believe I'd ever had an aversion to intimacy. It was as if, overnight—literally— she'd put me back together again and made it so her touch was a balm rather than a punishment. "Life was cruel to you, and it made you who you are. Beautiful. Justified. Vengeful. But only toward people who deserve it." Her eyes captured mine. "You're put together differently due to the circumstances life threw at you, but you're no less perfect."

I stroked her hair back from her face, brushing my knuckles against her soft skin. She was healing me without even realizing it.

Chapter Twenty-Five

IVY

Welcome to Rome.

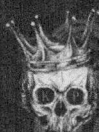

Narrow cobbled streets. Piazzas. Churches. Fountains.

Rome had over two thousand historic fountains, fifty monumental ones and hundreds of smaller ones—or so our driver told us when he picked us up on the tarmac. "More than any other city in the world," he'd called over his shoulder, his accent thick and jovial. I'd forever think of Rome as a city of fountains, thanks to Bernardino.

"I guess I don't understand the obsession," I muttered as we ducked under a balcony's drooping clothesline.

"The ancients took pride in them, I guess. And they do come in handy when it's hot out. Not to mention all the ones that act as coin collectors for gullible tourists."

"Like today." I pulled my hand out of Christian's and

wiped my sweaty palm on my jeans. "It's like we're baking in hell. And we're definitely not dressed for it."

He let out a dark chuckle. "It won't be us baking, angel. Want to stop and buy a dress?"

It was the hottest day recorded for December in Rome, and of course, we were here. I was dressed in jeans and an off-white hand-knit Aran jumper, boiling from the inside. Honestly, I marveled how my husband managed to look cool, not a bead of perspiration on him, while wearing a three-piece suit.

I rubbed my temple, annoyed that I was *still* feeling the effects of jet lag, even after several days. "Might be a good idea. Otherwise, my DNA will be all over this city and I'll end up in an Italian prison."

His eyes turned a shade of blue so deep it was almost black. "I'd sooner level this city before I'd let them put you there, angel."

"It'd be a crime to lose all the beautiful fountains," I remarked, smiling softly while my insides melted. Fuck, I loved the way he showed affection.

"It'd be a bigger tragedy to lose you." His eyes watched me with a possessiveness I was growing to love. "And trust me, angel. They'd be begging for death."

The soles of my Vans felt too heavy against the thousands-year-old stone. The sound of silverware and plates, running water from the open windows and cracked doors, reminded us that it was past lunchtime. It was the pocket of time in the afternoon when everyone was about to take their rest.

Christian stopped in front of a local shop. "Here, let's stop in here and see if you like anything."

A group of priests passed us, pulling drags from their cigarettes and speaking in rushed Italian. Their designer sunglasses and expensive watches caught the light and my attention.

"I thought joining the priesthood was about giving up material things," I whispered under my breath. "And living modestly."

Two looked up and smiled at us while Christian glared at them.

"Nothing modest about them," he gritted, and I squeezed his hand in comfort.

"Let's see what this shop has," I said, tugging him through the old wooden doors.

Ten minutes later, we exited the shop looking like locals: me wearing a white dress and a sunhat; Christian in a wide-brimmed hat and summer version of an old-time suit with suspenders over a white linen shirt, the buttons at the collar undone.

"You just need a mustache and you'll look like some twenties gangster," I teased as we eyed a café with outdoor seating that showed no signs of closing up.

"Then let this gangster buy you lunch." My eyes flashed to him, surprised to hear him crack a joke.

I bumped my shoulder against him as he held the wicker chair out for me.

"I didn't know you had a sense of humor."

He smirked. "I don't. Ask anyone who knows me."

Except, I didn't think there was anyone who actually knew him. Not truly, anyway. Not when he lived behind those thick, high walls. But I was slowly making my way through, and I wouldn't stop until we stood chest to chest, bare to each other with all our faults.

I intended to show him that I wasn't going anywhere.

He took a seat next to me and we looked out over the piazza. This café seemed built with the purpose of welcoming patrons following church service, with many in the area but the closest one at the center of the square. I peered at it and realized—unsurprisingly—a fountain with a wolf's head carved out of stone lay before it.

Compared to other churches we'd visited in the city, this one was almost unremarkable. But this was where Father Gabriel's trail had led us.

Our driver turned tour guide had been worth the money I knew Christian was paying him. Particularly when he'd taken us for an extended drive a few days ago and pointed out the Sistine Chapel and St. Peter's Basilica, pulling over to let us watch the Swiss guards change shifts. Christian and I had stayed silent when a Vatican Swiss guard wearing a striped tunic the colors of the Medici family—red, dark blue, and yellow—approached our black SUV and bent to scowl at Bernardino.

The guard took one look at us in the back seat and hissed, "No loitering," in perfect English.

Surprise shot through me and I blinked in confusion, about to argue when a folded note drifted through the window and landed at my feet.

Christian had read it and promptly requested our driver to get out of there, and that was how we found ourselves here, sipping our espressos and checking over our shoulders to ensure we had privacy.

He pulled the note from his pocket and unfolded it, elegant writing staring at us. It was the last known location of Father Gabriel.

"He must have done something bad to be placed in such an unremarkable location," I muttered.

"Close to headquarters but still too far away," Christian deadpanned. "They must have learned about his tendencies."

I'd come to the same conclusion.

"It's about time karma caught up," I whispered, eager to see my husband's vengeance delivered.

PRIEST

Stalking a prey and patience were two things I excelled at. As I sat in the little café with my wife, drinking coffee, I kept a watchful eye out.

It was no accident that I'd chosen this table. From our position, we could see every movement in and out of the church, and most importantly, we could see our target's figure shadowing the windows. Almost as if he could sense judgment day was coming.

We'd been following his every move for the past week, down to every activity the fucker packed into his pathetic little routine. We tailed him to the Vatican and the grocery store, even his coffee and cigarette breaks. His last mass was at seven in the evening, and we planned on slipping through the rectory door while he started his ritual of locking the doors. He always started with the front gate.

Leaning back in my chair, I drummed my fingers on the table. Any minute now.

And like clockwork, my target came into view: a pathetic excuse for a priest, hunched over, rushing across the square toward his little sanctuary. It was a dump, that's what it was. Not a church. And it was about to become his final resting place.

My mouth twisted into a smile, which was probably more like a grimace.

"Thank you," I said, my eyes never wavering from my target. I sensed Ivy's surprise, but I couldn't look over at her. Not now. Not when the object of my nightmares was so fucking close.

"For what?"

"For giving me *him*," I breathed. "You were right. I need him dead to get closure."

And I would finally get it.

The truth was that the Vatican should have done more than shove him away, out of sight. It wasn't enough of a punishment for all the pain he'd caused. Maybe they'd hit him where it hurt—his ambition and pride—but they should have flayed him until flesh ripped from his bones.

But not to worry, I was content on playing judge, jury, and executioner. This devil, the rotten apple, would be removed from their folds.

"You're welcome. Make him pay, baby." I grinned at the viciousness in her voice. It was what I loved about her. She wasn't soft, not in the classical way. She was like an avenging angel, stronger than I imagined most people gave her credit for. Her brothers made a mistake when they chose to keep her sheltered in that Irish castle. She was born to lead.

"Don't you worry, angel. He'll pay."

Father Gabriel was about to have a very bad day, and I'd make it even worse by informing him it'd be his last.

Even from here, I could smell the stench of desperation and foulness radiating off of him. I still remembered the fucker's cologne, even after all these years. It was burned into my nostrils.

But his demise was imminent, and it was for that reason and that reason alone that my shoulders felt lighter than they had in a decade.

I glanced down at my espresso with a curled lip, then stood up, extending my hand to my wife.

"Showtime."

Her hand in mine, we made our way across the piazza and into the church from the east-facing side as Father Gabriel struggled with the heavy door of the church. He never even glanced our way, unaware we were taking the back way that led into the rectory while Father Gabriel locked the front door of the church.

Once inside, I turned to my wife and asked, "Are you sure you want to be here?"

It was her last chance to run.

"Absolutely. We stick together through thick and thin. Like Bonnie and Clyde. Let's just aim for a better ending."

It was a cheesy comparison and she knew it. Still, it made my lips twitch in amusement.

Once inside the church, I locked the door behind us. It was now between God and me what I was about to do. Our footsteps were silent, making our way deeper into the rectory.

Taking a seat by the table, she crossed her legs.

We didn't have to wait long before Father Gabriel appeared in the doorway of the rectory.

"*Ma che*—"

I jammed my fist straight into his nose. He squealed like a stuck pig, tumbling to his feet and thrashing about dramatically. Before he could get his footing back, I punched him again. The crunching of bones signaled his nose breaking, and he wailed, his throat gurgling as blood gushed from his wailing mouth.

212

"*Non ho soldi,*" he screamed, clutching his bleeding nose. *I don't have any money.*

I yanked him by the back of the collar of his priesthood robe.

"We don't want your money." *Punch.* "I'm here to settle the score." *Punch.* "Remember me, Father Gabriel?"

He was on the ground, swishing in blood smeared with his spit, those beady black pools locked on me. His eyes widened in terror.

"Christian..." He choked on his words. "DiLustro."

I smiled viciously.

"Forgive me, Father, for I'm about to sin." My voice was cold, seeping from the depths of my soul. He was on all fours like the fucking cockroach he was. I kicked his ribs, making him cower and draw his hands up by his ears. "You should say your prayers now, Father. Tonight, you'll feel the icy grip of death."

I kicked him in the balls with all my strength.

He hunched over, vomiting blood and holding on to his groin.

"You won't be needing your cock anymore," I drawled, pulling out a knife from my ankle holster.

He stared up at me with bleary, unfocused eyes. "Wh-what?" It was only then that he saw my wife sitting casually at the table in the rectory. "*Ti prego, aiutami.*" Help me.

He reared back when I elbowed him in the mouth. "Don't look at my wife, you sick fucking pervert."

Ivy smiled, drumming her dainty fingernails against the wooden surface of the table. "Christian, love, make sure you let me know if you need my help. I'd love nothing more than to peel this poor excuse of a man's skin back, inch by inch."

Fuck, I was in love.

Father Gabriel crawled away from me, attempting to hide underneath the table. He reached for Ivy's leg, as if to beg her for mercy, but before he could touch her, I grabbed him and punched him so hard, he went flying across the floor.

"Don't you dare touch my wife with your filthy hands," I hissed and gripped his throat. His eyes bulged as I snarled into his face. "Now, fucking *pray*."

He swallowed violently, trembling as he looked up at me, his face ashen.

"P-please…" he choked, staring at me with undiluted terror.

My hand clamped hard around his throat, squeezing until his eyes rolled back in his head. "I didn't hear you pray, Father."

He squealed again as I grabbed the back of his robe and hauled him up, dragging him out of the rectory and into the nave, a part of the church similar to the one where I spent hours praying under the watchful eye of this sicko.

None of my prayers were answered. Father Gabriel's wouldn't be either.

Chapter Twenty-Six

IVY

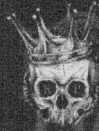

C runch of bones. Flaying of flesh. Whimpered prayers.

Just as I entered the nave, his confession echoed through the hollow church.

"I… It wasn't my fault," Father Gabriel pleaded, voice trembling. "She insisted. She told me it was God's will. You were a child of sin. You were too much of a temptation."

"I'm going to make you regret the day you were born." Christian's voice was sharp as a whip.

Father Gabriel's face twisted into something ugly, revealing the predator we already knew he was. "It was your fault. She was right about you, you are the devil's spawn." My chest twisted with disgust at this sick bastard. If Christian let him live, I'd be sure to kill him.

Slowly. Painfully. "Blame Vittoria. Blame *yourself.* You should have been born disfigured, the child of sin."

Christian's expression shuttered, pain he'd worked so hard to hide, plain as day. He breathed harshly, his chest rising and falling so fast I worried he'd succumb to an anxiety attack. I took several steps, stopping a small distance away, afraid I'd trigger him if I got any closer.

"You're not ugly." My voice was thick with emotion, hoping to get through to him. "And you're not a child of sin. None of this is on you. It's on him. We reap what we sow, Christian. When he dies, nothing will save him. Not his prayers. Not his God."

The priest laughed, the sound grating in the otherwise quiet space. "But I'll wait for you in hell, my boy."

Christian lifted a chair and brought it down on Father Gabriel's head, his cries echoing against the washed-out mosaics. The old wood splintered into pieces and he fell limp between the pews, his head sticking out at an awkward angle, stained with blood.

"May the Holy Spirit free you from this miserable life and your sins swallow you whole with the grace of the Holy Spirit. Amen, motherfucker."

Goose bumps rose on my skin. It was hard to get used to hearing him recite his last rites.

My husband's eyes found me, his breathing heavy.

"Angel?" My shoulder blades snapped together at the emptiness in his voice, the crazed look fixed on his face. I had to be strong right now. For him. No freaking out for some pedophile who didn't deserve any of my sympathy. "My angel, why are you crying?"

My brows furrowed and I touched my cheeks. They were damp. "I'm glad you made him pay, that's all."

"Only thanks to you." His voice softened, the crazy in his eyes slowly retreating. "I couldn't have done it without you."

He extended his blood-stained hand and I closed the distance, taking it without hesitation. After all, none of us were innocent in this world. Not my father. Not his. Not this priest who lay dead at our feet.

"Yes, you could have," I assured him, my gaze bouncing between his beautiful eyes. "But all that matters is that you got your justice and found your peace." My skin prickled for Christian and what was sure to be a long road of recovery ahead. "Shall we go?"

He nodded and stepped over the lump on the floor. "Let's get the fuck out of here."

Holding his hand in mine, we slipped into the dark the same way we entered and followed the shadows all the way to our hotel room.

Chapter Twenty-Seven

PRIEST

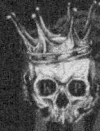

I was buying time: I knew it, my brother and cousins knew it, but she didn't.

While we followed Father Gabriel around Rome, my yacht had made its way to Italy. I had to ensure we had a way out of Italy. It proved the right thing to do.

The same night Father Gabriel took his last breath, we boarded my yacht in the small town at the mouth of the Tiber River. It was a major trading port, and during Mussolini's time, a small town, Lido di Ostia, expanded in the area around the beach.

We sailed to Monaco, where we stopped for a brief business deal with the Corsican mafia. It was the closest thing to neutral territory that neither the DiLustros nor the Corsican mafia owned, but I didn't want to take any chances.

After the rush of torturing Father Gabriel, dealing with the Corsicans felt like a nuisance. I didn't bother dragging anyone with me on the dinghy, opting to leave my guards to watch over Ivy who was sound asleep in our bed.

Our bed. Fuck, I never thought I'd like the idea of having someone share my bed.

My jaw set tightly as I entered a palace in the neighborhood that exuded luxury and exclusivity. It was situated in the Carre d'Or, or Golden Square which was a small area located between Avenue des Beaux-Arts, Avenue de Monte-Carlo, Boulevard des Moulins, and the Mediterranean Sea.

My usual rage-fueled instincts had dimmed, and it had everything to do with Vittoria and Father Gabriel no longer walking this earth. Although, one fear remained: that my wife would learn the secrets shrouding her athair's death. With everything she'd just done for me, I wanted to protect her from the pain that would inevitably come. She and Juliette... well, they were more than friends. They were like sisters.

The elevator stopped at the top floor and the gloomy thoughts vanished, and in their place was an expressionless mask. I stepped out into the lavish, gilded entryway, ready to face whatever came at me.

Jean-Baptiste sat in the corner, his pants at his ankles

and some bimbo on his lap. I couldn't help but roll my eyes. He was even dumber than I thought to be caught with his pants down. I was almost tempted to slice his throat right here and now so I'd never have to see his face again.

Unfortunately, I had to be smart about this alliance—what with him being the head of the Corsican mafia. And then there was the small matter of his armed guards scattered around every corner of this property.

"DiLustro," he greeted me, leaning over the table and snorting coke off a mirror, his woman grinding up and down on his dick. "Want some?"

I curled my hands into fists, shooting him a disgusted look. I didn't even bother to clarify what he was offering. "I'll pass."

Jean-Baptiste leaned back and wiped his nose, then smacked his whore's ass. It was then that I noticed his brother, who was Jean-Baptiste's enforcer. Sébastien Noël Blanchet. All my intel showed that while Jean-Baptiste partied like a tragic "where are they now" rockstar, it was Sébastien who kept their men in line. He was a force to be reckoned with, a thug in a suit with a lot more brains than he let on.

Although, at this moment, he looked bored and fucking angry.

"Let's get to work," I gritted.

Jean-Baptiste chuckled. "The king walks in and he's ready to hold court. Let's have fun first."

My molars ground. "Well, best not keep me waiting, then."

"Relax." Jean-Baptiste grinned like I'd just uttered a joke. "We have all the time in the world."

My fingers itched to shorten his lifespan.

Sébastien cleared his throat, ignoring his brother—still in the midst of fucking—and stepped forward, extending his hand. "Thank you for meeting us, Priest."

We shook, and I gave him a terse nod. "I don't discuss business in front of outsiders."

He nodded, then turned around, but not before shooting an annoyed look at his brother.

He guided me toward a separate room, the dramatized moans and groans following our steps until the door shut behind us.

"Just the two of us, then?" I asked.

"I hope you don't mind." Sébastien waved a hand around the beautiful old library, the floor-to-ceiling shelves filled with leather-bound books. "This meeting will go faster that way."

I nodded.

We both took seats on the couch, opposite each other. Rumor had it that Sébastien was as ruthless as Jean-Baptiste was lazy and impulsive.

"The French Ripper" was what people in the Corsican mafia called him.

Just like me, he was the product of a piece-of-shit

monster. The only difference: the cruelty lay at his father's hand.

Sébastien cleared his throat, almost as if he sensed my mind was elsewhere. It was hardly the time to be caught unaware.

"I'm all ears," I said. "Why did you drag me from my honeymoon bed for an urgent meeting, during which your brother's busy fucking a whore."

He cleared his throat again, rolling his shoulders and choosing not to comment. "Noted. Let's get you back to your woman."

I grunted, nodding. "Appreciate it."

"The Serbian mafia approached Jean-Baptiste. They want to use him as a way to penetrate the United States market. The problem is—"

"That Bogdan Dragović is a fucking lunatic," I grumbled. Everyone knew to stay away from the Serbs and Albanians. I was still on the fence about the mafia in Montenegro and Kosovo. For now, I'd been erring on the side of caution and not doing business with any of them.

Sébastien shifted in his seat, bringing up his ankle to rest on his opposite knee. "That, but even more so, he's a wild card, and I'm certain he has ulterior motives."

He looked grim.

"They've been calling him the young lion for a reason," I pointed out. "But what does any of this have to do with me?"

"Bogdan wants Philly." Alright, this was a problem.

"And Jean-Baptiste promised he'd get him the rule of the city. If he fails, he gets *our* territory in France."

"It sounds like you're going to lose your territory." Because there was no way in hell I'd let anyone into Philly. "I'm not exactly known for sharing."

Especially not with the Serbian crime family, who tended to behead their enemies if the situation even lightly called for it. They were ruthless, and Bogdan was at the helm of it all.

"I thought you might say that." He nodded to me coolly. "As a token of goodwill, and assurance that we all remain in business, I have an offer for you."

My brows shot up. "Okay... and what exactly is this offer?"

"Freedom to move products across our boundary lines. It's your way into Europe."

I tilted my head, studying him closely, but Sébastien kept his mask firmly in place. It was what made him a better criminal and businessman than his brother—and most heads of criminal organizations, come to think of it.

"I already have a way into Europe," I deadpanned. "Through my wife's connection to the Murphy mafia. I have my own property in Ireland."

The latter wasn't common knowledge since Aisling had only just gifted it to me. Of course, I wasn't going to accept it, but Sébastien didn't need to know that.

The corners of his lips tugged up.

"Ireland is its own island. Not exactly easy to

smuggle into continental Europe without having access to a port here." I shook my head. He must have anticipated it because he added, "This access would be for you, your family, and your brothers-in-law."

My jaw clenched, wanting to refuse, but he knew exactly what he was doing when he threw in the cherry on top. He was offering me the ace card and using the Murphy brothers to seal the deal.

The problem was that shit would be fucked up the moment we pinned the death of Ivy's father on Sofia Volkov. And something told me that was just the tip of the iceberg.

Money talked, and it was exactly that which made this song-and-dance game conclude: I might need this ace card one day.

We sailed the Tyrrhenian Sea into the Mediterranean, where my family descended on my yacht like a pack of hyenas. It took them all of five fucking days. Basilio and Dante even brought their wives and my papà along with his new wife who were entertaining Ivy at the moment. Or vice versa, who knew with those girls?

I sat behind the desk in my office on the yacht, my brother and cousins surrounding me. Silence held steady in the room with their dark, DiLustro eyes on me.

When I was a little boy, I wished my eyes were their

color. That I held more resemblance to the DiLustro features, but not anymore. A truth that had everything to do with my wife, who accepted me just the way I was.

They had something to say, and I knew what it concerned, but still, I waited.

Basilio spoke first. "We should tell her."

My muscles tightened, revolting against the idea of hurting my wife with the news that her athair was murdered by her best friend with the help of the DiLustro family.

Forcing myself not to react, I leaned back in my chair. "No."

I wouldn't risk losing her for her best friend's stupidity. I'd finally found the woman meant for me, a woman who didn't care about my past and my faults. She was mine, I wouldn't risk losing her.

"Secrets have a tendency of surfacing," Emory chimed in, watching me with those inquisitive eyes. She had always been able to see more than she should.

My gaze narrowed. "Speaking from experience?"

She looked away, obviously hiding her own secrets. "This isn't about me. It's about you doing right by your wife."

"I know her better than you." I sounded like a scolded child, but aggravation had lit a small fire in my chest. "I don't tell you what to do with your love life, so don't tell me what to do with mine."

The fear of losing my wife raged inside me, hot and

unrelenting. I was sure I could keep this secret from her. It'd be the only secret between us, but I was certain it'd spell our destruction. Sofia Volkov had committed many sins and offenses—what was the harm in one more?

Emory shook her head in disapproval. "Christian," she started softly, resorting to my legal name, which she rarely used. "Please be reasonable. If you tell her now, she'll probably hold it against Juliette, and maybe us, but she won't hold it against you. If she learns you knew and didn't tell her, she won't forgive you."

I had a better idea: Giving Ivy the satisfaction of killing Sofia and avenging her father's death.

"Once Sofia is dead, we'll be the only ones with the knowledge of who really killed Ivy's father," I reasoned. "And I trust that none of you will reveal it."

"I agree," Dante chimed in for the first time. "It's a sound plan. Let's just kill Sofia and move past this. She has to die anyhow."

"Will your wife confess to Ivy?" I questioned, but I knew the answer already.

"No."

"I'm guessing you never revealed what happened to Wynter. Right?" I asked my cousin. If he suddenly started blabbing Syndicate secrets, I would have to resort to some drastic measures.

"Wynter doesn't know," Basilio answered coldly.

"I cannot *believe* you," Emory hissed. "Ivy deserves

to know. Keeping it from her is fucked up and you all know it."

"Her brothers called," Basilio mentioned casually, not acknowledging his sister, which usually meant he thought she was right.

"What did they want?"

"You should ask your wife because apparently she felt comfortable asking them to help you two kill Sofia."

"I'm assuming they're on board," Dante grumbled. "Even though it would be better if we kept it between us."

Basilio shrugged. "They want revenge too."

I sighed. "I can see this going wrong in so many ways."

"Can you see the future now?" Dante drawled, and Emory rolled her eyes.

I was starting to regret their visit. "Why don't you all go find some hobbies?"

"Why don't you?" Emory retorted dryly.

"I have one," I told her coldly.

"Chopping people up doesn't count," Basilio said, a smile playing in his eyes.

"Only the sick, irredeemable ones," I pointed out.

"You all are twice as fucked up as I am," Emory grumbled. "Can we get back to the point of our conversation?"

My expression darkened, telling her the topic was off the table. And if she didn't stop pushing, I'd shift the focus of this family group discussion to her. I knew exactly what secrets she was keeping these days.

Her gaze hardened and a smile touched my lips.

She was so touchy when it came to Killian Brennan. Not that she was ever a sharer before, but now with whatever was going on between the two of them, her lips were sewn shut.

I never thought I'd see the day.

"Okay, you two. Stop your staring contest. We all know who'll win," Basilio said. "What am I telling your wife's brothers, Priest?"

I drummed my fingers against the table, holding his gaze. "Tell them to join us, and when we spot Sofia Volkov, we'll shoot her before she can say a word."

"Doesn't it bother you that you will have to kill your great-grandmother?" Emory asked.

I rocked back in my chair. "No."

I didn't think of Sofia as my family just as I didn't think of Aisling as my mother. It took a lot more than genetics to be a family, and neither one of those women ticked the boxes for me. They were nowhere to be found when I needed them, so they missed their chance.

"Charming." Emory smiled wryly. "We sure as fuck turned out like a gravy family."

"Basilio seems to be happy with his ice princess, and my brother has found happiness with Juliette." My eyes settled on Emory. "So fucking sue me for wanting the same."

Emory's shoulders slumped.

"You deserve the same and you're getting it, Christian. I just don't want you to lose it." She stood and stopped in front of the door of my office before turning to me. "I'd strongly advise you to come clean with your wife before it all comes back and bites you in the ass." Her eyes darted to Dante and Basilio. "All of you."

I held in my response. So did Basilio and Dante.

As soon as she left, I kicked my feet up on my desk.

"You gotta love family meetings." *Fucking not.*

A whisper of tension tightened in my body, almost as if I sensed a dark cloud following this yacht drifting toward Montenegro.

Chapter Twenty-Eight

IVY

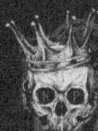

Hanging out on a 30-meter mega-yacht with split-level decks and a pool with your best friends and your dog wasn't a bad way to spend your afternoon. Not. At. All.

Up top was the master suite complete with a jacuzzi and access to the helipad, and down through the main cabin's corridor—where all ten luxury full-service cabins were now occupied by friends, family, and various staff —was a glass-bottom floor with a view to the ocean below. Each room was more impressive than the last. Large living spaces, lounges, three full bathrooms, and a main pool area in the rear.

Of course, Wynter, Juliette, and I immediately parked ourselves on the pool deck. Christian's father and Aisling —I couldn't get used to calling them my in-laws—opted to retreat back to their bedroom. And Cobra hung next to me, her head against my thigh, staring at me like I was the best thing that'd ever happened to her.

Fuck, I was happy. I had a husband who was lighter than I'd ever seen him and a dog who was chipping away at my heart one lick at a time.

"That dog is scary," Juliette muttered when she reached for me too suddenly. Cobra growled softly at her sudden movement, watching her like she was ready to maul her. I'd never let it go that far, but it felt good to know I was safe with Cobra. I might've finally found the one bodyguard I would never try to ditch.

"Wynter, do you think it's a good idea your mom's here?" I asked hesitantly. "Christian's still coming to terms with Aisling being his biological mother."

She chewed on her bottom lip. "I thought maybe it'd force them to talk it out."

I didn't think it was that simple, but I didn't voice my opinion. Juliette, on the other hand, didn't hold back. "Maybe Aunt Aisling needs to acknowledge that her decisions have fucked up a few lives."

I shot her a glare, urging her to proceed with caution. Considering she and Dante had finally reached a stage of mutual trust, I assumed he'd shared a thing or two about his and Christian's childhood.

Wynter's delicate eyebrows furrowed. "She fucked up her own life, nobody else's."

I shook my head at my friend. She couldn't be *that*

naive. But then, maybe she needed to believe that in order to move on.

"Just let them deal with whatever's going on in their own time," I recommended.

Juliette glanced away, her voice dry as gin as she muttered, "Yeah, give them another decade or two, I'm sure they'll work shit out."

"Jules," Wynter and I scolded, and she raised her palms up in surrender.

She hesitated, thick emotion laced through her voice.

"I'm sorry." I shot her a surprised look to find her face lost all color, and her voice was so quiet I almost missed her next words, "I'm the last person on this earth that should judge her."

Silence stretched out with a volatile edge, consuming and confusing.

"What do you mean?" I asked, frowning.

She waved her hand. "Oh, nothing."

Azure water surrounded us as far as we could see. The soft sound of waves crashing against the yacht as the boat bobbed, almost as if hovering above the water, contrasted with the strained conversation among us.

"If I knew my brother owned a yacht like this, I would have begged to borrow it months ago," Wynter remarked, breaking the tense silence and shifting away from the topic. She was wearing oversized sunglasses and a pink sundress, looking relaxed and serene. We didn't bother with bathing suits, instead just soaking up the sun and occasionally dipping our feet in the pool water.

"I'm so happy to see you both," I said, smiling wide.

"Same," Juliette said. "Plus, hanging out on a yacht is always a good idea."

Wynter and Juliette talked excitedly for the next few minutes while I watched them from my lounge chair, letting my mind drift to thoughts of Christian. I was infatuated with his smell, his hands, his voice, his rare smiles, the way he always seemed to appear when I found myself missing him.

What we had was complicated, but it worked for us. Life was good, and I was beginning to see that loving him was inevitable.

"You and my brother..." Wynter smirked, pulling me out of my happy thoughts. "You seem happy."

"Don't grill her," Juliette chastised. "They're gorgeous together. Let them be."

"I'm not grilling them. I'm just excited to see them happy," Wynter protested, her eyes growing soft. "And the way my brother looks at you, it makes me melt."

"Everything makes you melt." Juliette smirked. "Probably because of the hormones."

I gasped and sat up in my chair, crisscrossing my legs. "You're pregnant?"

Wynter sighed, then nodded her confirmation.

"I know, it didn't take long. You can say it," she muttered.

I let out a loud squeak. "That's amazing. I'm so tickled for you. Davina is having a baby. You're following right behind her. I hope—" Laughing, I stood up, grabbing her hand and pulling her into an embrace. "I'm just so ecstatic. You're going to be the best mom."

"This might be almost as good as stealing money," Juliette stated matter-of-factly as she joined the hug. "Maybe we can steal this yacht and turn it into a girls' trip. We might not have many more opportunities with Davina about to pop out a boy."

"No, this is better," I said, smiling. "Much, much better. Nothing compares."

"Besides, we'll be better at having babies than stealing," Wynter agreed.

Chapter Twenty-Nine

PRIEST

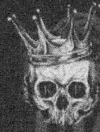

"You called the family meeting, Pa. Speak," I said, gritting my teeth while my eyes were locked on Aisling.

It wasn't often that my papà demanded a family meeting, but when he did, there was no denying him. So here we all were, piled up in the office on my fucking *honeymoon*.

I sat behind my desk, Papà and Aisling on the sofa, twin frowns on their faces, and Juliette sat stiffly in the chair with a staunch-looking Dante at her back.

"I've never sat in on a family meeting like this," Ivy remarked nervously. She was propped on the edge of my desk, her legs crossed and her bottom lip between her teeth. "Does this happen when someone's in trouble?"

"No, not necessarily," my papà answered. "But we need to address some recent hostilities."

I glared at him, then turned my eyes on Aisling. Ever since that woman had barged back into his life, he'd been getting increasingly involved. I liked him better when he was checked out of family affairs and out of my business.

"Let me guess. Mother dearest can't handle the DiLustro family dynamic." You'd be hard-pressed to miss the sarcasm in my voice. My papà clenched his teeth so hard I could hear his molars grinding. He glared at me while I feigned nonchalance. "But pardon me, you called the meeting, so please tell us what's troubling you."

"Watch it, son," he snapped.

"Okay, let's cool it, everyone," Dante cut in, trying to be the peacekeeper.

I leaned back in my seat, placing one hand around my wife's ankle. It was strange, but touching her always soothed me.

"I'm cool," I said, flicking a glance at Ivy. "You good, angel?"

She glanced between us, obviously not sure where any of this was heading. Her slim, pale neck shifted as she swallowed.

"Yeah, I'm good, thank you." She laughed, but it came out awkward.

"Good. Then, Dante and Christian, it's high time we addressed the elephant in the room," Papà insisted.

"We can't keep avoiding each other," Aisling pleaded, her voice brittle and her eyes falling downward. "Please. Whatever I need to do, just tell me."

"Well, that's easy." For a moment, Aisling's eyes flickered with hope, but I quickly extinguished it. "Stop trying. Stop coming around here at all, actually."

Aisling's gasp filled the room, and I felt Ivy's body tense. It took no time at all for Aisling's sniffles to start and crocodile tears to stream down her porcelain face.

Fuck her. Fuck my papà.

I really wasn't in the mood for family drama.

I was getting ready to scoop Ivy up and get out of here when my papà's booming voice stopped me.

"Enough!" His face turned red, his hand flexing on Aisling's shoulder. "We cannot go on as a family. Not like this."

"You can't force people to get along," Juliette said, her voice trembling.

"But I gave birth to him," Aisling protested, her voice cracking. "My heart already broke once, and now he's breaking it every time he treats me like a stranger."

More tears streamed down her face. Maybe I should feel something, but I didn't. Absolutely nothing. Although, judging by Ivy's trembling lip, Aisling was getting to her. That alone showed how manipulative she'd become.

"Why do you both hate me so much?" Aisling cried.

I stared at her while Dante watched her, his brows bent.

"Hate is a strong word," he remarked, clearly not comfortable with her show of emotion.

"I feel it," she protested. "You both hate me, but—"

She didn't finish her sentence, her eyes darting to our papà, and he finished for her. "But we think family therapy might be in order."

"Fuck that," I scoffed, standing up. "Ivy and I are leaving. In case it's not clear, we're not interested."

I threw one last glare at Aisling before ushering my wife out of this joke of a family gathering.

Thirty minutes I'd never get back.

I dragged her down the hallway and pulled her into our cabin, my muscles taut and the need to possess her clawing at me. I pinned Ivy against the door the moment it shut behind us. Tension in my shoulders still lingered, and it didn't take much to realize that I was quickly exchanging my old coping methods for a new one. We'd had a sex marathon, ensuring we christened every corner of this yacht in every position. I liked to take her from behind, sometimes with her all on fours, sometimes kneeling with my hands on her breasts. She loved it in any way, but I believed her favorite was missionary, our mouths molded together.

So I ensured at least once a day, I fucked her that way.

"Lock the door," she breathed against my lips. A soft click and I gripped the indent of her waist, which was so small I could probably connect my fingers if I tried.

I dropped a soft kiss to her mouth as she kissed me hungrily.

She yelped when I bit down on her bottom lip, drawing blood, but there was nothing but desire and love in them. I never wanted that look to vanish from her eyes.

"You okay?" she murmured against my lips.

Cupping her face, I tucked strands of her red hair behind her ears. "Yeah, just glad to have you alone."

I wondered if she'd be scandalized to know my thoughts, to discover what I wanted to do to her, but I dismissed it. She was my wife. She could handle a bit of scandal.

I rocked my hips against her warm cunt as I resumed tracing my lips along her soft skin, over her cheek, up her jaw.

"I want to own all of you," I rasped into her ear, unbuckling my pants. Goose bumps rose on her skin and her eyelids lowered. Her chest rose and fell with each heavy breath as I cut a path toward her gorgeous ass and kneaded at her through her sundress. "One day, I'm going to make this mine."

My shaft ached at the thought of it, already dripping with precum.

"Not today," she breathed.

"I agree." I trailed my palm up her thigh until her dress was draped over my arm. "But soon."

She swallowed and tipped her head back. "I can't decide if you're trying to seduce me or scare me."

"Maybe both," I said, snatching the neck of her sundress. The sound of shredding followed, her beautiful breasts spilling free. Sliding my lips to the shell of her ear, I tsked softly. "No bra. My wife's a temptress."

A shiver rolled through her, but she refused to acknowledge my words.

I lowered my head, palming the weight of her bare breasts. I squeezed the soft flesh and ran my thumb around her nipple, then sucked the pulse point on her throat, pulling the skin between my teeth to leave another mark behind.

I bit her nipple hard, then immediately eased the sting with my tongue.

"Fuck, you smell so good," she said in a husky voice.

I ran my thumb across her nipple and her ragged exhale pushed between her parted lips. Fuck, she was so sexy.

I slid my hand down her stomach, between her legs, and pressed my thumb against her clit, applying the slightest amount of pressure. She closed her eyes tight, rolling her hips.

"Please, Christian," she breathed, her ruined dress falling to the ground. Her panties soon followed. "I need you inside me."

It was all the encouragement I needed. I sank inside her soaked pussy, stretching her wide. Her head fell back against the door, banging it lightly.

"Fuck, that feels—"

"So. Fucking. Good." I punctuated each word with a thrust of my hips, driving deeper inside her with every stroke.

"Yes!"

Her legs wrapped snugly around my waist and I buried my face against her neck, inhaling her sweet scent while I pistoned in and out of her.

Her muscles clamped around me, milking me as she moaned my name. The sight of her flooded thick heat through my veins, curling down my spine and settling heavily in my cock. My blood began to pound in my ears.

I watched her eyes roll back, a pink flush warming her cheeks as she orgasmed, clenching around me. I lost all control, following right behind her and finding my own release.

For a long while, we panted, breathing heavily as we came down from the high. I ran my nose along her jawline, inhaling her scent like the worst kind of addict.

And the need to claim her again awoke my veins like an inferno.

Chapter Thirty

IVY

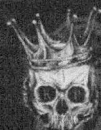

We heard the helicopter before we saw it.

"Ah, they're here," Basilio murmured, and Christian gave him a terse nod.

"This is sure to turn into a shit show," Dante grumbled.

"Who's here?" I asked, shielding my eyes from the sun.

"Come on, you'll see." Christian stood and offered me his hand. By the time we wandered over to the helipad, the chopper had touched down and a familiar figure emerged, closely followed by two more.

"Hey there, sis," greeted Aemon.

The familiar Gaelic words slid down my spine and

my hand slipped from my husband's as I ran across the deck and into my brothers' arms.

"Never expected such a warm welcome." Bren and Caelan laughed. "Did you miss us?"

"Of course," I said, happy tears stinging my eyes. "I always miss you."

"You just don't want to be holed up in Ireland," Aemon remarked half-jokingly.

I rolled my eyes, not bothering to correct him. I loved Ireland, but they knew I thought it was suffocating.

"What brings you here?" I asked instead.

"Sofia Volkov has been spotted in Montenegro," Bren explained, and my stomach knotted painfully. Sofia would remain a shameful secret until we laid her to rest, but first she had to pay for Athair's death. And there was a part of me that wanted to learn more about my twin sisters—the piece of this nightmare puzzle that my brothers still didn't think I knew about.

"It's time we kill the bitch," Caelan hissed, his eyes darting over my shoulder to Christian as he approached us. He must've hung back to let us catch up, but I could feel the weight of his stare on me now. "I still cannot believe your husband is related to that woman."

Christian's expression was unreadable. While he had strong feelings about his biological mother and step-mother, he remained unmoved about Sofia Volkov. Not surprising I guess, considering he never had the displeasure of meeting her.

"I can't control my blood relations any more than you can," Christian stated simply, watching my brothers with those inquisitive eyes that I had a feeling saw more than they should. "I'm sure your father has done a thing or two that you're ashamed of."

Bren's gaze narrowed. "But our father wasn't some psychotic bitch. There seems to be no shortage of those in your bloodline."

"I certainly hope it's not part of your DNA," Caelan added, studying Christian as if he was some kind of test subject. A lesser man might've shriveled under his returning gaze, but my brother was either oblivious to it or flat-out ignored it as he nudged my brothers and said, "We have future nephews and nieces to consider, don't we, gentlemen."

Christian's body stiffened beside me and aggravation lit in my chest, but I kept my voice indifferent. "You three are guests on his boat—"

"*Our*," he corrected, and I raised my brow. "It's our yacht, angel."

I flashed him a smile, my cheeks flushing, then returned my attention to my brothers and started over. "You're guests on our yacht, so I'd ask that you refrain from insulting my husband. Besides, he's doing us a favor."

Aemon, who could rage when the occasion called for it but also had the most rational head on his shoulders, finally chimed in. "You're right, little sister. Forgive us."

Eager to break the tension, I smiled and nodded. "Want a tour? Or want to join us at the pool?"

Aemon's gaze locked on Christian. "Actually, I'd like to go over the plan of attack."

My other brothers nodded in agreement.

"I fucking hate surprises," Bren muttered. "And right now, everything will be a surprise."

"Maybe you should stay behind, then." Caelan snickered, slapping him on the shoulder. "Sunbathe on this yacht in the nude."

I was making a puking face as my other two brothers cracked up when one of the crew members arrived with a tray of drinks.

"Bren, if I catch you in the nude, you're a dead man," Christian warned casually, and everyone snickered. "As far as a plan, there isn't one. We catch Sofia off guard, end her, and that'll be the end of that."

Bren nodded, completely unfazed by the unsubtle threat he'd just received, then grabbed a drink from the tray and shoved an hors d'oeuvre into his mouth.

"We want to question her," Aemon stated. Waves of ice rolled from Christian, threatening to swallow this entire yacht, but Aemon ignored it. "I want to know why exactly she killed our father."

And how far back their business and personal relationship went, was his unspoken intention.

"I won't risk Sofia slipping through our fingers so you can have a conversation with the woman."

Aemon frowned, studying my husband as if trying to uncover his angle. Truthfully, I was surprised at his response too. I knew it was common in our world to extract information from captives; killing first and asking questions later left you blind to schemes.

And Christian knew that. So why take that approach?

"Fuck that," Bren hissed. He'd always been the loose cannon in our family, but we didn't fault him for it since we knew he had a heart of gold. "How will we uncover her agenda?"

"Sofia's agenda is fucking people over," Christian deadpanned. "Nothing more. Nothing less."

"She kills with a purpose," Bren argued. "So unless you and your family are hiding something, we'll be holding her for questioning." His tone was dismissive, almost challenging.

Fury reflected in Christian's gaze when he spoke again. "Are you accusing me and my family of something?"

Caelan jumped in to try to smooth out the situation. "Absolutely not, but you have to admit, it's unusual that none of you would want answers from Sofia, especially considering your familial connections to the woman."

Uncertainty tugged at my throat and nervousness radiated in my every cell, pouring out of me.

"Let's leave this for now," Aemon ended up chiming in, his brow rising in humor. "We are guests after all."

And just like that, my other two brothers fell in line.

251

Except nobody was fooled—at least I wasn't—that they'd dropped the subject.

Priest

A few minutes before seven, everyone gathered for dinner. Ivy was glowing from a day spent in the sun, her hazel eyes shining. I hadn't seen her like this yet—so content and free-spirited.

Her brothers' visit wasn't exactly a welcomed one, but it was either that or risk them getting to Sofia before us. They'd been on their way to Montenegro following a tip from Danil Popov's father, who'd arranged a meeting with Sofia.

I couldn't let that happen without me, so I invited them here. Everything they said about keeping your friends close and your enemies closer... well, it applied to family too.

My gaze flicked to my sister-in-law, slightly agitated that she'd put us all in this position. Of course, she couldn't have known when she set out on her revenge path that Ivy's father would be on the list.

Ivy said something to Juliette who was seated on the other side of her, and the latter smiled, but if you looked carefully, you'd notice the steady worry in Juliette's eyes. She was going out of her way to be there for Ivy, probably plagued by her guilt and fear that her secret would come out. If it did, it'd destroy more than one life.

Fuck, if only Dante wasn't so obsessed with her.

Ivy was seated next to me, and thankfully all my cousins, brothers, and brothers-in-law worked to distract me from my birth mother's presence, who sat next to my papà on the opposite side of the dining room table.

"The gelato we ate in Rome was so delicious." My wife beamed, speaking about our honeymoon, leaving out the main reason we were there. It was just who Ivy was. A softy with a positive outlook on life. She made it too easy to feel comfortable around her. "And the cappuccinos are to die for."

"Let's not talk about gelato and cappuccinos until later," Aisling said. "Otherwise, we might spoil everyone's dinner."

My hand on Ivy's thigh tightened, and she gave me a curious look, but she didn't say anything.

"I'm always in the mood to talk about gelato," Juliette commented, slicing off a chunk of her filet mignon and popping it into her mouth.

"Give me gelato anytime," Wynter teased, grinning at her husband with a smug look in her eyes. "Anywhere, anytime."

"Ivy can talk about anything her heart desires," I said, offering Aisling a tight smile. "In fact, if she or anyone else at this table is interested in eating ice cream right here and now, please feel free to do so." I narrowed my eyes. "Ivy is a grown woman and certainly doesn't need any permission from guests."

Was it skirting the "passive" and going straight to aggressive? Probably. Did I care? Fuck no.

Aisling pursed her lips, flashing me an uneasy smile, while my father looked about ready to explode. *Good.*

"It's okay, darling," she assured, patting his hand.

Ivy glanced at me, then at Aisling, uncertainty in her wrinkled brow. I kept my gaze locked on my father, a muscle in his face twitching. Just as he opened his mouth to say something, Dante jumped in.

"Maybe we can sample some ice cream after dinner." He smiled at Aisling with too much gusto. "Heck, maybe even eat it all night."

"I vote yes," Juliette said, once again going out of her way to take Ivy's side. "Let's take a vote, shall we?"

Aisling went perfectly still, her eyes bouncing between Ivy and me before standing to her feet.

"I'm going to call it a night," she said with a strained smile, my father taking her lead. It wasn't until the two of them left the dining room that the tension left the room. The commotion and jokes started, turning our dinner unexpectedly lively and full of discussions on the best and worst desserts while I remained quiet, observing.

Ivy and her friends threw around some jokes about the extra-curricular activities that'd put them on our radar two years ago. Ivy's brothers grumbled, unamused.

"Clearly we should have brought our sister back to Ireland a long time ago," Bren muttered.

I drew her hand to my mouth and pressed a kiss to it. "Too late. She's mine now."

And I wouldn't let anyone take her from me.

Ready to get this dinner over with, I gave Ivy a look and we stood as one, wishing our guests a good night. I'd become greedy for my wife, and I couldn't wait to get her alone.

She followed me down the hallway, but before we could even reach our cabin, I spun her to face me, grabbed the back of her neck, and kissed her deeply as her body molded to me and her arms wrapped around my neck.

"You must have a fetish for dark hallways," she murmured into my mouth, her voice breathless.

"Only when it comes to you," I admitted.

I brought my hands to her breasts, groaning at the feel of them in my palms, my hips grinding against her soft, welcoming body. Achingly hard and ready to fuck her, I grasped her upper thighs and hoisted her up.

She met my gaze, bearing down on my shaft and chasing her pleasure, and it had to be the most beautiful sight I'd ever seen. I bit down on her throat, then licked the spot, soothing the sting while she moaned.

It was then that the sound of footsteps registered and Aisling's voice rang through in the distance.

"Frank, we can't—"

"Bed, now," I hissed, dragging her toward the side of the yacht where our cabin was while she giggled softly.

Once there, I turned around, cupped her face, and ran a thumb across her cheek. "You're my salvation, angel. I want to fuck you nice and slow, but I also want to take you fast and dirty."

Her lips parted, a blush rising to her cheeks. She rose to her tiptoes and breathed three words against my lips: "Then do it."

Satisfaction ran hot through my blood. I wanted everything from her—every thought, every breath, every kiss.

I picked her up and carried her to the bed, then undressed her, leaving her in nothing but a bra, heels, and panties. And something about seeing her sprawled there almost naked had my chest growing tight. I didn't deserve her, but I was going to spend the rest of my life working on it.

"I love you, wife." It was surprisingly easy to admit, something about it making me feel lighter.

She shifted up onto her elbows. "You do?"

"I do. It's almost an annoying feeling, because it's all I think about. Somehow you sneak between my every heartbeat. Every word, every thought, every breath becomes yours. It's an exasperating feeling, and it's bad for business, if I'm being honest." Her mouth curved into a smile and I couldn't help rolling my eyes. "Luckily for me, my brother has been picking up the slack now that *his* lovesickness has worn off slightly. So yes, I love you,

Ivy DiLustro. I love your loyalty. I love that you're soft and strong. I love that you don't run from my crazy."

I sat here, professing my love. It wasn't ideal, but fuck it. Nothing in this relationship had been ideal, but it was so fucking right.

Chapter Thirty-One

IVY

Every word that passed Christian's lips filled my heart to the point of bursting. This man seemed to know my deepest desires and fears. He accepted them both.

"You're not crazy," I breathed. "Far from it." In a short span of time, he'd come to know me better than anyone. He'd faced his demons for me—for us—and made our connection stronger. *I loved him.* "I meant every one of my vows. Ours might've been an unconventional beginning, but I wouldn't have it any other way. I love you, Christian. I'm yours."

"And I'm yours."

Then he kissed me, rough and consuming, as I ripped open his shirt, sending the buttons clattering to the wood floor. He yanked it off while I fumbled with his belt and pants, my desire boiling to a frenzy.

He shed the remainder of his clothes and then he stilled, watching me with reverence in his eyes.

"Fuck, angel… Wife… You're beautiful."

I lowered my gaze to my emerald lacy bra, matching panties, and pair of nude heels, then returned to look at him. "I'm glad you think so," I murmured. "Because you're stuck with me."

The corners of his lips lifted. "Thank God for that."

He slid his calloused hand down my inner thigh, only to trace it back up and cup my sex over the silky material of my thong. His free hand tugged my strapless bra down, freeing my breasts so they sat atop the padded cups. For several heartbeats, he just stared at them before he brought his half-lidded, lust-filled gaze up to mine and removed my bra.

He bent his head and took a nipple in his mouth, his other hand dragging my thong down my legs. Lowering himself to his knees, he threw them to the side, his gaze focused on the little patch of hair between my thighs.

His eyes darkened and a shiver rolled through me.

He shouldered my legs apart, leaving me open to him, and began to devour me. When he came up for air, his eyes dazed, he draped my legs over his back, then stood up with me seated on his shoulders.

My back pressed against the wall for support while his face buried in my pussy, he made the most erotic sounds. Like he was eating delicious, ripe fruit. He was loving every second of this moment just as much as I was.

The growl of satisfaction that escaped him vibrated against me. I grabbed a fistful of his hair, grinding myself against his mouth.

The pleasure was overwhelming. All-consuming. My thighs trembled, resisting the orgasm that was just out of reach, wanting to stay like this for the rest of my days.

"Christian… Oh, God…" I breathed, a bead of sweat trickling down my breasts. "I'm so close."

A scrape of teeth against my clit and the orgasm barreled into me. My eyes rolled back in my head, my spine arching off the wall.

Waves of pleasure short-circuited every single cell in my body.

Pulsing. Vibrating. Energizing.

Until I was floating on a cloud, blissfully unaware of my surroundings. My feet hit the ground but Christian steadied me, offering me his strength. It was a good thing too because my quivering legs didn't stand a chance of holding me upright.

"I want to reciprocate," I murmured into the crook of his neck. Nervous jitters buzzed through me, and Christian, being who he was, picked up on it.

"You don't have to."

I smiled and watched him, my gaze heavy.

"There's nothing I want more," I whispered, hesitating only for a moment. "It's just that I... I haven't done it before."

I swallowed as awareness settled between us and I slid to the floor. His hand gently—*painfully* gently— came to the back of my neck, gathering up my hair with his deft fingers.

Tension rolled through him and I paused, locking eyes with him. "You'll tell me if you don't like it. Right?"

I was scared I'd be a disappointment. Or even worse, set him back in his healing. Over the past weeks, I noticed Christian getting more comfortable with touch. It made me hopeful that he craved me as much as I did him. But I knew we hadn't crossed all the bridges, and there were still ghosts haunting him. I witnessed the occasional bad dream or look full of old ghosts.

"I like everything you do, wife."

I studied every inch of his beautiful body, from the strong column of his throat down to his muscular abdomen. And then there was the tattoo on his abs that resembled the skull in his club in Philly, right below the Kingpins of the Syndicate sign. It made me drool as I explored it, trailing my fingers over his hard muscles all the way down to his erection.

My hand trembled as I wrapped my fingers around his erection. And it was then that I noticed the ink etched on his cock.

"What is that?" I rasped, leaning forward. His cock

was tattooed with vines, the evergreen climbing over the length of his shaft, blue, black, and red ink swirling around it like... *ivy.*

"You told me to get a tattoo." He shrugged, but his blue eyes were blazing.

I had no words, the implications of this hitting me all at once. When had he...? "I didn't mean on your dick."

"If you want me to tattoo you on my chest, I'll do that too. Want my entire body inked in ivy and the letters of your name? Just say the word."

Holy. Fucking. Shit. That was hot as hell.

"No, don't," I murmured, pressing a soft kiss to the tip of his cock. "I like it just like this. Our own little secret."

"Forever," he breathed, and I drowned in his gaze. Emotions threatened to swallow me whole as I leaned forward, rubbing my cheek against his length. Hard and thick. Smooth and warm.

A shiver racked his body before he brought the head of his shaft to my lips.

I licked him from base to tip and he pulled in a strained breath as he watched me with eyes that had grown hazy. I laved at him with my tongue, humming with approval. I ran my tongue across his crown and then finally slid him into my mouth.

"Fuck." His head fell back, before he returned his eyes on me and cupped my face, caressing my cheek with his thumb. "Suck," he demanded.

My pulse drummed between my thighs at his command, and sparks of pleasure fluttered through me. I sucked him, taking him deeper into my mouth, gliding up and down.

"Look at me," he ordered roughly, and my gaze instantly flicked to his. "That's it, angel. Fuck, I love you so much."

A raw wave of warmth flickered in my chest at the tender look in his eyes. Wisps of eternal love settled in and sealed our fates.

He inched deeper and my eyes watered. I stilled and he held my face as he fucked my mouth. He gave me everything, holding nothing back.

I moaned around his cock, and he started thrusting into my mouth, faster and faster. Harder. Flesh slapped against flesh. Gurgles rose up my throat and then he pulled out at the last second and came all over my face— thick, salty ropes of cum coating my skin.

I watched him with his cum dripping off my face and darted my tongue out to lick as much of it as I could.

"Jesus fucking Christ, angel," he breathed, running a thumb across my bottom lip. "Are you trying to give me a heart attack?"

A small squeal escaped me when he suddenly lifted me by the backs of my thighs and laid me back on the bed.

"What are you doing to me?"

"Loving you."

He made a noise of contentment and I banded my arms around his neck, my legs around his middle.

"Fuck, I love this," he breathed before pushing inside me so deeply it tore a gasp from my throat. He angled his hips so he hit that spot inside me, making me see stars. He kept surging deeper—rougher, harder, faster—again… and again… and again until he was reaching into the depths of my soul.

"Oh God, Christian, it's so good… I'm gonna—"

I clenched around him, my breathing ragged, and cried out his name as my pleasure detonated, my inner muscles spasming around him.

"Fuck," he grunted as his orgasm hit him. I clung to him as he came inside of me, his warm cum filling me up, dripping down my leg and making a mess of the sheets. When we came down from our high, I found his eyes on me, his hand flexing around my throat. And nothing had ever felt so right.

"Shower with me," he said roughly, a hint of something I couldn't decipher in his tone.

I followed him into the bathroom, and this time, when he pressed me up against the shower wall and slid into me, his movements were slower, gentler. Almost as if he were savoring every moment.

That night, as I drifted off to sleep, I couldn't ward off the sliver of worry that something was wrong.

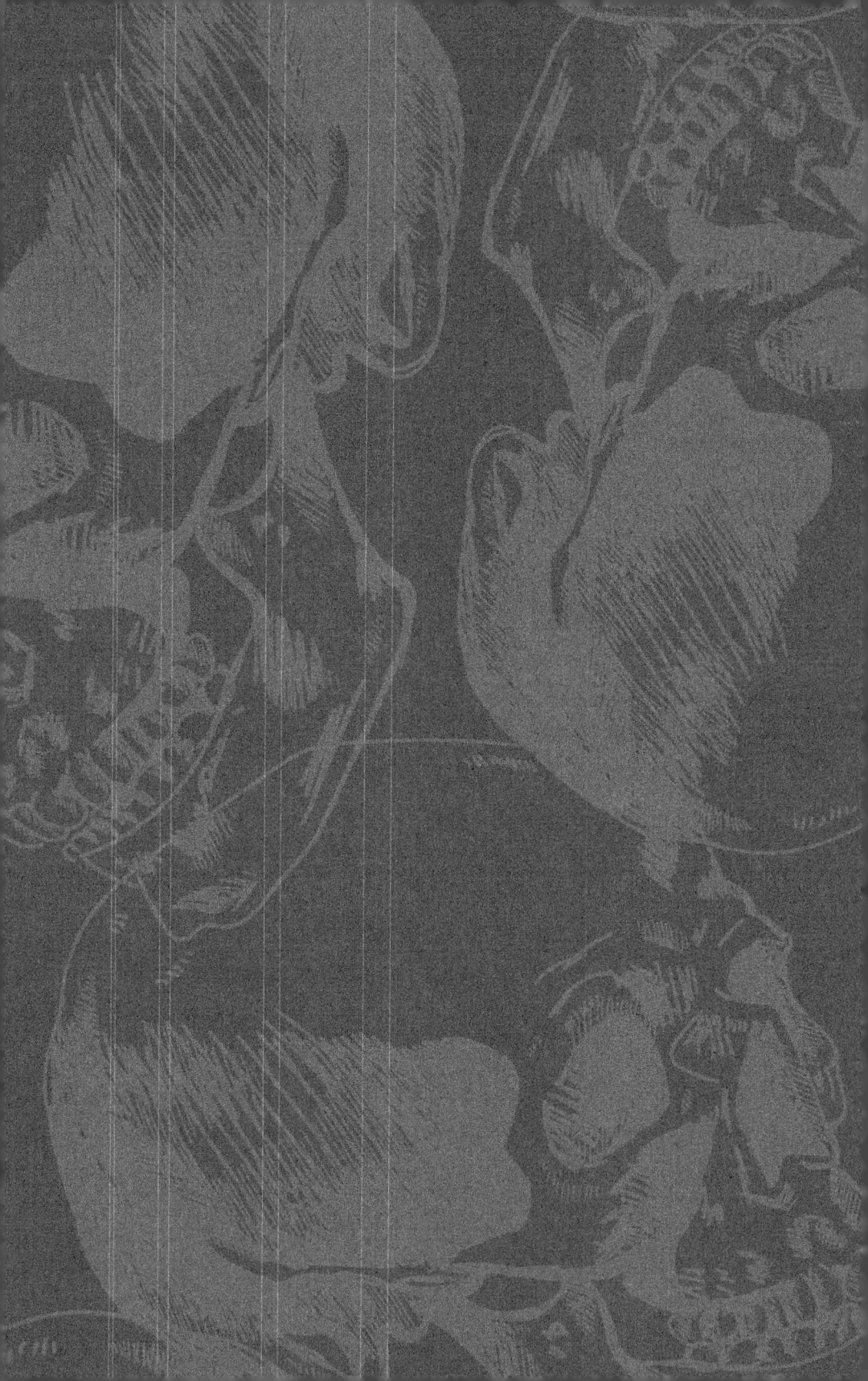

Chapter Thirty-Two

IVY

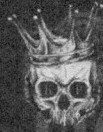

The DiLustros and my brothers wanted to leave me behind, insisting it was too dangerous for me and I wasn't the killer type, but I wouldn't hear it.

"I'm going," I stated stubbornly.

"Ivy—" Christian protested while his cousins' and Dante's eyes cut to him, as if imploring him to leave me behind. "Your brothers and I will be too distracted to ensure your safety."

Bren tried to grab my elbow, but before he could, I shoved it into his ribs. "I said I'm going."

"Stay with Wynter and I promise we'll handle it and be back before you even think to miss us." Christian tried to nudge me back onto his yacht, but I stepped away from him.

"I'm not going back on that boat."

I wanted to see the revenge delivered to Sofia Volkov. Besides, I hoped to question her about my sisters too.

"Ivy, let us handle it," Aemon reasoned, stepping forward to stand in front of me. "We'll all be distracted with your safety—"

I sidestepped him and fixed Christian with a stare. "Either I go with you guys, or I'll find my own way there."

Dante's dark gaze locked on me, something unnerving in it. "Ivy, I think you need to stay."

"I don't care what you think," I snapped, knowing I sounded like a stubborn child. "I'm going." Christian shook his head, but the remainder of the DiLustro family watched us closely, murmuring that I needed to stay. "You'll have to kill me to leave me behind," I whispered, locking eyes with my husband.

Christian looked back to his family and for a moment they simply stared at each other, until he said, "She's coming."

My brothers appeared at my side. "No weapons for her," Aemon grumbled, while my attention was locked on the DiLustros and Juliette, something in their expressions giving me pause.

But I had gotten my way, so whatever was going on there would have to wait.

Somewhere on the outskirts of the Budva Riviera in Montenegro, I stood with my husband, my brothers, Juliette and her husband, Basilio, and Emory. All of them were armed to the teeth, except for me.

It wasn't the smart call now that I thought about it as we stared at Alexei Nikolaev, Kingston Ashford, and a young woman who watched me warily. We'd had a run-in with Alexei during one of our heists, but unlike his brother Sasha, Alexei was standoffish. And right now, he looked none too happy to see us.

Well, too fucking bad.

My father deserved justice and, lovers or not, Sofia would pay for it with her life for fucking with him.

I let my gaze travel over the young girls who were filthy and evidently in shock, huddled around the three of them, almost as if they expected us to attack. Then the old memory sent a wave of fury down my spine along with heavy sorrow as realization dawned on me. Sofia Volkov was heavily involved in human trafficking. These girls must have been part of that ring.

I stared at the group of battered girls. My heart raced, but my mind was numb. My athair helped Sofia traffic girls, and this was the result of it. Simple as that. *Goddammit*. Acid coiled in the pit of my stomach that he'd willingly participate in such an event—blackmail or not.

Christian turned my head to him, his silent gaze boring into me, wordlessly asking me if I was okay. I gave him a terse nod, unable to admit out loud that my own athair could have had a role in something so grim. That these young, terrified women had been put through who knew what.

"You better have a good reason for being here." Alexei broke the silence.

"The kingpins and Murphys together," Kingston stated coldly, his eyes roving over us. "Something's afoot."

"My intel indicated Sofia Volkov would be here," Christian responded, his voice cold and his demeanor unperturbed.

"So you brought an army," Kingston snickered. "Sofia's not here."

"It appears your intel was all wrong, DiLustros and Murphys," the young woman who looked incredibly badass snapped, clutching her weapon in one hand and holding the shivering girl protectively with the other. "Now get lost."

Basilio chuckled. "You must have some balls on you. How about you start with introducing yourself?"

"Fuck. You."

"It's only fair," Dante chimed in. "Since you seem to know who we are."

"I'm Kingston," the dark-haired one answered. "And this is Alexei."

Christian scoffed. "We know who you two are. Who is she? And what's with the girl hanging off her like she's Mother Teresa?"

Kingston didn't look thrilled about my husband's reply, and I sensed a retort when the woman beat him to it. "I'm Lilith. And I'm going to kill you all if you don't move out of our fucking way. We have somewhere we need to be."

Their faces remained impassive masks, yet I couldn't shake off the feeling that the woman was lying. Not about killing us—she definitely meant that—but about who she was.

"Badass," Juliette commented. "I'm impressed."

The woman's jaw clenched, her eyes flashing with fury at my best friend.

"Sofia Volkov killed my father," I chimed in, but the woman didn't spare me a glance.

Instead, her eyes locked on Juliette. "No, she didn't. The person who killed Edward Murphy is standing right there next to you."

"What—"

"How—"

Every cell in me froze while my ears started to ring, her words on repeat. Who did she mean? Surely she was wrong. Then the woman smiled ferally. "Didn't you know?"

How could a woman with such a beautiful face deliver such horrible news?

"What do you mean?" My voice shook violently, my teeth clattering.

"Juliette DiLustro killed your father, Ivy." The chaos around us suddenly reflected what I felt inside me too. "Now, if you'll excuse us…"

Alexei shook his head. "Listen, we have to get these girls to safety. It's our priority. You guys figure this shit out," Alexei said in a cold voice, but I had a hard time hearing it. My world spun and spun until it landed upside down.

The woman, Alexei, and Kingston started moving, keeping the rescued girls surrounded, when the woman who just destroyed me glanced over her shoulder. "By the way, Sofia's not yours to kill. She's Kingston's." Her gaze met mine, unspoken words swimming in her eyes. "So back the fuck off, or you'll answer to me."

The three of them disappeared, but the rushing in my ears didn't.

I turned to stare at my best friend, her ghostly pale face a silent confession. But I needed to hear it. I *deserved* to hear it.

"Is it true?"

Everyone around us stood frozen as we watched each other.

"Ivy, please let me—"

"Is. It. True?" Tears glimmered in her eyes. "Tell me… please."

I stared at her, waiting. Willing her to shake my shoulders and tell me it was all a misunderstanding.

"Yes."

One fucking word and it stomped on my heart. All these months. All the conversations we'd had and time we'd spent together and she let me believe Sofia was the killer. Was she laughing at me behind my back?

Awkward silence followed while Juliette and I stared at each other. Years of friendship and loyalty turned into dust until all I saw in front of me was fakeness oozing from her.

She shifted and I realized she was growing uncomfortable beneath my stare.

Juliette glanced away, seeking out her husband. Basilio and his sister stood emotionless while Emory's gaze shimmered with pity, but she refused to get involved.

"I would have told you sooner—" Juliette started, but I didn't let her finish.

I gritted my teeth as a wave of resentment crashed over me.

"Let me guess, it slipped your mind," I spat, my gaze narrowing.

"Well, no… but I didn't want to lose you. I can't lose you too."

For a second, I was reminded of all the times we'd stuck by each other, through thick and thin, her difficulty coming to terms in learning her parentage, but I refused to let her pull on my heartstrings.

I snapped, the pain and deceit blurring my vision. I moved almost robotically, like I was watching this version of me from above, as I grabbed a chunk of her dark hair and pulled, jerking her head to the side. She looked at me, shocked, and lifted her hands on instinct. Ready to fight back.

From my peripheral vision, I noticed Dante trying to cut in to help his wife, but Christian held him back. "Let them work it out."

Basilio and Emory kept my brothers contained, though they didn't seem too concerned with my safety. I must look feral to have earned their confidence.

She pulled at my shirt, throwing us off-balance, and we fell to the ground. Amid the wreckage caused by the destruction left behind by Sofia Volkov, I straddled her and knocked her head against the ground.

Juliette screeched. "Ivy, stop."

"Get your hands off my wife," Dante growled.

"Stay out of this," Juliette and I hissed at him at the same time while Dante fought against Christian's hold.

"I'm going to murder you," Aemon growled at Juliette, but unlike Dante, he stood stoic, unwilling to fight against Emory—any woman, for that matter.

"You try, and I'll end your entire fucking family," Dante glowered at him while Basilio struggled to keep my other brothers at bay.

"I can't believe you would keep this from me!" I slapped Juliette's cheek. We might have all come as one force, but there was no fucking way we'd leave as one.

"If you would just let me explain," she said, shoving me to the side with her knee. A breath left my lungs while Juliette tugged my hair so hard my scalp burned.

"What is there to explain?" I growled, digging my nails into her wrist until she released my hair. Her body shoved me away, leaving me lying on my back, trying to catch my breath.

"You *killed* my dad, you fucking psycho."

She turned her head to look at me. "And *he* killed my father."

Something in the tone of her voice made me falter. She let out a bitter laugh. "What? You don't see me bitching about that, do you? Besides, your husband could have let you know."

I froze. "What?"

"Shut the fuck up, Juliette," Christian seethed, the fury vibrating from his every pore as he pulled me up off my best friend. Correction, *ex*-best friend.

"I want to hear what she has to say," I returned, a volcano full of betrayal threatening to explode in my chest.

"He knew," Juliette breathed heavily. "Your husband knew and he chose not to tell you."

My chest heaved from the exertion, though the anger was long gone, leaving only a cold detachment behind.

Ringing in my ears drowned out the bickering between my brothers and the DiLustro family.

They seethed, the indignation visible in their expressions. Aemon had his gun trained on Emory, but I knew he wouldn't shoot her. Bren wrestled against Basilio while Dante kept Caelan restrained.

"I'm sorry, Ivy," Juliette cried, like I was the one who'd torn up her heart today. Like I was the one who lied and pretended for fucking months that she was my friend, despite the fact that she killed my father. "I just didn't want to lose you. Please believe me."

Ignoring the nausea her words induced, I lifted my eyes and locked them with my husband. Surely he wouldn't deceive me like that. I stood by him, never judging. He'd never betray me like that.

Yet, the answer was right there, in his blue eyes I loved so much.

"And things were finally going well," Emory muttered under her breath.

I didn't bother asking her what she meant by that. Instead, I stared at Christian, his touch burning like frostbite and betrayal twisting my heart in a brutal grip.

The world was spinning. I needed to get away from here. From him. From her. From everyone.

Christian turned me to face him, his chest brushing against mine, and I flinched.

"Don't touch me," I hissed. This pain clawing at me

was too much. The people I loved—and trusted—the most, hurt me.

"Please, angel, let me—" I shook my head, and his words faltered. I couldn't do this. I just couldn't. I promised him forever, but he betrayed me. Lied to me. He must have seen something in my eyes because he released me.

I walked over to my brothers who stood waiting for guidance on what to do. *Yeah, there's a lot of that going around.* Their eyes met mine and worry crept into their expressions.

"I want to go home with you," I choked out.

They didn't hesitate. Their anger took a back seat to their concern for me.

"Let's go," Aemon gritted, glaring at my husband and his family. "And this isn't over."

"Not by a long shot," Bren added.

A coldness radiated from my chest, ready to consume me whole as I walked away from my husband and best friend.

It wasn't until we were back in lush green Ireland and far away from the DiLustros that the tears began to fall. For the loss of my athair, my best friend… and most of all, my husband who'd betrayed me.

Chapter Thirty-Three

PRIEST

I watched her leave, my chest hollow and my eyes burning. I wanted to run after her, yet I found myself frozen to my spot.

With the last glimpse of her as she disappeared from my view, her brothers in tow, something cold settled in my stomach.

"Priest, you can't let her go," Juliette cried, shivering against her husband. I couldn't look at her. I couldn't look at any of them. Not without risking going on a killing spree that started with my own family.

The worst part was that it was all my fucking fault. I should have been honest and told her what I knew. Should have. Could have. Would have.

And now it was too fucking late.

"Short of killing her brothers, he can't force her to

stay," Emory murmured. It was the closest to *I told you so* she could get.

I felt empty. Something tightened in my throat and pierced me in the fucking chest.

I rolled my shoulders to push the odd sensation and tension away. I inhaled deeply, and with an unnatural calmness, I turned around and faced my family.

"Let's go," I rasped, then gritted my teeth before adding, "We're done here."

The trip back to the yacht was a blur. I waited until I was alone, in the cabin where her scent still lingered, to unleash. Before I knew it, items were flying across the room. Hitting the wall and crumbling to pieces at my feet.

I swept all the toiletries off the bathroom counter and reveled in the sound of glass shattering and skidding across the hardwood.

I scrubbed a palm down my face and invited a dangerous calm to settle over me as bitterness bit into my chest.

This wasn't over. Not by a long shot.

Chapter Thirty-Four

IVY

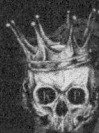

I was numb. Or maybe I felt too much. It didn't really matter because nothing would ever be the same.

My mood was gloomy which wasn't helping the affairs of my heart.

My eyes strayed to the sky and I hated that the usual gray, dreary English weather refused to cooperate today. I would prefer anything that would spare me from the blue.

The past twenty-four hours were dominated by my broken heartbeats, sending a raw ache through my chest. Everything seemed surreal. My best friend killed my father. The fact that Juliette could even do something like that—kill in cold blood—flabbergasted me. Now that I'd gotten some space and time to think about it, I couldn't stop my mind. Juliette wasn't who I thought she was. I questioned every word she'd ever spoken to me, everything she'd ever done. I kept thinking I would wake up and it would all be a bad dream, but I never did.

And my husband had kept it from me.

My vision blurred, the shimmer of the sun against the lush green grass contrasting my gloomy mood. But no tears came.

My brothers hadn't said a peep about my husband or friend, only exchanging worried glances whenever they thought I wasn't looking. They didn't try to tell me lies or feed me platitudes. Their motto was usually keeping things from me, accustomed to their idea of protecting me. After all, it was how I learned of Sofia and my twin sisters.

Instead, they let me sit in silence, staring at the beautiful landscape and deceiving weather that invited me to go outside. But I didn't. It was all deceitful, just like *they* were.

"You should get away from the window," Aemon urged. "You'll catch a cold."

"In a moment," I said. My voice sounded strange to my ears.

"Ivy, you can't keep—" Aemon broke off with a grunt when Bren punched him in the stomach.

"It's okay, sis. You do what you need to get over that douchebag and move on. You deserve so much more than that fucker. And we'll ensure the DiLustros and Juliette pay for what they've done."

All my pent-up emotions from the past twenty-four hours burst forth, and I was swept up in a tsunami of hurt, anger, and betrayal, but most of all heartbreak. I let it all wash over me and broke down into sobs. I cried until my eyes burned and my body ached.

Somehow, I found myself crying into my brothers' chests, all three of them wrapped around me in a protective cocoon.

Juliette lied to me. Christian lied by omission. For fucking *months*.

I'd lost a best friend and the love of my life in one fell swoop.

I knew I'd never be the same.

I finally depleted all my tears. After the grueling journey from Montenegro to Ireland, I had little left in my tank.

Two weeks had gone by since I walked away, and this ache in my chest refused to ease. Juliette had been blowing up my phone with messages and calls. I ignored them all. The news traveled fast because it didn't take long for Davina and Wynter to follow suit, but I ignored their calls too.

And soon a string of emails, voicemails, and messages followed through. It was all the same though.

They gave excuses and reasons why I should see the reason and forgive my best friend and husband.

But there had been nothing but silence from Christian, making my chest feel like it had been ripped out. It wasn't that I would have forgiven him, but maybe everything about us had been a lie.

My phone pinged on the table, but I ignored it. I didn't want to deal with anything in my empty-headed state. The sense of loss I could deal with. The betrayal, I couldn't. Ironically enough, Athair's betrayal didn't sting as much as my husband's and best friend's.

Instead of dealing with it, I avoided the world around me and lost myself in the Murphy library, rereading my old favorite thrillers and steering clear of anything romance-adjacent.

The cacophony of stomping boots and whispered voices came from another room, signaling my brothers were approaching. *Great.* I was thankful I had my brothers' support, but I needed space. Time. Answers.

If only I wasn't so afraid of them.

"Look what I found," Caelan announced when he stepped through the open door.

He grinned at me where I was cuddled up near the crackling fireplace, nothing but leather-bound books surrounding us. This used to be our parents' favorite room in the house and all of us had always gravitated to it when we were troubled. The only thing missing was

Cobra, who I yearned for with a fierceness I hadn't expected.

No sooner had Caelan walked in than my other two brothers followed, wide grins splitting their cheeks.

My brow furrowed at their appearance.

Caelan looked downright ridiculous with a bowl of popcorn in one hand and a bowl of ice cream in the other, a set of rubbery pink eyes stuck haphazardly on his cheeks. Aemon and Bren weren't far off, although their grumbling expressions offset the apparent spa-night accessories.

My brothers tried their best to put on happy faces around me, but I heard their whispers and saw their side-long glances. They were worried. Really worried. And then there was their fury: at Juliette and at the DiLustros.

"We need to talk," I said, folding my legs under me. My brothers exchanged glances before returning to stare at me with concern scrawled all over their faces. "First, what in the hell are you wearing?"

Bren slapped a hand to his face, pulling off the ridiculous pink sleeping mask and shaking his head. "I told you this was stupid," he grumbled.

"Pink makes girls happy," Caelan muttered. "I read that somewhere. Pajama parties, bubble baths, junk food, and chick flicks are how girls get over a breakup."

"And you're a fucking expert, right?" Aemon followed suit, tossing his mask on a nearby desk. "I should beat your ass for making me wear that shit."

Caelan rolled his eyes. "You can give it your best shot."

"I should just smother you both so you'll shut the fuck up," Bren grumbled. "This is about Ivy, remember?"

I sighed, pinching the bridge of my nose. I'd been seeing a therapist to help me talk things through, although I was starting to think that maybe a talk right now wasn't the best idea. There was nothing I wanted more than to seek oblivion in sleep. If only I'd stop dreaming about *him*. Maybe lying in the dark and listening to a sad-girl playlist was the answer.

I stood up, but before I could make a single step, Aemon came up to me. "Nope. You're not running off and hiding in your bedroom."

Bren nodded. "You wanted to talk, and we think that's a great idea."

They sat down, Bren and Caelan taking the sofa that protested under their weight and Aemon the leather recliner.

Resigned, I settled in and met my brothers' determined gazes.

"Okay, now let's talk," Bren demanded.

I didn't know where to start. Truthfully, I wasn't even sure where all this would end either. Sometimes oblivion was a blessed state, but I couldn't bury my head in the sand anymore.

"Athair had an affair with Sofia Volkov," I began,

taking a deep breath and meeting their eyes one by one. "And I know it went on long enough to produce twin daughters, who are now adults and around my age."

The oxygen in the room thinned, every breath was downright painful.

Aemon's shoulders tensed and he shared a glance with our brothers before meeting my eyes. "How do you know?"

I rolled my eyes. "I overheard you two talking."

"I didn't want you learning that about Athair." Aemon's face softened a smidge. "You idolized him so much."

I shook my head. "You all have to stop shielding me. I'm sick and tired of being treated with delicate gloves. After all, I didn't lose my shit when I learned about Sofia Volkov, did I?" My brothers seemed stunned into silence. "Now, tell me what you know."

"I don't know much. Just that the twins are older than you." My eyes shot to Aemon, and for the first time in weeks, I spotted fatigue in his expression. "They're a few years older than you."

"Alive?"

"One is," Bren answered.

"At least we think so," Caelan chimed in.

"It turns out Lilith, the woman we just met..." Bren started, and my mind traveled back to that fateful day when I learned of the betrayal and the strange group that consisted of Kingston, Alexei, and a woman who were rescuing trafficked women. "She's one of Athair's twin daughters, her name is Louisa."

I waited for the pain to come. And waited some more. Maybe I was too numb for it.

"I thought she said her name was Lilith."

Caelan let out an exasperated breath at the same time Bren grumbled, "Well, obviously she lied. No daughter of Sofia Volkov can be trusted."

I raised a skeptical brow. "You all lied too. Are you telling me none of you can be trusted?"

Aemon smacked Bren on the head and hissed, "Stop talking, you fool."

"I'd rather wear a pink onesie and a sleeping mask than sit here with you two talking buffoons," Caelan muttered, his warm eyes settling on me. "Listen, Ivy. It's as good a time as any for you to learn that men are idiots. Athair loved us, but if you're looking for answers as to why he strayed, you'll never know peace. That shit happens in this world."

He was right. Even mistresses were cheated on. I was naive to think Athair would be different, regardless of how attentive and caring he was toward Mama and us kids. Of course, had I understood who Sofia Volkov was when I met her, I would've put it all together a lot sooner.

"I know." I twisted my wrist nervously. "A memory came back to me when I overheard you three whispering about Sofia Volkov."

Bren shot Caelan a glare. "See? You're a talking buffoon too."

"You three really need to grow up," I said tiredly. "Stay focused so I can tell you what I know. I expect you to tell me the same." Aemon opened his mouth to protest and I raised my palm, silencing him. "I'm not asking for your business contacts and offshore bank account details. I just want to know about our family's fuckups."

Caelan snickered. "Well, men. You heard her."

Aemon shook his head. "Okay, little princess. Tell us what you remembered so we can air out Athair's dirty little secrets."

My life seemed to revolve around dirty little secrets, but now was not the time to ponder on that.

"I was maybe five," I started. "Athair took me with him to some docks. I got scared because there were kids there. Some were crying, others were hurt. He met with Sofia, and they mentioned the twins." I recounted the entire conversation, at least the way I remembered it, while my brothers listened. "He made me promise it was our secret, and honestly, by the next day, I'd forgotten."

Aemon muttered a curse, and Bren and Caelan didn't look any more pleased.

"Athair went too far," Aemon finally said. "Taking you there. He put you at risk."

I shrugged. "It's in the past now. The fact is we have two siblings out there—"

"They're not our family," Bren spat bitterly.

"They didn't ask to be put in this situation any more than we did," I protested. "We owe it to them to at least meet. If they don't support Sofia and her twisted business, I want to have them in my life. If they'll have me as their sister."

They reacted as predicted. Bren's scowl was deep, Caelan looked lost in thought, and Aemon kept his face a blank mask, giving nothing away.

When the silence stretched like a rubber band, I was the one to snap first. "Well, is anyone going to say anything?"

"I can reach out and coordinate a meeting with Kingston and the twin, whichever one's alive," Aemon finally said.

"How did the other twin die?" I asked, grief striking at the loss of a sister I never got the chance to meet.

"Not sure," Bren answered. "Not much is known about them, and the only information we could gather was on the one twin. Lilith, as she calls herself. Her real name is Louisa. Her twin's name is… was Liana."

"We should reach out to her," I suggested. "Try and make amends. Athair should have been there for them. Who knows what it would've been like to grow up under the care of Sofia Volkov." I shuddered just thinking of the horrors.

"And what if it's too late for her?" Aemon challenged, and I heard the unspoken words. *What if she's a monster like her mother?*

I bit the inside of my cheek, then quickly shook my head. "I don't think so. If she was, Alexei Nikolaev would have ended her."

"Or Kingston Ashford," Caelan added.

We shared glances, determination on our faces. "Then it's set," I said, ready to wrap things up. "We'll arrange a meeting."

"Not so fast, sister." Aemon sat back and crossed his arms, and I shot him a confused look. "We have to talk about your husband and your friend."

That stinging in my eyes was back, but still no tears. Maybe there were only so many allowed in a lifetime and I'd spent all mine. I dragged in a deep breath and steeled myself for what was to come. Christian didn't deserve my time and energy after the hurtful betrayal and lies, nor did Juliette.

If only my heart was on the same page.

"What about them?" My voice was surprisingly steady.

"We can't let them get away with what they did," Aemon stated matter-of-factly. "She killed Athair, and he..." His fists clenched and unclenched as if picturing beating Christian up. "He hurt you. You barely sleep, barely eat. All you do is stare into space. I should kill them."

My brothers were pains in the ass sometimes, but I still loved them. Still, that didn't mean they could go around killing people. Not to mention the mafia war it would start.

"I told you what I remembered of Athair's meeting with Sofia Volkov." I swallowed, unsure why I would even bother defending Juliette. These days she was the bane of my existence, every message received causing my insides to blaze like hellfire. I shoved the feelings somewhere deep and dark, hoping it'd cool off. "It's obvious he had something to do with the death of her birth parents."

Caelan leaned forward, his brow wrinkling as he studied me. "And what's your scumbag husband's excuse for lying to you?"

He wasn't wrong. He had a choice, and he opted to lie and shove the blame onto Sofia Volkov. The woman was a far cry from innocent, but she didn't murder our father.

What stung the most was that he took Dante and Juliette's side but kept me in the dark. It was obvious that whatever Christian's feelings were toward me, they weren't strong enough to stick by me through thick and thin.

Maybe it's for the best, I tried to comfort myself. At least I learned it early on rather than ten years down the road. There were no children involved—a thought that brought me almost as much comfort as it did pain.

"So your husband is fair game," Bren stated calmly, and my spine straightened.

"No." The word shot out of me like a bullet while my heart raced in my chest with images of a dead Christian. No, I couldn't live with that. "None of you will kill him. Understood?"

They shared glances, not saying a word, then nodded.

"Noted," Aemon said. "We won't kill him, we'll just make him hurt a bit."

I stood up, tsking. "*Do not* kill him." I handed out pointed looks, then headed for the door when a thought occurred to me and I stopped, throwing a glance over my shoulder. "But I would like my dog back."

Chapter Thirty-Five

PRIEST

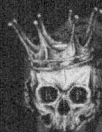

Aemon's fist slammed into my face, and I barely had a chance to catch myself before stumbling back onto my ass.

I'd been expecting this visit since the moment I heard Ivy's brother had landed in Philadelphia. Still, I made no move to avoid him or to defend myself. I deserved to have my ass handed to me by the head of the Murphy mafia.

"You. Motherfucking. Bastard," he hissed, his eyes wild as he kneed my stomach. I doubled over, the breath stolen from my lungs. Another punch followed, this time to the side of my ribs, and I still did nothing.

The pummeling continued until I dropped to my knees. Fucking ironic, considering this entire thing started with me on my knees in front of Ivy, teaching her a lesson for her shenanigans in my brother's casino. And now here her brother was, at the scene of that first encounter, laying me out.

But the physical pain was nothing compared to the pain I felt in my chest. I welcomed it. Relished it. It was what I deserved.

"What?" he snarled, looking at me like I was filth under his fingernails. He wasn't far off. "Too much of a coward to punch me back?"

"Something like that," I rasped.

Aemon hauled me up by my collar.

"You made my sister cry." His words sliced through me. "You sick psychopath. Maybe you should have stuck to your nickname and become a priest."

No physical beating could hurt more than the thoughts that'd been plaguing me. She accepted all my flaws and brokenness while I kept crucial information about her athair from her.

I dreamed of her face every night, of her expression before she walked away from me.

My stomach roiled.

I wanted her back. I wanted her in my city, in my house, in my bed. And she couldn't stand to even look at me.

One bad judgment call had cost me the one thing I couldn't live without.

And now I'd lost her, along with every other piece of

me that mattered. It all lay scattered around her feet, following her around wherever she went.

"Fucking hit me," Aemon growled. "Fight back so I can keep my promise to her and kill you fair and square."

I flashed a grim smile. "If she wants me dead, kill me."

His next blow sent a fresh burst of pain straight to my skull.

"She made me promise not to, you fucking asshole." His mouth twisted, and he shoved me away with disgust, his jaw flexing. "You don't deserve a place on this earth, never mind in her heart. Why in the fuck she still loves you, I'll never understand."

He was right. It would be easier if he killed me. But then his words sunk in and hope sparked like a flicker of light in the dark of a nightmare. Her heart... It was mine.

He kicked me, but I was too high on the realization that Ivy's heart was still mine. *She still loves me.*

"I will fucking end you and your entire family. Tell Juliette I'm coming for her too for betraying her best friend." His voice cracked on the words, his sister's pain as raw as if it were his own. "We'll never forgive you. Any of you DiLustros."

That makes two of us. But as I said before, I wasn't a good man, and I refused to give my wife up. I physically couldn't.

So I would fight for her. It had nothing to do with the Murphy brothers. My loyalties lay firmly with the only woman who'd ever accepted me for what and who I was. All my faults and invisible scars. She loved—possibly still did—all of me.

Aemon's face hardened. "If I ever see you near my sister again, I'll kill you."

Just the idea had my stomach churning all over again.

"Or we can make a business arrangement," I offered, coughing out blood and wiping my shirt sleeve over my face.

He shook his head. "You have nothing of interest to us, not unless you're ready to offer up your brother and his scheming wife."

I wasn't proud to admit—to myself at least—that if I didn't have an ace card, I would consider offering him precisely that.

"How about something better?"

He scoffed. "Such as?"

Shifting to kneel on my knees, I gripped both my hips with white-knuckled fists. "A way to smuggle your product into continental Europe."

He stilled. "Who said we want a way in there?"

I shrugged. "It's what got your athair into bed with Sofia. He always wanted to expand, but she double-crossed him." Surprise flashed across his expression. It wasn't a well-known fact. There were only three individuals who knew that fact, and two were now dead. How did I learn it, you might ask? I hacked into my dear great-grandmother's database that she kept away from her regular businesses. It was one of the most code-protected pieces of information I'd ever encountered. "She got knocked up, my guess on purpose, and instead used his little corner of coastal Ireland to move flesh from Europe to Russia and the States."

I watched Aemon process the information, seconds stretching into minutes.

"And what do you want in return?" Before I could answer, he added, "Not my sister."

It was a matter of saying the right thing. Words were currency in these parts. "Of course, if your sister doesn't want me, I won't force her."

"Get me the contacts and a way to move my product," he gritted. "And get me the dog my sister wants."

He shot one last disgusted glance in my direction before he left. The door banged shut, and I knelt there, staring out the window for what felt like hours while a single thought played on repeat.

I planned on taking what was mine if it killed me. I'd get on my knees and get my wife back and show her exactly how sorry I was.

I couldn't live without her light.

———————————

Three weeks of pure hell.

I didn't know how to get rid of this pain, this edginess beneath my skin, without resorting to violence. But for Ivy, I'd try anything.

It was how I'd found myself in Ireland, with my binoculars and a pair of Wellingtons, reduced to collecting intel from Murphy Castle's tree line like some Peeping Tom.

But as per usual, after trekking an hour each way through the woods, I only glimpsed my wife when she passed a window or stepped onto her balcony with her afternoon tea. I didn't fucking like it. Why couldn't she come onto the grounds and enjoy some fresh air?

"You look like shit." Dante sank into the chair opposite of me outside the dingy little inn on the outskirts of Dublin.

"Why are you here?" I muttered, my eyes locked on the fire flickering in the massive fireplace, not bothering to look up at him. "Aren't you breaking some mafia alliance or some shit?"

"No more than you are," he pointed out. "Besides, the Irish pricks know I'm here. They called me."

Now that piqued my interest. "What about?"

Dante arched his eyebrows. "Seriously?"

"Yes."

"Hm, let's think about it." I groaned. God, please rid me of my annoying family. "My wife killed their father, which, somehow, they've come to terms with. My brother is lurking on their territory. And no, before you ask, they haven't come to terms with that."

"I don't have time for this. Get to the point," I spat. I'd been in a foul mood since my wife left me, so it was best Dante stayed away. Unless he wanted to die.

He rubbed the back of his neck. "From where I'm standing, you have nothing but time. You haven't been to Philly in weeks, apparently happy letting the Corsicans poach your territory."

It would seem among this clusterfuck, I forgot to mention the agreement I reached with Sébastien. No matter. I didn't give a shit about anything anymore.

I picked up my glass of Macallan whiskey and shot him a dry look. "Dante, whatever it is you have to say, do it quickly and then get lost. I'm a busy man."

I drained the whiskey in one gulp. "First things first, Wynter asked me to deliver your package."

It didn't surprise me that she sent someone in her stead. Basilio mentioned she had been feeling sick in these early weeks of her pregnancy. I just wished she'd sent her husband rather than my brother. At least if I decided to kidnap my wife, Bas would be on board. Dante not so much.

"Thanks."

"Jean-Baptiste teamed up with Bogdan."

I arched my brow. "Your point?"

"Fuck, brother. We can't have the Serbian mafia roaming Philly, and Jean-Baptiste is up to no good. Rumor is he's running an underage prostitution ring."

Now that perked me up. Finally, a good excuse to

dish out some beatings. Maybe I'd pop back to my city and torture Jean-Baptiste a bit. Fuck, that sounded like a good plan, but first, I had to go back and get a glimpse of *her*.

I stared at my empty glass, wishing the alcohol would numb these feelings. It was so much better when I felt nothing.

"It's still morning," Dante remarked, nodding at my empty tumbler. "Don't you think it's a bit early for that?"

I didn't give two fucks.

"It's five o'clock somewhere."

He stared at me, then rolled his eyes. "Not funny."

"I thought it was."

Dante's face was calm, but disappointment washed over him and slammed into me. "This is not how you're going to get her back."

I drummed my fingers on the arm of my chair, contemplating whether I should have another shot of whiskey. "And pray tell. How do I get her back? Or maybe your wife knows?"

"For Christ's sake. Between both of you moping like you're headed for your own funerals, I'm going to lose my fucking cool."

I drummed my fingers on the glass. "When did you get so fucking dramatic?"

"Since I've been getting daily calls from the Irish pricks threatening to kill our entire family, since my wife's routine of crying herself to sleep began, and since my brother has given up on life altogether. Like I told Juliette, crying—or in your case, stalking—won't fix this. Do something."

Fuck, I needed another drink. I raised my hand and flagged the waiter-slash-inn owner for a refill. He appeared within a minute. At least he understood the assignment.

"Christian, are you even listening?"

I snorted. "The whole fucking inn is listening."

Dante's face fell and he stood up. "Fair warning: if they catch you on their property or territory after tomorrow, they'll kill you."

My jaw clenched and a vein throbbed in my temple. I downed my whiskey and got to my feet. Hope flickered on my brother's face, but my next words instantly extinguished it.

"I guess I better make the most of tonight."

I shrugged on my jacket. There was no time to waste; I had a promise to keep.

For better or for worse, she was my wife, and while she might not want to be around me right now, I'd be there for her.

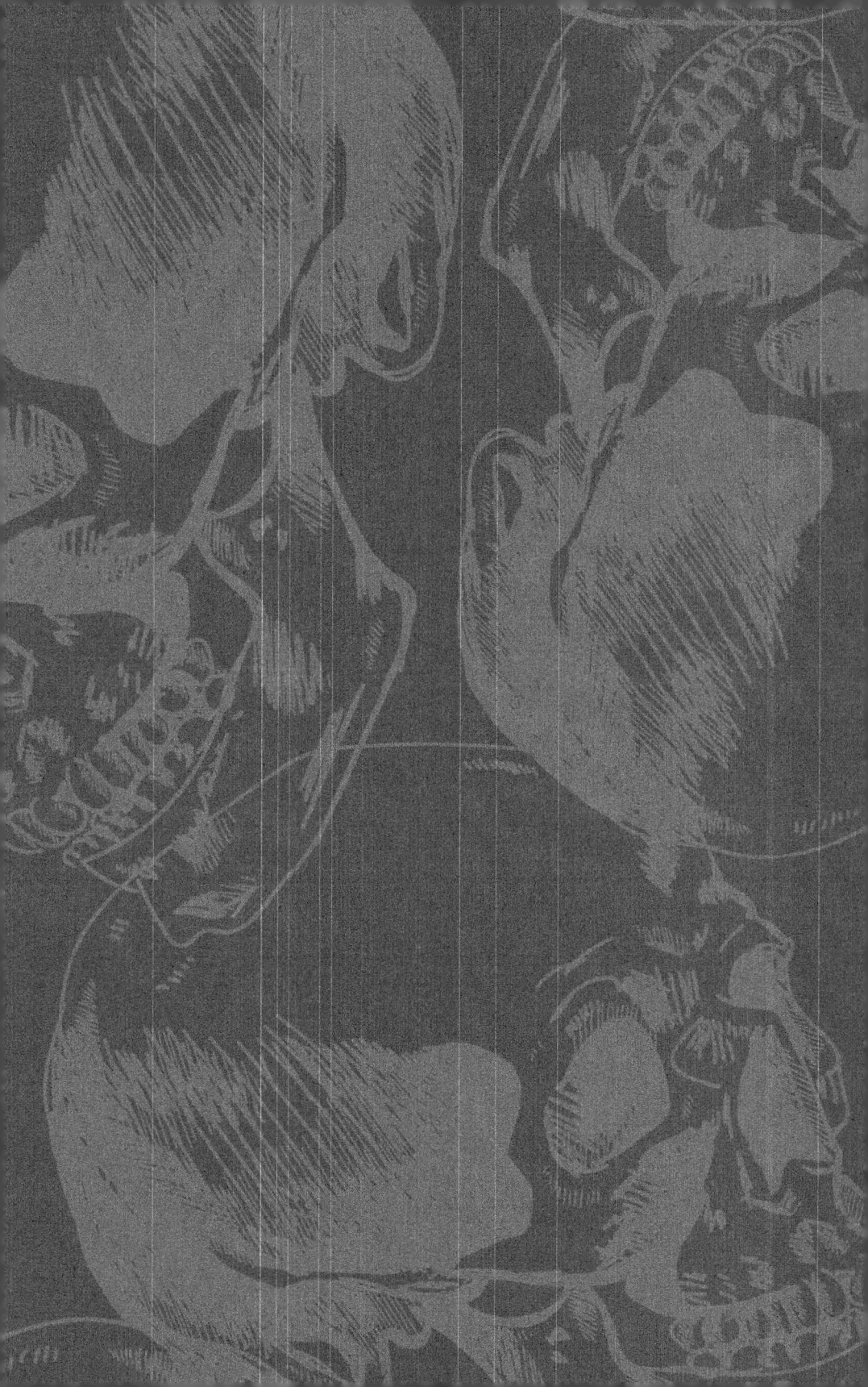

Chapter Thirty-Six

IVY

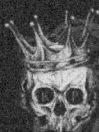

I caught a glimpse of a familiar shadow at the forest's edge and fury blasted through me, shocking me out of my stupor.

The months following my wedding should have been the best time of my life. Instead, they'd been the most heartbreaking. My only distraction from moping around like a brokenhearted, idiotic teenager was my search for my sisters.

And this… this *stalker* of mine who cowered in the shadows.

I was sick of it. Sick of people who didn't deserve me. Messages upon messages had been pouring in from Juliette, Wynter, Davina… all asking—no, demanding we talk it over. Expecting I should forgive and forget.

Wynter was mad at me because Christian was upset. I

understood he was her brother, but what about me? Davina remained neutral, and at this point it agitated me that she refused to pick a side. And Juliette… well, it wasn't worth getting into it again. She knew what she did.

I was fucking done allowing people to have this kind of hold over me.

Anger and indignation rushed through my veins, compelling me to go out there and face my husband. I forced myself out of bed, took a shower, and brushed my teeth, then stomped out of the bedroom in sweatpants and a hoodie. At the entrance, I shoved my feet into green boots and was just about to make my way outside when my brother's voice boomed.

"Where are you going?" I slowly turned around to find Aemon's stoic, watchful face.

"Outside."

"It's not a good time."

I gritted my teeth. Our entire household was aware of Christian lurking in the woods surrounding our estate, but nobody spoke about it. Like if we pretended it wasn't happening, it might eventually stop.

"I have to talk to him."

"I'll come—"

"Alone."

A small frown took over his face. "I don't think—"

I shook my head. "I mean it, Aemon. This is something I have to do on my own." I took a deep breath, smothering the snappy comment that fought to make its way out of my mouth. "I appreciate everything you've done. I'm so lucky to have brothers who care so much. But this... my husband... my marriage..." Shit, I was getting choked up. "I need to do this. For me. You can watch us from the window if it makes you feel better, but you'll just have to trust me."

There was a long bout of silence before my brother finally broke it.

"Give him hell, sister," he said softly. "Keep your phone on you. If you need me, I'll come running."

His words caused a knot of emotion to form in my throat. My brothers would never fully understand how much they meant to me. They'd all been my rocks this past month.

I swallowed the lump in my throat and huffed out a small breath, hoping to ease this tightness in my chest. "Thank you. I'll be right back."

I grabbed a jacket and stepped out into the fresh air. My boots squeaked in the mud as I made my way across the lawn, feeling the heat of my brother's worried gaze on my back and my husband's electric gaze on my face.

My pulse quickened, and with each step closer to him, I couldn't help but hope that he was only a figment of my imagination. He still wreaked havoc on my heart, looking like an Adonis in black jeans and a green jacket, his blue eyes fevered.

Four feet... three... two... He was too much. Those

eyes were pulling me in as oxygen grew scarce. I could barely breathe, my chest tightening to the point I worried there was a heart attack sneaking up on me.

Or maybe they were just the symptoms of a broken heart.

My feet faltered, a mere half a foot away from him, but the familiar scent of his cologne was all it took for feelings I thought had dissipated to come flooding in. My thunderous pulse roared in my ears as we stood in silence, staring at each other, enveloped in the Irish fog.

"Hi," he said softly, his gaze locked on my face as if memorizing each line.

"You have to stop." My own voice sounded blessedly calm. "You can't keep hanging around here."

He swallowed hard. "I miss you, angel."

The words were a punch to the gut. I'd rather he didn't say anything at all, because the betrayal wounds opened, threatening to bleed again.

I wrapped my arms around myself, glancing to the side. Looking at him was just too much.

"You have to leave, Christian," I murmured.

"Please give me another chance." I shook my head, scared my lips would betray me. "Our vows were forever, angel. For better or for worse. In sickness and in health."

I exhaled a shaky breath, the memory of our wedding day tearing me apart. I meant those promises, but even then, he'd been holding back secrets of my athair's death and my best friend's betrayal.

"The trust is broken. How could I ever trust you again?"

"I thought I was sparing you from pain, but I can see now that I was wrong." He swallowed hard, clearly struggling. But I couldn't give him what he needed. If we didn't have each other's backs, what did we have? As if he could read my thoughts, he added, "I'll do anything for a second chance, angel. Anything."

A small part of me—okay, a big part of me—wanted to fall into his arms and put it all behind us. But deep down, call it woman's intuition or whatever, I sensed there were more secrets, and I just couldn't continue doing this for years to come only to end up in this same exact spot.

"I'm sorry, Christian, I can't," I murmured, and he exhaled a shaky breath, his brows drawn tight.

"I thought I was protecting you."

"But you weren't," I whispered. "You were protecting your brother and Juliette. You didn't trust my judgment. Would I have been upset? Probably. But at least I wouldn't have felt betrayed by you. This isn't even about Juliette. It's about us. You." He stared at me, his face stony. "You have buried yourself so deep into your shell that this"—I motioned with my hand between us—"will keep happening over and over again." His face darkened while emotions flickered in his eyes. "Until I wake up one day hating you."

Christian flinched. "You hate me?"

"*No.*" Tears blurred my eyes and emotions clogged my throat. "And I don't want to hate you. But you ruined the fragile thing we had, this bond of trust, and I can't just pretend all is well. You need to work out your own problems and secrets. For your sake, Christian. So you can find happiness."

I felt naked and vulnerable as we stared at each other. It wasn't only him I had to resist but my own body that craved to hold him in my arms once more.

It turned out the therapy sessions I'd started attending after the whole ordeal were paying off, although every time I thought of Juliette, I wanted to start punching something. It wouldn't be this man. He'd suffered enough. I immediately scolded myself for even caring. Christian was a big boy and he could take care of himself just fine.

"I don't want children." My eyebrows furrowed at the sudden, seemingly irrelevant admission. "I had a vasectomy done to ensure that. You said you wanted family, children, and I said nothing." He reached for me, but before he touched my face, his hand curled into a fist before stuffing it into his pocket. "I didn't tell you for fear of losing you, but I was an idiot." A tiny tremble in his shoulder caught my eyes. "I should have told you about your athair, but I thought it'd—" Hurt filled his face and the veins in his neck pulsed, tension stretching his muscles. "You're my happiness. My light. The reason my heart beats. Don't leave me in the darkness."

His eyes burned into mine, bright with pain and love. But there were ghosts there too, and I knew I couldn't help him with those.

I shook my head, my whole being swelling with exhaustion. "You deserve to be happy, but I finally understand that I can't give you what you need."

He rubbed a fist over his chest, his heart. "I'll wait."

I couldn't do this anymore. Fearing I'd cave, I shifted away from him. "It's for the best that we don't see each other anymore. We need to move on, meet new people."

He grabbed my wrist, his warm fingers curling tightly around my skin. I looked at where we were connected, then slowly lifted my eyes to his face to find his had darkened to stormy skies.

"I can't accept that. I'll wait for you no matter how long it takes, but if I find you looking at any man, I'll kill him." The muscles in his jaw flexed. "I fucked up, but I'll fix it. Fix myself. And you *will* be mine, Ivy. If it kills us both."

My mouth dropped, but before I could say another word, he released my wrist and whistled. Then I heard the familiar bark and rustle of leaves getting closer and closer before Cobra slammed into me. I fell to my knees, laughing and hugging her to me as she licked my face.

"This isn't goodbye, wife. I will see you soon."

With a solemn nod, he turned around, and it was only then that I noticed another figure deeper in the woods: Dante DiLustro.

Throat thick and heart heavy, a single tear rolled down my cheek. Cobra nudged me with her head, and I cuddled into her as I watched my husband disappear into the dark.

Chapter Thirty-Seven

PRIEST

Therapy with Dr. Anna Violet Freud, who for unknown reasons sometimes went by Violet and other times as Anna, was no small or cheap feat.

Her Ph.D. from Harvard hung behind her, the evidence of her accomplishments undeniable. Nobody else between the States and Italy was good enough to deal with this shit. Or maybe Dr. Freud's forays into the minds running the criminal underworld gave her a specific set of skills. From the sounds of it, she'd been treating more than a few people in my circles.

A week had passed since I left Ireland and my wife behind. It wasn't a goodbye, though. I meant what I said to her that day. But it *was* the reason I found myself sitting in this room in Trieste, Italy, working out my shit so I could see her—have her—again.

Until then, I'd watch her from a distance. I'd purchased the Irish security company that had a monopoly in the country and could penetrate every corner of the island with the exception of people's homes. It was the best thing—for now—to contain my restlessness and worry over her.

Dr. Freud's voice interrupted my thoughts with her next request.

"If you could say one thing to your parents, with no consequences or judgment, what would it be?"

The clock's ticking was the only sound in the room while Aisling, Papà, Dante, and I sat in a semicircle.

I reclined in my chair, resting an ankle on my knee as I contemplated her exercise. The air around me was thick with the unspoken deeds that were trapped in my soul.

Just as I opened my mouth to utter a white lie, my eyes narrowed. *You need to work out your own problems and secrets. For your sake, Christian. So you can find happiness.*

I would do this for her. For us. For *me*.

Running a thoughtful hand across my jaw, I admitted the truth.

"I hated Vittoria. I hate Aisling too." It was the truth, but not the whole truth. Dr. Freud couldn't stop a spark of surprise from lighting in her eyes. Aisling's lip quivered, but she remained seated, clutching her skirt. "A discontent between children and parents is hardly a novelty," I mocked lightly.

Dr. Freud's lips quirked, and to hide her reaction, she dropped her attention to her lap where an empty file lay.

"Tell me why, Christian," Aisling asked, her eyes locked on me. "I'm tired of tiptoeing around you, desperate to get into your good graces. Yet, the only thing I'm running into are brick walls." I gave her a blank look and her gaze wavered, but she powered on. "You're buried so deep into your shell, I don't know how to reach you."

I focused on a dot on the wall right behind her and suddenly hated myself. Aisling's last sentence fucked me over, an echo of similar words that Ivy uttered.

I hadn't been a good man for a long time. However, I'd learned at too young of an age that the world was a dark place. I'd become so tainted that I started to believe darkness was the status quo. Only... as I sat here, my ears ringing, I realized I could get back to the light, and maybe this world I ruled could be gray.

"When children lack protection, or their parents are absent in times of need, resentment can form and follow them into adulthood," Dr. Freud supplied tentatively.

Papà raised a brow. "That's impossible. My sons were protected at all costs."

Dr. Freud didn't even spare him a glance, her eyes locked on me. "I'd like to give your sons the floor."

When I didn't answer, Dante cleared his voice.

"Mother... Vittoria... was a vindictive bitch. She hated Christian because he was a reminder of Papà's infidelity, and she hated me because I looked like him. She... wielded her power over us, as you shrinks might say. But really, she fucking terrorized us." He cleared his throat and brushed a nonexistent piece of lint off his shirt. He might seem unaffected, but I knew my brother.

"Physical abuse?" Dr. Freud asked while Papà and Aisling sat frozen, unable to process Dante's words. "Or sexual?"

"Physical," gritted Dante at the same time I clenched my teeth and said, "Both."

And there it was, out in the open. There was no retracting those words.

Aisling's gaze whipped to Papà's, but he just turned to me and then Dante, horrified. A sardonic feeling pulled in my chest that he could have been so fucking blind. We were rough as boys, but not even the clumsiest person in the world got as many bruises as we had growing up.

"How is that possible?" Aisling questioned, her eyes darting between Papà and me, then back to Papà. "Frank, you promised nothing would happen to him." Her breathing labored slightly. "You promised."

Before he had a chance to answer, I did. "She gave carte blanche to Father Gabriel."

Dr. Freud fidgeted, averting her gaze and crossing her legs. For a moment, we simply stared at each other in silence as unspoken words bounced off the walls. I could almost hear the pitter-patter of every heart as we all stared at each other in thick silence.

This was me no longer hiding. This was me going for the heart: my wife's. The fire in my chest stole my breath.

"Why didn't you say something?" Papà's voice shook and so did his hands.

I looked out the window, running a hand across my jaw while Dante's thoughtful gaze settled on my face.

"Vittoria swore she'd kill you if we did," my brother answered. "Kill us too."

"No wonder you hate me," Aisling whispered. "Did Vittoria—" She swallowed, then tried again. "Did she—" An audible gulp sounded in the room. "Did she touch you too?"

One corner of my lips lifted, although there wasn't an ounce of humor in my body. "Don't worry. Every person who touched me without my permission is dead."

The bomb dropped, and in its wake were harsh breaths and soft sobs. I didn't want anyone's pity. I wanted—needed—to get my mind fixed so I could win my wife back. The alternative was unfathomable. Dangerous.

"You should have told me," Papà said, suddenly sounding decades older. "I would have ended that bitch."

I shared a look with my brother and could see my thoughts reflected in his eyes. *We can't change the past.*

All we could focus on was on the future. But we both knew it was easier said than done.

"Not to worry," I grumbled. "She got hers." *For fucking years.* But there was no need to get into specifics.

Papà stared at us for a silent beat. "Her death... the fire... wasn't an accident?"

I raised a brow but remained silent. It was best he came to his own conclusions. Plus, I knew enough about doctor-patient confidentiality to trust Dr. Freud, but I wasn't in the mood to test her limits.

"Good, she deserved nothing better," Aisling said breathlessly, her thoughtful gaze settled on my face.

My eyes met hers. "I need you to stop trying so hard. I can't give you what you want."

"You don't even know what I want."

My jaw tightened. "You want a son, a relationship. But every time I look at you, I remember Vittoria and all the shit she put Dante and me through. And you're the one who put us in that position in the first place."

"Maybe I can help," offered Dr. Freud.

"I don't need help." I'd never uttered a more ridiculous lie.

"Maybe. Though your behavior contradicts your words, Christian," Dr. Freud said with a slight lift to her lips. "In order to help yourself, you need to come to terms with your past. Once you do, you'll be better equipped to move past it and accept your normal human emotions. Only then can you start building a relationship with your mother and father."

"And if I don't want a relationship with them?"

"Then how about with your wife?" Dr. Freud smiled sadly. "Unless you learn that a relationship is the constant work of two people sharing and negotiating, you'll lose everything and everyone you love." A sardonic breath left me. "But then you already know that, don't you?"

For the next hour, words were spoken and tears were spilled—mainly by Aisling—before the session concluded and steps forward were taken.

It wasn't until I crossed the parking lot and slid into the driver's seat of my Aston Martin that I understood why the damn doctor came so highly recommended.

Chapter Thirty-Eight

FRANK

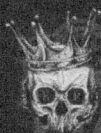

Being born into the Syndicate didn't come without responsibilities.

I was raised to believe in strength and power. The result of my parents' strict expectations. My own father prepared to banish me for taking an Irish mafia princess for a mistress. Not because I cheated on my wife whose family had a pull with the mafia in Italy.

Oh, no. They all had plenty of mistresses lined up and were none so discreet.

Much of it stemmed from the Irish being unfairly considered an enemy of the Syndicate.

What my father didn't know was that when I saw Aisling, I came alive. She made me feel something other than darkness. When she fell pregnant, she begged me to keep the baby. It wasn't hard to convince me because life with her was the only thing I wanted. Christian was our miracle. I'd never felt prouder than I did the moment when I met my beautiful boy. A product of Aisling's and my life. The boys and Aisling were *it*.

But then my father and the Syndicate learned of the child. If it had been a girl, he would have dismissed the whole ordeal.

But it was a boy. A beautiful baby boy who looked like an angel.

We ran.

We got caught.

We were judged.

In the eyes of the Syndicate and the DiLustro family, it was a betrayal, and we were given two options: die together or live apart. My first wife's family would ensure if we took the first option, the entire DiLustro line would be wiped out.

So neither Aisling nor I had a choice once Christian was born. In order to ensure his survival—and ours—she had to give him up.

Aisling got the short end of the stick. I had Dante and Christian, and the Syndicate. She was left with only this secret to keep from her family.

My boys and I were always close. Connected. They sought me out regardless of whether I was busy.

Then they stopped, seemingly overnight.

Just like that, the walls went up. I chalked that up to hormones, and while it stung, I left them to their own devices. Perhaps I was scared they'd closed themselves off to me like I'd done with my father.

I knew too well how strained relationships worked in our family. I didn't want to repeat that with my sons.

But after everything, and hearing it all spill out onto the therapist's office floor, I understood.

I recalled how both boys would shut down whenever Vittoria was around. She'd always fuss over me, distracting me from my sons' discomfort.

My sons had been hiding their pain for decades. I never imagined my wife would ever torture them, abuse them.

Fuck, I should have seen it. Hell hath no fury like a woman scorned. Vittoria perfected that fucking motto on my boys. My. Boys.

Nothing could forgive the fact that I let my sons down. They needed their father, and I wasn't there for them.

I expected Aisling's resentment—hell, I almost welcomed it. She left Christian under my protection and I'd let her down. I'd let them all down.

Maybe I could fix everything. Starting with my sons. Maybe then, they'd forgive me and we could be a family.

A real family.

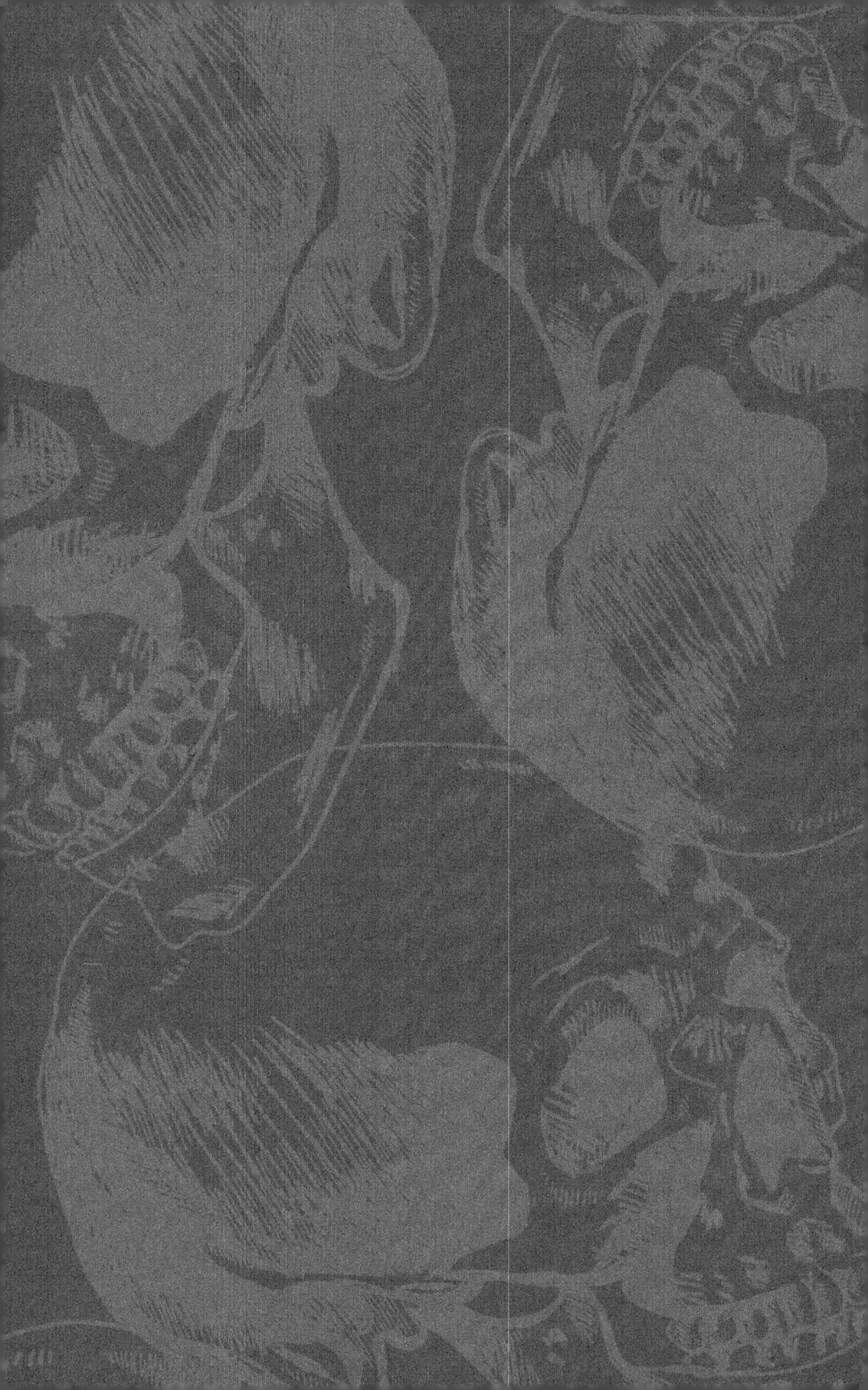

Chapter Thirty-Nine

PRIEST

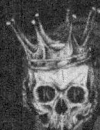

The wound in my chest—invisible to outsiders—bled with each passing day, festering without my wife in my life.

I couldn't come to terms that she left me. Refused to talk to me. Refused to see me.

But as Dr. Freud talked and I went through the motions of pretending to listen, I decided my wife was mine. She couldn't fucking leave me. We'd spoken vows in front of God. Church. Family and friends.

There was no fucking way we'd spend our lives apart.

I was done giving her space.

I'd been going through this for weeks, trying to time it perfectly. How long did a woman take to cool off?

Maybe I could ask Wynter? No, she and Ivy were too close.

"Are you listening to me, Christian?" Dr. Freud's voice pulled me back from my latest silent rant.

I locked eyes with the young doctor and nodded my head, although I'd bet a pretty penny she didn't believe me. I'd lost count of how many appointments I'd sat through. And while I hated group sessions, I detested one-on-ones because there was no escaping her keen eye.

"How long does it take a woman to come to her senses?" I asked, figuring I had nothing to lose. At least this woman didn't know Ivy and couldn't run to her and blab.

Dr. Freud smiled. "Ah, your wife."

I kept my face expressionless. "It was a general question."

I was tempted to applaud her for keeping a straight face. "Well, Christian. It depends on what happened."

I just shrugged. "It doesn't matter."

Her gaze met mine, her eyes narrowed and lips slightly pursed as if contemplating how to get me to divulge my secrets.

"Tell me how long you've been married," she finally said, pulling the charm on her necklace back and forth. It was her only tell.

I sat back, eyeing her warily.

"That's an interesting piece," I stated calmly, tilting my chin toward her charm. "Want to know what it is?"

Hesitation flickered across her expression, but she inhaled a breath and took the bait. "Yes."

"Marabella Mobster arrangements. It's an auction of human flesh." Conflict danced in her eyes before she masked it. "Girls and women sold off to criminals all around the world."

She stared at the file in her lap, the charm on her necklace tugged on back and forth, back and forth. She swallowed and after several heartbeats looked up.

"Ask," I said.

She dropped the necklace and her hand went to her thighs, and I watched her knuckles turn white from the force of her grip.

"Does your family participate in that kind of thing?"

"No."

"Do you know a family that does?"

I ran a thumb across my bottom lip. "I know of them."

She accepted my answer and continued her probing. Maybe I should charge *her* for this session. "Do you have their last names?"

"You shouldn't go looking for those answers, Doctor." I held her gaze, watching emotions pass across it. She realized she'd dug deeper than she should've. My phone vibrated in my pocket and I looked at the clock.

Standing, I buttoned my jacket and headed to the door.

"Not knowing is worse," she said, jumping to her

feet, her hand loose by her side while her eyes burned with desperation.

I paused with one hand on the doorknob and glanced back at her. "You won't find what you're looking for. You'll only get yourself killed."

Thirty minutes later, I ran into my papà and Aisling in the office of the club I named after my wife, The Angel. They had yet to visit, but it surprised me to see them here today of all days.

"Shouldn't you two be in Chicago? Or New York?" I raised my brow.

"Your mother wanted to see how you were after your... session," Papà stated, slightly uncomfortable. "Just in case you needed us."

A sardonic feeling pulled in my chest. We'd been on *slightly* better but not quite caring terms.

"As you can see, Aisling, I made it out alive."

Papà's phone rang and he let out a string of curses, darting a look to his wife who assured him wordlessly that she'd be okay.

"I'll be right back," he assured, kissing her on the cheek and then disappearing.

Aisling and I remained quiet. She held her head high but clutched her pearls, betraying her nervousness. She was desperate to start anew but also scared of learning about the dark shit that occurred over the past twenty-seven years of my life.

She continued pulling at her necklace, the tic reminding me of Dr. Freud.

And then I remembered the question. "Aisling?" A glimmer of hope flared in her eyes. "How long might a woman hold a grudge?"

Her delicate brows furrowed.

"Are we talking about your wife's grudge?" The woman was too perceptive. I nodded. "Have you apologized?"

"Of course," I answered quickly, then immediately frowned. Didn't I?

"Then depending on the woman, I'd say a few months. Three, to be safe." My self-doubt was immediately forgotten, and I straightened up. "Why do you ask?"

Because I'm going to kidnap my wife. Again.

I went to turn around but Aisling sidestepped me, something she saw on my face alarming her.

"Why, Christian?" she demanded to know.

I shrugged. "No reason."

She shook her head frantically.

"Oh my God. You're planning on doing it again." It wasn't even a question. Damn it, I should have never asked her. I stepped forward, but to her credit, she didn't cower. "Aren't you, Christian?"

"I'll give her a bit more time," I said slowly. "But you won't say anything to anyone."

She sighed tiredly. "I won't, but I really think you should—"

"I'll handle my wife," I cut her off.

The next time I tried to leave, she didn't stop me.

Ivy

I glanced out the jet's window as it landed on the tarmac of a small private airport in Lisbon.

My stomach was in knots as various scenarios played in my mind. I was about to meet my sister, courtesy of Alexei Nikolaev's coordination with Kingston Ashford. Our last encounter didn't exactly go peachy, so I could only hope for improvements.

Meanwhile, one feeling superseded all others. *Fear.*

I was scared that she'd hate me and I'd lose my chance at having a sister. It was ridiculous to fear losing a sister I'd never met, but fear wasn't supposed to be rational. Plus, there were the rumors of Louisa's ruthlessness.

"Juliette will be here," Caelan warned under his breath. "Are you up for it?"

It was Alexei's condition for arranging a meeting with my sister. Apparently the man decided to become a mediator or some shit like that.

Fury savaged my insides, blazing along the familiar path at the mention of Juliette, obliterating everything else until I was scorched earth, incapable of harboring any other emotion.

My therapist told me I had to learn to let go and stop expecting others to handle their emotions and actions the way I would. It wasn't so much the control I wanted, but I'd settle for less lies and deception.

"Ivy?" Caelan's voice pulled me back. "You're not going to start beating her again, are you?"

I brushed off the idea, no matter how tempting, and smiled.

"Please." I waved my hand casually. "My yearly quota of beatdowns has been met," I said breezily.

A smooth smile spread across his face. "I'll be sure not to get on your list for next year."

"We're in Portugal," Bren announced, getting up off the couch and ending our discussion. Cobra looked up, watching him tensely as usual. "God, this dog is looking at me like she wants to eat me."

I raised a brow. "Scared?"

"No, but I don't know why we're keeping a dog trained by Christian DiLustro," complained Bren. "I'd stake my life on him having this killer trained to attack us."

"She's my dog and she stays with me," I stated calmly. "And if you come for me, she'll protect me, regardless of who you are."

"She shouldn't attack the family," Bren grumbled,

referring to when he chased me around the house after I threw the last pack of his cigarettes into the fireplace.

"Cobra is a born protector," Aemon said as he stood up, never looking up from the screen of his phone. "She protects Ivy, and that makes her an excellent bodyguard."

"I hope she attacks those DiLustros," Bren muttered under his breath. "I'd give her a steak dinner for a week straight, bone and all."

"Bribes don't work on her," I told him.

"There's a first time for everything," he retorted dryly, glancing at Cobra. "Right, girly?"

A black Cadillac waited for us as we exited the plane, along with a driver who looked like he was ex-military.

"Murphy family," he greeted us. "Welcome to Lisbon. I will take you to your destination."

I nodded my thanks and he opened the door. Cobra jumped into the back seat without waiting for permission.

Aemon grumbled and I stifled a laugh as I slid in right behind my girl.

"That's right," Bren mocked. "In case you missed the memo, we work for the dog. Now drive her around Lisbon."

"There's still room for you in the back with us," I told them, then shot Bren a look. "You, on the other hand, have to get in the front."

Bren glared at me but got into the front seat without

further complaint. We were all tense, not sure what to expect of the upcoming meeting.

As we drove through the busy streets, I sat on the edge of my seat to take in the sights. I'd never been to Lisbon before, and it was a good distraction to the nervous energy pumping through my veins.

A million thoughts ran through my head as we passed the popular tourist sights—Torre de Belém, Torre Paroquial, and Mosteiro dos Jerónimos—before the car came to a stop way too soon.

A familiar figure stood on a lawn, her dark hair blowing in the wind as our eyes locked. Juliette was here. Of course I knew she would be, but I thought I had more time.

The car door opened, and for a moment, I sat frozen, the wicked voice in the back of my mind hissing that I wasn't ready to face her. As I watched her standing there, her husband's arm protectively around her, it was a painful reminder that my own chose to protect her too.

Not me, but her.

I tried to reason with myself that after everything Juliette had been through when she learned about her birth parents, their murder, and the abuse she'd endured, she deserved all the happiness and affection.

But envy and bitterness were a dangerous company. They seeped into my bloodstream, poisoning me.

With my brothers' help and Cobra close at my heel, I

exited the vehicle and felt torturously alone despite being in this big city.

I stared at my best friend, tangled in a mess of emotions.

Wynter, Juliette, and Davina had been my family from the moment I stepped foot on the Yale campus. We'd been through so much that letting go was proving to be more difficult than I could've ever anticipated.

As if summoned by my thoughts, the phone in my purse started to vibrate and I pulled it out. There were messages from Wynter, Davina, and even Aisling.

> Wynter: Just checking in to see if you're okay. I'm sorry about everything. We love you, Ivy. And miss you so goddamn much.

> Davina: No matter what, we love you.

I read Aisling's message last.

> Aisling: I don't know what happened between you and my son, but I know that you're healing him and he loves you. Forgetting is impossible, but I'm hoping you'll find it in your heart to forgive.

I stared at the text and bit back my tears. There was still the bitterness of betrayal, which I doubted would ever fully go away, and the echo of my own shame that I hadn't been there for her when she discovered my athair played a part in her pain.

I was about to move when I caught a glimpse of the very same woman we ran into amid the debris of Montenegro. Louisa Volkov. She walked out of the house, guided by Kingston Ashford, known as the Ghost, one of the most dangerous men in the underworld. Correction: *the* most dangerous man.

My brothers tensed but didn't move as the two of them approached us. Alexei moved like a panther behind them, but stopped next to Juliette and Dante.

I returned my eyes to my sister, studying her, yet the only Murphy genes I could see in her were her eyes. They were a beautiful golden color, speckled with hazel. Very much like my own. Her golden hair, on the other hand, definitely didn't fit the mold. She had her mother's hair.

She came to a stop in front of me, several inches taller than me and undoubtedly stronger. She wore white shorts and a green T-shirt with flip-flops, a stark contrast to my yellow dress that barely reached my knees.

We studied each other for several seconds before her eyes darted to my brothers.

She's sizing us up, I realized. Our strengths. Weaknesses. Fuck, I certainly hoped I didn't bring my brothers into a spider's web. Kingston's dark, blank expression was trained on us, his hand around Louisa's tense shoul-

335

ders while he appeared relaxed and stoic, offering his support and comfort.

Kind of like my brothers.

Then I saw the little girl behind Louisa, clutching her arm. It was the girl they rescued from Montenegro several months ago now, and it hit me like lightning.

Louisa was nothing like her mother.

The evidence was right in front of me. She'd taken a vulnerable girl under her wing, and by the looks of it, she'd transformed her into a swan by giving her safety and a home. Unlike Kingston, she fixed me with a half-terrified, half-feral look that told me she'd tear me to pieces—or at least try to—if I so much as hurt her guardian.

"Hi there," I greeted her softly, extending my hand. "I'm Ivy."

She eyed my hand and Louisa froze for a moment before giving her an encouraging nudge.

I watched with bated breath as the young girl took my hand. "Lara."

"Nice to meet you, Lara." I turned toward my sister. "Ah, thank you for meeting us." I swept my tongue over my lips nervously. "I... We..."

Fuck, I had the entire speech prepared in my head on the flight over, and now it had completely vanished from my mind.

My eyes met Caelan's for a fraction of a second and the assurance I saw in his eyes was all I needed.

336

I took a deep breath and said, "We learned about our connection to you and your twin only recently, and... well, you're family." I swallowed a lump in my throat. "If you want to be, that is."

"And the fact that I'm Sofia Volkov's daughter doesn't bother you?" she all but snapped at me.

Bren and Aemon growled, their upper bodies leaning forward, and I pushed them back. "Stop it, you two, or I swear to God, I'm going to—"

"No, it doesn't bother us," Caelan cut me off. "None of us can choose our parents. Besides, a blind man can see you're not your mother. Just as we are not our father."

She didn't show much, but something promising lit up in her eyes.

I took a hesitant step, placing my hand on her forearm, and smiled sadly.

"We all think so, even though Aemon and Bren act all tough. They're overprotective, so don't be surprised if they start that macho stuff with you." I glanced over my shoulder at my brothers who rolled their eyes, but the truth was written all over their faces. "I hope you won't judge us for Athair's betrayal."

Her delicate throat shifted. "I'll admit, I'm... I *was*... jealous." She looked over to Kingston and Lara, her eyes softening. "But now... I have my family." She turned her attention back to me. "But there's room for more people in it."

"I agree," I rasped, the lump in my throat growing until I thought it'd suffocate me. I blinked rapidly and wiped my cheeks with the back of my hand.

"I'm glad." Louisa smiled, her expression softening. "Because good friends are just as important as family, and I hear that you're... or were... very close with Juliette?"

My eyes darted back to where Juliette stood with her husband, her shoulders slumped. I couldn't comprehend what she had to do with any of this.

"Until I dropped the bomb on you," she added.

I stiffened. "You only told the truth."

"Yes, but maybe not the whole truth."

"Explain, please," Aemon demanded, very much the head of the Irish mafia in this moment.

Louisa tilted her head, studying him pensively.

"You look like him." There was no need to ask who *him* was. Aemon was a spitting image of our athair. "Demanding, never asking."

It was a harsh accusation, and not entirely incorrect, but she didn't know him like I did. Aemon was a big teddy bear once you got to know him.

"Not always," I jumped in, defending him.

She nodded, seemingly accepting my words at face value.

"What I meant is that I should have explained that she killed your... eerrr, our... father—" Her words said more than she realized. She didn't consider Athair her

338

father, and I couldn't blame her. "She did it because he arranged the Cullens' executions. He attempted to burn her birth parents alive. As you know, the Cullen children survived, thanks to Liam Brennan. But if he hadn't shown up…"

My brothers spat out curses in Gaelic, clearly disturbed with the images Louisa's words created. I was overwhelmed with it too. My own throat felt tight, clogged with emotions while my stomach roiled. How could Athair ever allow such a thing to happen?

"It doesn't excuse the lies," I whispered. I wished Juliette all the best, I really did, but I didn't know if I'd ever be close with her again. I didn't know if I had the strength to face the demons she represented.

"It doesn't," she agreed. "But we're all human, and to be human is to make mistakes. And trust me, life's too short to hold grudges."

I hesitated. She was right, life was short, and maybe the whole betrayal had more to do with my husband and the fact that he took Juliette's side over mine.

Or maybe it was my fault as much as hers that it had come to this. I hadn't given her a proper chance to explain herself, nor did I attempt to explain what I had learned about my athair either.

"Let's go inside," Louisa recommended, sliding her hand around my elbow while taking Lara's hand as we made our way into the charming white-stone house. She flicked a glance over her shoulder to Kingston. "Are you guys coming or are you planning on standing out here all day?"

She didn't wait for their answer, stopping by Juliette, whose red-rimmed eyes betrayed her state of mind. She looked tired, that usual mischievous, slightly crazy gleam in her eyes gone with her rumpled hair and faint purple smudges beneath her eyes. If her physical appearance was anything to go by, she was just as heartbroken about the state of our friendship as I was.

My steps faltered and we stared at each other, the world stopping in its tracks.

"I'm sorry." Her voice cracked. "I was an idiot to think my revenge was the most important thing."

A sob rose in my throat. "Your betrayal hit hard."

"I'm so sorry," she said again, tears streaming down her face. Agony scraped her voice raw, making my own soul bleed. "You're more important to me than anything else. I'll do anything—"

Her voice broke and I sucked in another shallow inhale. "Juliette, I…"

She froze, her breaths heavy with regret.

"If you can't forgive me, at least forgive him." I couldn't breathe. I needed to think. How could I forgive the scars Christian and Juliette caused? There was too much going on. I was here for my sister, not for Juliette and Christian. "I'll be sorry until the day I die," she said hoarsely. "For not coming clean. For not choosing our friendship first. For using Christian's loyalty to his brother to keep a secret from you. You deserved better than that."

I was slightly overwhelmed with everything, but suddenly my sister's words filtered in. *Life's too short to hold grudges.* I knew Louisa was right. After weeks of emotional turmoil, I was exhausted, and Juliette was right here in front of me, offering an olive branch.

A slightly desperate look in her eyes told me she meant it, begging me to accept her apology.

A small sob rose in my throat and my resolve crumbled. I fell into her arms. We cried, hugging each other while dampness soaked our cheeks.

Things weren't solved and they might never go back to the way they were, but this step felt like a move in the right direction.

Chapter Forty

PRIEST

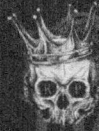

I sat in the office of my penthouse in Philadelphia, nursing a bottle of alcohol, and smoking which I gave up the day I tied the knot with Ivy. I kept watching the security monitors. Certain screens showed surveillance footage of Ireland, and on another, footage of when I first touched Ivy in the hallway of my club played. I'd watched it on repeat for the past two hours.

And all the while I waited for my purchase of Lisbon Telecommunications to go through so I'd have access to the surveillance of Lisbon where Ivy currently was.

I threw my head back as images from that night flew through my mind.

Upon learning the call I received was phony, I returned to the club, irritated and ready to make someone pay for the fuckup. As I stepped inside, hordes of people parted like the Red Sea and others scattered like chickens.

I made my way to the private corridor that led to my office when I came to a slow stop. I narrowed my eyes on the woman who'd captured my interest mere weeks ago when she and her friends strutted into my brother's casino in Chicago and wreaked havoc.

I strolled toward her silently, and the moment she spotted me, she went still. Despite her nervousness, the little minx didn't run. Instead, she continued staring at me, likely aware of the fact that I had her cornered.

Despite our height difference, she looked me straight in the eyes. High cheekbones, petite nose, and full lips, almond-shaped hazel eyes, exquisite body and skin that would tempt a saint, never mind a devil.

Lucky for her, I was a broken man, and tonight I was in the mood to teach her a lesson.

The delicate skin of her throat worked up and down as she swallowed. The motion made the viselike grip in my chest tighten, stealing my fucking breath.

A subtle blush ran up her neck and she cleared her throat. "I don't even know your name."

"Forget about pleasantries." I grunted, inhaling her scent. She nodded, almost as if in a trance. "Now look at me."

She lifted her head, staring up at me with those beautiful eyes as I sunk to my knees and tasted her. It was game over right there and then. She would forever be imprinted in my mind and my heart.

I just didn't know it then.

A beeping sound pulled me from my reverie and images of Lisbon finally filtered in. I typed in her sister's address—being a good hacker had its advantages–and the barrage of footage filtered in, making it difficult to process anything. It wasn't until I saw her that my brain cells slowed down.

Long red curls. Yellow dress. She was a vision.

I leaned in, hungry to see every line of her body, my heart heavy. I didn't think it was possible to miss someone so much. Surprisingly, all the shit that was coming out in therapy was helping with every aspect of my life *except for* my love life.

I scoffed softly. If it could even be called a *love* life with this constant presence of ache in my heart.

Occasionally—okay, every second of the day—it made me contemplate kidnapping Ivy. I could bring her back by force and wait patiently for her to come around to the idea of us, but the thought of causing her more pain was bothersome.

Fuck, therapy really had softened me.

It might be over for her, but it would never be over for me. I couldn't think without her near—her smell, her smile, the feel of her hands on me. I missed it like the desert missed the rain.

My throat tightened.

I slammed my fist against the table and reveled in the shock that reverberated up my arm.

I returned my attention to the screen, watching Ivy disappear into the house, her brothers and Kingston right behind her.

"At least there wasn't another catfight." Emory showed up out of nowhere, distracting me. It was temporary, but it was better than nothing.

"It's not over yet." My words came out slightly slurred, and as I turned over, I saw a double image of my cousin. One Emory on this planet was plenty. Two might just level it.

I blinked, trying to clear my head.

"You should call it a night, Priest," she suggested, taking a seat next to me, having a perfect view of the monitors. I swiftly exited out of our encounter in the hallway.

I stood up and walked to the window, releasing a heavy breath as I stared at the dark garden outside, the soft hum of the surveillance monitors barely soothing.

"Just admit you want her back," she said when I remained silent.

"I've never denied it, but I need her to *want* to be here with me."

"Yes, but maybe you should consider being *there* with her, because I don't think Ivy's coming here and watching hours upon hours of this crap." She waved a hand toward the monitors. "It's a waste of time." My brain was too woozy thanks to the alcohol, making it hard to think. "You know what they say. It won't happen unless you make it happen."

"You could use that advice right now, cousin," I muttered.

She crossed her legs and flipped her hair over her shoulder. "We are not talking about me right now."

Despite wearing jeans with combat boots most of the time, there was no shortage of men pining after Emory. Of course, good luck to any fucker who tried to get close to her. He would have to get through her brother, Dante, and me first.

"I have an idea," she offered, but I was too lost in my own thoughts. I tapped my finger against my thigh, then halted as an idea of my own flickered in my foggy mind.

"Do you want to hear it or—" Suddenly, she leaned over, her eyes narrowing on the monitor.

"What is it?" I asked as I strode toward her and retook my seat. But before she could answer, I saw it. Or him, rather. "What in the fuck is Jean-Baptiste doing in Lisbon?"

"My thoughts exactly," she said.

After a few clicks, I zoomed in and hacked into the public CCTV files too, just to be sure.

"Can we get facial recognition on this?" I asked, and after a few clicks, she had it up.

"It's him," she whispered, our eyes darting between two images. It was the same profile, same height and same build.

I tapped the screen. "And he's got his sights set on my wife."

Chapter Forty-One

IVY

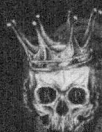

L ouisa's story—what little she shared with me —was heart-wrenching. Even my brothers, who were rarely affected, appeared to be shaken. Athair had made a grave mistake by leaving the twins—our sisters—amidst wolves. They deserved better.

We were all piled around the massive living room in Louisa and Kingston's house in Lisbon, where we'd spent the past six hours eating and getting to know each other.

Juliette and Dante had long since given us privacy, although something had them tense, and I didn't think it had anything to do with our awkward situation over here. Dante received a call about a half hour ago, and ever since then, he'd been roaming the living room, checking every window. It wasn't long before Kingston was doing the same.

Ignoring their odd behavior, I returned my attention to Louisa, feeling grateful that we'd fallen into a kind of comfort. "I want to help find your twin. Our sister."

We locked eyes, a wordless exchange of regrets and our parents' sins swirling around us. I wanted to right the wrongs. Even more, I wanted my sisters to be a real part of my life.

"I'm not sure what we'll find," Louisa admitted. "After so many years—"

Her voice cracked and I reached for her hand, squeezing it gently. "From what you've told me, she's strong. A fighter. A survivor."

"But so many years of torture," she murmured. "Nobody can come out of that sane."

"You did," I pointed out. Her eyes darted to me in surprise. "It might not be the same kind of torture, but it's just as painful. Your mother put you through hell, mentally abused you, and you survived."

The ghosts I'd often seen in Christian's eyes came to life in Louisa's and my heart ached for the suffering they'd both endured. Fuck, even Christian's cousins. They'd all paid for their parents' sins, and I couldn't help but realize how lucky I was.

Athair wronged so many, but he did right by me and my brothers. Of course, that didn't forgive his mistakes, and it would be naive not to acknowledge he wasn't the man I always thought him to be, but he was gone. He could no longer cause any heartache, and that had to be the work of something bigger.

Louisa's gaze flicked to Kingston's and she softened. *Interesting.*

Before I could formulate a question, she uttered the answer to it. "It was thanks to Kingston. He's the reason for my being. My everything."

And there it was. She had found her rock.

My eyes darted to Juliette and Dante, who were discussing something with Kingston and my brothers, glancing out the window every so often.

"I hope Liana found someone too," I whispered absentmindedly while another man invaded my own thoughts.

"If she hasn't, I'll see to it that she does."

My head whipped to her in confusion. "What do you mean?"

She smiled, her eyes shining with slight mischief. "A friend—" She rolled her eyes and I straightened in my seat, my hand falling to my side. "I guess he's a friend, I only met him recently. He's going to help me find my twin."

My eyes darted to Kingston before returning them to my sister and I flashed her a hesitant smile, unsure where she was going with this.

"Ummm, is Kingston on board with this *friend*?"

Louisa chuckled softly. "He is. We came up with the plan together and reached out to him."

"Oh." She seemed to know what she was doing. "Who is he and when did you meet him?"

She took my hand. Her excitement had me leaning in. "We met with Giovanni Agosti yesterday. He's head of the Cortes empire now, which means we finally have a way in."

My eyebrows scrunched. "Way in where?"

"Into human trafficking." I stared at her in shock, my mouth gaped open. "Before Sofia was... executed..." She looked at me as if to judge my reaction, but she'd be waiting a lifetime; I grew up in this world. I knew how to school my features better than anyone else. "She said to get to Liana, we'd need a way in with a trusted family that participates in human trafficking."

The latter was a hard drawn line for me. I hated nothing greater than the flesh trade. I'd come to accept certain illegal acts of the mafia, but there were certain things my brothers and I wouldn't stand for. There might not be a lot of decency among the criminals, but this was one area most of us were in agreement on.

"I don't follow," I admitted, hoping I'd heard wrong. "What does Giovanni Agosti have to do with it?"

She gave me a pointed look. "He's the head of the Cortes empire since his uncle Perez's death."

My mind whirled, and realization struck like lightning. "And he's involved via the Marabella Mobster arrangements."

"Exactly." Then she added, "Well, Perez Cortes no longer participates in anything since I killed him." Her lips curled in a savage smile. "Revenge is sweet."

I told myself not to judge her. One had to do what it took to survive in the underworld, but I found myself unable to bite back my next words.

"But doesn't that... bother you? That Giovanni's your friend and he has a hand in human trafficking. All the innocent—"

"Giovanni doesn't support human trafficking," she cut me off, slightly appalled. "He's been working from different angles to undermine it for years." My shoulders sagged in relief as she continued. "The whole thing with him is complicated. He only recently learned of his connection to the Cortes family. He was going to end it all when I killed his uncle, but then I asked him not to. Not yet, anyhow."

My hands shook at the thought of her playing any part in such a sick industry, no matter her justification.

"I see."

Louisa's hand squeezed mine. "I know. It's horrible that I'm standing by and watching it continue for another day, but I need to..."

Her words faltered and I covered her hand with my free one.

"I understand." I would try to, anyway. "And I—" I glanced at my brothers. "We're going to help you. That's what family is for."

Chapter Forty-Two

PRIEST

I was already angry when I arrived at the entrance of the underground gambling club that had been "given" to the Corsicans. After I was kept waiting there for ten minutes by Jean-Baptiste's men, I was fucking furious.

When I stepped from the dock and followed the path that led inside, I blinked several times to chase away the red mist. It wouldn't do to reduce the fucking club to ashes… yet.

First I needed answers from Sébastien.

The moment I spotted him next to Bogdan, the Serbian mafia don, the red mist returned with a vengeance and my anger turned into rage.

He sat at one of the tables as he scanned the crowd, wearing a dark suit and a smirk on his face, and it was immediately clear. This club wasn't Jean-Baptiste's. It was Bogdan's through and through.

I made my way deeper into the club to find the two facing off and I stilled, listening.

"...supposed to do? Giving him her name and location was stupid and reckless," Sébastien snarled.

"Ivy DiLustro is well protected." My anger ramped up and I had to take a step back or risk attacking them to the point of no return. And I needed to hear everything concerning my wife. "She'll be fine."

Sébastien punched the wall. "And if she's not? Jean-Baptiste is a fucking animal, and if he so much as touches—"

He spotted me and I swore that even under the poor lighting of the club, he paled.

"Fuck," he cursed, running a hand through his hair. "Here we go."

I was so fucking tempted to just plow through the guards I could see closing in on me in my periphery. I'd end them all and leave Sébastien and Bogdan for last. But that might delay me from reaching Ivy, which was not an option.

"I think it's in your best interest to tell me why Jean-Baptiste, your fucked-up business associate, is stalking my wife," I said with apathetic calm while my ears buzzed with rage.

Noting the icy look on my face, Bogdan raised his brows, stroking his chin.

"Would you like to sit down, DiLustro?" he invited in his deep baritone. "Maybe a drink?"

"This won't take long," I snapped, seething. "Start talking. Why is Jean-Baptiste anywhere near my wife?"

"You sure you don't want a drink?"

"Tell me," I roared. "Or I swear to God, I'm going to level this entire city only to ensure you are both dead."

"Suit yourself." Bogdan flagged a waitress over. "I'm getting a drink."

Glaring daggers at him, I ignored the waitress who showed up, throwing heated glances my way. I hadn't noticed another woman in the two years I'd known Ivy, and I wasn't about to start now. Once she filled Bogdan's glass, he dismissed her and she disappeared.

"Start talking or I'll—"

Bogdan's face darkened, his eyes flashing as they pierced into mine.

"Pick us off, one by one?" He chuckled quietly. His lips curled savagely. "But then you won't know what Jean-Baptiste is planning."

"*Merde*, I feel like we need dueling pistols." Sébastien sighed, raking a hand over his head. "Maybe I should just kill Jean-Baptiste myself."

I didn't give two shits whether Sébastien lived or died. Yes, he was better at his job than his brother, but he let him get away with way too much, and now the fucker was sidling up to my wife?

He exhaled. "What I'm trying to say is that he leads

with his dick. Though, I'm sure I don't need to remind you of that." I scoffed, of course I'd remember the way he tried to hold a conversation with me while a woman bounced up and down on his dick. It was an image I prayed I'd forget.

"There are millions of women on this planet," I gritted. If that fucker even dared to inhale Ivy's scent, I would destroy him. Demolish him. Scatter his ashes in opposite corners of this planet so he'd never find peace. "My wife shouldn't even be on his radar."

"She got on his radar the moment you married her." Sébastien chuckled bitterly. "He always wants what he can't have. The fact you took Philly from him is an added bonus, and makes her that much more desirable."

"I fucking *let* you back in," I growled, walking toward him and jabbing a finger in his chest. It didn't matter that I had guns pointed at me. Fear was a mild inconvenience when you were scared out of your mind for the love of your life. "You have the dock, don't you?"

"I hoped it would be enough." To his credit, he stood his ground. "So back the fuck off."

I turned to Bogdan, who acted as if this was all some great performance, taking another sip of his whiskey and looking bored. But I saw past it; he was taking stock. Evaluating me.

"Jean-Baptiste means to use her as a pawn to fuck with you and get his territory back," he said coldly, his voice venomous.

"And what do *you* want?" I growled back. "Some kind of pissing contest to see who's better, faster, stronger?"

Bogdan chuckled, but it didn't reach his dark eyes. "A 'pissing contest' is fucking a rival's woman." When I stiffened, Bogdan cocked his head, arching a cold brow. "What I want is docks in every major port on the East and West coasts of the United States."

I narrowed my eyes. "And what does that have to do with me?"

"Don't mistake me for a blind or stupid man."

I released a long breath, choosing to ignore his insolence for now. Ivy was all that mattered to me.

"The DiLustro family only has access to New York and Philly." I splayed my palms out wide. "You're already in Philadelphia, in case you're confused."

My eyes locked with his. A second ticked by. Then another. "We'll start with New York. Then you'll reach out to your distant family member in Toronto." My brow furrowed. Our connection to Alessio Russo, recently changed to Ashford, was barely known. "Yes, to Alessio. And from there, we'll slowly make our way down the coastline."

"You're fucking crazy," I snarled.

"Maybe." He chuckled, the darkness in his soul filling his eyes with black. "But unless you agree to it, the bomb I have surrounding Kingston Ashford's home will explode with your wife inside it."

Harsh breaths burned my lungs.

I knew there was no life without Ivy. The moment we crossed paths, I began experiencing feelings that were so foreign I had to look them up. She'd healed parts of me that I thought were gone for good.

Yes, I desired her, but it was so much more than that. It was an obsession. It was love. It was an emotion so strong that it dug under my skin and buried itself into my DNA.

"It's yours," I finally said. He cocked his head as if debating whether to believe me. He must have never known love, otherwise he'd understand. The thought of Ivy perishing into ashes made my chest squeeze worse than anything else. "And Jean-Baptiste is mine," I stated coldly, challenging either man to disagree.

They didn't.

I was nearly at the exit when Bogdan's voice stopped me.

"Priest?" Turning my head, I caught his eye. "If you ever step foot on my territory without an invitation again, I'll cut your fucking head off."

I left Bogdan and Sébastien in Philly twenty-four hours ago to board a jet bound for Lisbon. Right after I'd given the Serbian asshole access to another dock in Philadelphia and one in New York.

Speeding down the highway on my motorcycle, I was eager to make Jean-Baptiste history and head to the part of town where Ivy currently slept. Parking my bike at the end of the street where my intel showed Jean-Baptiste was hiding, I continued on foot. My steps were silent as I wound my way past charming villas. They were small but private, with tiny courtyards in between. The lights slowly started to flick on as I reached the last house on the street.

My phone flashed and I lowered my gaze to find Basilio's name on the screen. I ignored his call, but no sooner had it stopped ringing than it started again.

Sighing, I answered it. "I should have checked in with you first."

"Oh, you fucking think?" Basilio roared. "What good is the Syndicate if we're just doing things on our own terms?" I scowled as I studied the blueprints of the home, memorizing each room. "Are you listening to me, Priest?"

"Yes, but I'm kind of in the middle of something," I hurled back.

"Bogdan is a fucking enemy, dipshit!"

I pinched the bridge of my nose. I hadn't slept in forty-eight hours and it was starting to take its toll.

"You know what they say, keep your friends close and your enemies closer."

"I want to barge into that fucking dock, guns blazing, and level him," he bellowed so loud I was certain his voice carried over the ocean and not via the phone line.

"Bas, I really am busy—"

"Oh, fuck off," he snapped angrily. "And what are you busy doing? Drinking yourself to death and staring at security footage?"

For fuck's sake, I just wanted to kill Jean-Baptiste and get Ivy back.

"I gotta go, jackass," I said, then hung up sharply. He'd get over all this. Eventually.

Before he could call me again, I turned off my phone and tucked it away.

I checked my gun to ensure it was loaded, then started forward. Jean-Baptiste's guard was waiting in a car with the engine on and window down. I stayed low, keeping out of sight of the rearview and side mirrors as I moved toward the open window, then in one swift move, I sliced his throat.

The guard tried to sit up, clutching at his ruined skin, but it was too late. He gurgled, the life slowly leaving his body. I stayed there, reciting his last rites with a whisper, until the light extinguished in his eyes.

The street was quiet as I crept toward the front door of the villa. There was a stone wall surrounding the front, which would provide decent cover for what was about to go down.

My heart beat in a steady rhythm as I reached for the knob, but it couldn't be so easy. *Locked.* I dug for a tension tool in the pocket of my pants and worked it until I heard a soft click.

Lifting my pistol, I slowly pushed the door open, checking the area was clear. Then I crept into the house, my shoes soundless on the tile floor. It took less than two minutes to ensure every room on the ground floor was empty.

I paused at the landing of the second floor, the sound of grunting and cries reaching me. The bedroom door was ajar.

"Please, stop. Please, plea—"

I peered inside the bedroom, my blood froze. A little boy, who couldn't be older than nine, sat cornered in the room, his head buried in his hands as Jean-Baptiste approached him, unbuttoning his pants and dragging his zipper down.

Sick fucking *prick*.

Images of my own childhood flashed through my mind like a broken Polaroid.

Fire licked my skin and blood roared in my ears. And then came the rage.

I had no idea how the door splintered, flying off the hinges. At the sudden explosive sound, the boy looked up and scrambled to his feet, bursting past me through the door. Jean-Baptiste reached around his waistband for his gun, but I was quicker, pressing the barrel of mine against his temple.

"Move and I'll blow your fucking brains out." The

defeated look in his eyes was one I hoped I wouldn't soon forget. "Now, Jean-Baptiste, would you like your last rites read?"

His skin flushed and his chest heaved with the force of his breaths. "You won't kill me. It'll start a war."

"Move," I hissed, shoving him toward the chair.

He fastened his pants and walked to the chair.

When he didn't move, I shoved him down the rest of the way. "I said sit the fuck down."

His eyes kept darting behind me, and I smirked. The fool was waiting for his guard to show up.

I pulled out a bunch of zip ties and began strapping him to the wooden chair with efficiency. First his ankles, then his wrists.

"You've been stalking my wife," I said casually as I retrieved a switchblade from my pocket and flicked it open.

"I don't know what you're talking about," he roared.

I held the knife up to his cheek. "By the time this session is over, you will."

He tried to edge away, but it was all in vain. I swiped the blade across his cheek and a stream of red ran down the side of his face. He screamed.

"And how many boys have you hurt? How many girls?"

He didn't answer and I cut his other cheek, deeper this time. The coppery scent of blood perfumed the air.

"How many?" I gritted.

"None, I swear," he cried like the fucking coward he was.

I pointed the tip of the switchblade at his crotch and he began to struggle against his binds.

"Don't lie to me," I warned.

"I swear, I didn't—" I sliced the tops of each thigh, then I pressed the knife into his balls. He writhed in the chair, tears streaming down his face and turning pink from all the blood.

"Tell me," I shouted in his face.

"I don't know," he cried. "I don't keep a tally of filthy children."

Putting my mouth near his ear, I said, "You're the filthy one." I lunged and rammed the knife into his groin. I worked the blade, the screams echoing off the walls filling me with a new sense of peace.

I jammed the blade deeper, then twisted it into his flesh. He howled and I yanked it out, only to shove it in again, slightly higher. He roared, shouting curses in French and every fucking language he knew while I repeated the movement, blood dripping all over my hand.

"Please... stop," he whimpered. "P-please."

"Did you stop when the boy begged you?" I asked. "Tell the truth or I'll prolong your suffering. I tortured my adoptive mother for over a decade, so trust me when I tell you, it won't be pretty."

Terror entered his eyes at the prospect. "I... I didn't... stop."

"That's what I thought. Now, take a good last look at your balls before I shove them into your mouth," I said casually, ice settling in my chest.

By the time I was finished with him, blood stained my clothes and skin, and my body buzzed from the torture I dished on him. It was a high like nothing else. There was only one thing that was better and that was Ivy underneath me, on top of me, in front of me. Fucking anywhere.

As I made my way out on the peaceful street, the edge of my mouth curled.

"It's time I take my wife back."

Chapter Forty-Three

IVY

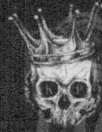

I'm *dreaming of him again*, I thought through the sleepy fog in my brain.

Strong hands wrapped around me, carrying me, holding me tight. That feeling I used to have in my girlish fantasies. A prince rescuing his fairy princess.

But then the sound of an engine punctured my haze and my body jerked. My eyes snapped open and I found a familiar figure hovering over me. Those hard features and that calm facade.

Stubble covered Christian's cheeks, adding a slightly rough edge to his aura. He looked like he'd just gotten out of the shower, droplets of water rolling down those gorgeous bare abs, his skull tattoo glistening and tempting me to trace it with my tongue.

Then my gaze dropped to his gray sweatpants and my lips parted on a sharp exhale. *He's hard.*

I had no business looking in that general area, so I shook my head, lifting my gaze to his face where those intense blue eyes that had haunted me every minute of every day and night watched me with a gleam in them.

"Finally awake, angel." His voice was like velvet as his gaze traveled the length of my body. "I missed seeing those hazel eyes looking up at me." A smile spread on his lips.

"What—" My gaze darted around, panic slowly rising at the unfamiliar surroundings. "Why am I not in my room at Louisa's?"

It was a stupid question because the answer was evident. He had kidnapped me. Again.

I finally registered the humming noise. We were on a plane.

Overwhelming rage flooded my veins and I shot to my feet. Well, I attempted to, only to be yanked back by the seat belt.

"Safety first," he said.

How dare he mock me? I thought in my rattled state. It was all too much. To go from dreaming about him to waking up in the sky and seeing him in the flesh. And worst of all, he looked good. Gorgeous even.

"Take me back. Right now. Or I swear, I'll unleash my brothers and my sister—who's Sofia Volkov's daughter, by the way—on you," I snapped, shameless to use my brothers and newfound sister as my connection. Then, just in case he didn't get the point, I added, "She's super badass."

He laughed, the sound vaguely amused at best. "Your brothers and newfound sister encouraged us to bury the hatchet and work out our problems." I scoffed, but then immediately tensed as he leaned over. I watched his movements as he unbuckled me, noting the wedding ring on his finger.

He must have caught me staring at it because he dug into the pocket of those sinful sweatpants and took my hand into his. "It's about time you put yours back on."

I snorted. "I see you're still breaking and entering."

The last time I saw my wedding ring was when I shoved it in the drawer of my bedroom back in Ireland.

"Only when it comes to you, wife."

My stupid heart fluttered, but instead of falling under his spell, I rolled my eyes and stood, needing to put distance between us.

"So damn cliché."

"If that's what it takes to win you back." His tone was light, amused, but shadows danced in his eyes.

"Christian, I thought we decided to move on." My chin trembled at the thought of him with another woman.

"We did not," he stated calmly. I inhaled and exhaled heavily in a hopeless attempt to return my heartbeat to normal. "I told you I'll kill any man who gets near you. You are *my* wife. *My* life. And I've been going fucking crazy without you. Not even therapy is helping."

"You went to..." My voice broke before I recovered it. "You've been seeing a therapist?"

He nodded somberly.

"I will do fucking anything for our marriage. For us." He took a step forward, reaching a hand to my face and cupping my cheek. "You're my wife, we belong at each other's side. We've made vows."

My heart that had been aching for months suddenly shuddered with ideas of its own.

"There was no mention of kidnappings in our vows," I pointed out, my teeth grinding. "And I don't believe that my brothers and sister would allow you to take me just like that."

Fear held me back. Juliette's betrayal hurt, but Christian's just about tore me apart. I didn't want to love someone that much to give them such power.

"Divorce is perfectly acceptable."

His jaw clenched and his eyes darkened to the deepest oceans.

"Til death do us part." His voice lowered to a frightening edge. "Remember?"

"No," I lied. "Shouldn't there be an apology or some groveling buried somewhere among your words?"

"I'll spend my life groveling, angel." The depths of his blue eyes flickered with so many emotions, it was terrifying and thrilling at the same time. "But first, I'm taking you home."

Christian brought me home, but not to the one I expected.

We were in an old manor located along the craggy cliffs of Ballyhack in Ireland. It was his mother's wedding present—a home and land of our own. Unlike the Murphy estate, which was surrounded by woods and soothing sounds of forests, this manor had the view of cliffs and the Atlantic Ocean on one side and green pastures as far as the eye could see on the other.

We ended up in my homeland with an uneasy truce, if it could even be called that. He was with me from morning to night, rarely leaving my sight.

On top of that, he had gifts delivered on a daily basis. Sometimes even hourly. Chocolates. Cakes. Flowers. Jewelry. A *car*.

Everything but the one thing I really wanted.

An apology.

Compromise.

Promises kept.

And then there was the sexual frustration. By the end of the first week, I was torn between dragging him to my bed and banishing him.

"We need to talk," I said Saturday night as we both

sat in the living room, the television on with the girliest rom-com I could find: *Legally Blonde*.

"Okay." Christian turned to face me and I instantly regretted starting a conversation. My eyes fell to his bare torso, those abs tempting me like a glass of water on a hot summer day. He wore nothing but sweatpants, the outline of his hard length clearly visible. I had to ask the question that'd been plaguing me since I woke up on the plane last week.

"Why do you insist on wearing sweatpants?" I blurted, forcing my gaze away from his body and locking it on his face.

"Your Pinterest." His mouth twitched when I glared at him.

"Stalker," I muttered. I had completely forgotten that I had a mood board dedicated to men in loungewear.

"Just so you know, I'm strongly considering working through that list of models and ending them all."

My mouth gaped, unable to find words. Then I gave my head a subtle shake.

"I'm going to take that as a joke. A lame one," I mumbled. "Anyhow, I want you to stop with the gifts." Then, because I was genuinely worried, I added, "And my sweatpants models are not to be touched."

Christian raised an eyebrow. "Delete the board, then."

I threw my hands up in frustration. "Fine, but I want your word that you won't go after them."

His smile faded. "I told you, no other men for you."

Yes, he was a psychopath, but his obsessive madness was doing stuff to me and I worried I was going to cave into temptation and jump him right now. *Sex on the couch seems like a great idea.*

I launched myself off the couch, terrified I'd follow through if I didn't get away.

"Just stop sending me gifts," I said over my shoulder, then ran like the devil was at my heel.

For the remainder of the evening, I hid in my bedroom like a coward, sprawled on the bed with a pulse throbbing between my legs. I stared at the ceiling, stubbornly ignoring the desire coursing through my veins.

The clock's soft ticks and tocks filled the space. I'd just dozed off when suddenly my wrists were pinned above my head.

Despite the dark, I could make out the outline of the beautiful face. Those intense eyes and the set of his jaw. My husband.

My body slackened under his weight and my legs fell apart. I moaned something incoherent and licked my lips, watching his eyes blaze as his free hand wrenched off my underwear. He slammed inside me with a feral force, and I glimpsed his vulnerable expression before his movements wiped all thoughts from my mind.

I cried out, my back arching off the bed as he proceeded to ram into me, owning every inch of me with every ruthless thrust. His groin slapped against my flesh, his hips crashing against me with the savage power.

"My wife likes when I fuck her hard." His voice was raspy, and when I opened my mouth to speak, he covered it with his palm. "Don't deny it. I can feel it in the way your cunt is strangling my cock."

With every word out of his sinful mouth, my core tingled. My brain turned fuzzy, world spinning as his rhythm took on a feral momentum. He fucked me like it was the last thing we'd get to experience in this life and the next. Like it was our final act. Like I was his.

My walls clenched and pleasure started to gather in my core, shooting all the way up my spine before submerging my entire body.

"Christian..." I moaned. "So... good."

"There she is." Dark tones coated his voice as he leaned down and trapped the lobe of my ear between his teeth and whispered hot words, "Let go, angel. I'll catch you."

I gripped the sheets, my orgasm *so close*. Just a little more and...

I shot up from my pillow, panting hard.

For a second, I was lost to the steadily retreating images, but then I looked around and found my fingers were inside my panties.

Fuck. I was dreaming.

My damp hair stuck to my temples and my heart was thundering erratically against my rib cage.

I went to yank my hand from my aching pussy with a jerk, when a voice froze my movement.

"I want to see more."

My eyes widened and my cheeks heated as I turned my head to the side. Embarrassment flooded me as I found my husband seated on the chair next to the bed, his legs crossed at the ankles.

He's still wearing those damn pants.

My eyes fell to his taut forearms, the soft moonlight throwing shadows over his features. The look in his eyes was dark, a thousand words spoken without him uttering a single sound.

His gaze zeroed in on my hand still frozen between my parted legs.

"What are you doing here?" I whispered.

"Watching you. Wishing my tongue could replace those fingers."

I looked down, my glistening pussy on full display. When in the hell did I get rid of my panties? Mortification filled me and my cheeks burned as I returned my gaze to him.

"Care for a toy?" he suggested.

I paused, my heart thundering at the tempting idea. When I remained silent, he stood up and closed the distance to the bed, taking my hand in his—the same one that was on my most intimate parts—and lifted it to his face.

Then he inhaled my scent deeply into his lungs. *"Fuck."*

My feelings dispersed, my heart buzzing, thundering, with nothing to anchor it. It desperately wanted to flee to *him*.

"Will you let me eat you out, wife?" he whispered darkly. "Like that first day."

My nipples instantly peaked into tight buds under his merciless gaze.

"Just that?" I asked cautiously, almost hopefully.

He remained there, watching, looming, waiting.

"Anything you want."

His long, masculine fingers wrapped around a taut nipple and twisted, gently at first, then harshly. A sharp inhale echoed in the silence, pleasure zapping straight to my core. It was so strong that my entire body shuddered, my every nerve coming alive under his touch.

He pinched both nipples and I nearly levitated off the bed with a yelp. "Mmm… again."

"So demanding." His voice was low, like the cool silk surrounding me.

He twisted them again, more forcefully this time, and I released an anguished cry.

"Yes, yes… ahhh…" I whimpered when he massaged the aching nipples with the pads of his rough thumbs. He continued twisting and pinching my nipples, then ran the pad of his thumb over the tips as if soothing them, giving them a slight reprieve before he went back to torturing them again. He knew exactly what to do with my body to bring it to release.

My core throbbed in sync with the rhythm of his fingers. Hard and fast, then slow and agonizing. My thighs rubbed together, hungry for his hand. Then, as if reading my mind, he released my one breast, tracing his hand down my stomach all the way to my soaked pussy.

At the same time he pinched my nipple, hard enough to elicit a whimper of pain, he thrust his finger inside me and a shiver shot through my body.

"Ohhh…" I moaned throaty sounds.

"Mmm. You're dripping, angel." Christian ran a finger through my folds. Pleasure coupled with pain and my lips parted in a wordless cry. "Look at me."

He thrust two fingers inside me and I almost blacked out from the sensation. "Ahhh…"

"Your walls are strangling my fingers," he rasped, his eyes locked on me. "Do you wish you had my cock?"

I moaned my answer.

Lust shone in his eyes, harsh and out of control. He pinched again and I gasped, the sensation and rhythm overwhelming and savage. He was working me like we'd done this a million times.

He rammed his fingers a few more times, the heel of his palm slapping against my clit with every move and it took no time for stars to burst behind my eyelids.

My back pushed off the mattress, meeting his fingers on my nipples and inside me. He curled them, and a scream tore from my lips as the ecstasy hit me from all directions.

"Ahhh… I'm… I'm… *ahhh.*"

I raised my hips, riding the wave. Riding his hand. It felt like dying and going to heaven. Sheer pleasure racked my body, tearing me apart only to put me back together.

Christian wrenched his fingers from me and placed them at my mouth. "Suck them clean."

My eyes widened in confusion or shock, I wasn't sure, but I had no time to contemplate because he pushed them between my lips.

"Mmm…" I lapped at his fingers, my face burning and my thighs clenching. The orgasm vanished, but a new one rose to the surface under my husband's penetrating eyes as I continued to slowly lick his fingers, curling my tongue around them.

"Such a good wife," he praised, heat flaring in his eyes.

I released them with a pop, a line of saliva sticking to them.

Then I watched with utter bewilderment as he walked out, leaving me sated and sprawled on the bed.

All alone.

Chapter Forty-Four

IVY

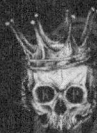

My phone rang in my hand, and Wynter's name popped up on the screen. I hesitated. She was my confidant, my best friend, but she was Christian's sister first and my friend second. After all, blood was thicker than water, and it made me leery about confiding in her.

Juliette would regularly be my go-to, but we'd barely mended our bond and I wasn't ready to resume as if nothing happened.

It was spiteful and unhealthy, but I had to do things my way.

"Wynter," I answered as I moved from my walk-in closet into the bedroom.

The glass doors to the balcony were open, so I moved through them to the fresh grass-scent air of the back garden. I had been sleeping in the manor's master bedroom because Christian didn't sleep in it, even though all his personal belongings were in this room.

Probably why he caught me red-handed last night. My cheeks heated at the memory, and a deep, deprived part of me wanted an encore. Except Christian was nowhere to be found.

It was for the best, I told myself.

"Hey, I wanted to check how you're doing," Wynter said warmly. "I heard my brother... umm... took you to Ireland."

Translation: I heard my brother kidnapped you again.

I bit my lip as I took a seat in a cushioned chair. The air was brisk this early in the morning, and wearing only my wool socks, shorts, and a crew-neck top, I pulled the knitted afghan off the vacant chair and wrapped it around my shoulders.

"Well, you heard right."

"So you're okay? You're not mad at him? Us?" She sounded deeply morose about the idea, which surprised me. To my knowledge, Christian was the only one who'd had a hand in my kidnaping.

"I don't know," I answered truthfully.

"I really thought when we helped him break your engagement to Aiden that it was for the best. But we didn't help him this time, I promise."

Surprise flared in me as I chewed my lower lip.

"I didn't know you helped him the first time."

"You're good for him," she muttered over the line.

"As his kidnapee?" I said.

"No, as his wife. Don't tell me you disagree."

"How would you know?" I stalled. She blew air through her lips and clucked her tongue.

"You glow when you're around him. And he doesn't have eyes for anyone else. Just you. And since you left him, he's let the Syndicate business fall to the wayside, giving away docks to the Serbian mafia and purchasing damn surveillance companies in every country you step foot in."

I sighed. Of course he did.

"You're hardly objective in this matter."

"Ivy, don't insult me, okay? We've known each other long enough to know better."

I sighed. "We have some things to discuss, secrets to come clean on." There was a pregnant pause, static with things unsaid on both ends of the phone.

"But you love him?" she questioned softly.

"Yes."

"I knew it. And he loves you," she murmured.

"What?" I blinked as the wind swept in from the cliffs.

"He loves you," she repeated, clapping in the background. "When I see you two together, I see chaos and peace. You make each other feel alive."

So alive I burned.

I traced my wedding ring with my thumb. I hadn't taken it off since Christian slid it back on.

"How did you know?"

"Because I experienced it with Bas. Because I've seen it with Juliette and Davina. Because I see it whenever you're with my brother. You are fierce and strong, but also kind and gentle. It's exactly what he needs."

"And what do I need?" I asked pointedly.

"A man who challenges your heart and your soul." She was utterly and completely right. "If anyone can give him what he needs, it's you. And if I may be so bold, I think he gives you exactly what *you* need."

"You're the youngest. You're supposed to be the reckless one, and here you are giving me sound advice."

Without hesitation, she said, "Juliette was reckless enough for the both of us. I had to balance us out."

"She came and saw me," I admitted. "In Lisbon."

"She fucked up, but I believe if she could go back, she wouldn't have done what she did," she said softly, the words waterlogged with timeless sorrow.

"I'm struggling to move past it," I murmured, the admission escaping me without permission. "Why would he protect *her* secret when I protected his?"

"Because Dante protected him when they were little," she pointed out softly. "It had less to do with protecting Juliette than it did with his loyalty to Dante."

"It hurts," I whispered, tears stinging my eyes. "It's stupid, but I can't help it."

"Just tell him," she said, her voice thick. "Although, I think moving forward, he's done with secrets. This is a cycle that will be broken because he's scared of losing you more than losing his own life. This shit with Juliette was—"

"A clusterfuck," I finished for her.

"Yes, a clusterfuck." Then she added tentatively, "Besides, we all need to get past this. The success of the school we're putting together hinges on it."

"Maybe this was a test," I croaked. "Didn't we take a class on business conflict and amicable resolutions?"

"I think I skipped that class," she joked.

"I definitely did."

"Love you," she said, and I blinked, my lonely heart warmed by the reminder that no matter what, even an entire ocean away from them, I was lucky to have friends and family who loved me and would always have my back.

Even when mistakes were made.

Chapter Forty-Five

PRIEST

The great thing about having morally questionable values was how much could be accomplished. I kidnapped my wife, but there was no fucking way I would apologize. She belonged with me, and for better or worse, we would work out our issues.

Her brothers didn't object to me taking Ivy because I threatened a war. After all, she was no longer a Murphy but had my name attached to her. And Louisa… well, she needed a bit more persuading. But I had the information she needed to find her sister and she couldn't bypass it.

Not that I'd cut her away from them.

They were family, and if she wanted to help her sister find her twin, I'd do everything in my power to find her too. With Ivy at my side.

Instead of going back to Philly, I'd taken us to Ireland and the property Aisling had gifted us. I even secured Cobra's transport so Ivy wouldn't feel alone, although a small part of me worried she'd sic her on me.

I stood by the large glass door that looked out onto the craggy cliffs of Ballyhack to the waves crashing on the beach. Strong. Powerful. Deadly. A combination so familiar it would usually bring me some comfort.

But not today.

I'd had my wife back at my side for a week now. She'd finally stopped asking me to take her back, but she refused to talk to me.

She just needs time to cool off, I told myself, yet as the back of my neck itched and tension crept up my spine, I had to roll my shoulders to push away my obsessive thoughts.

The months of therapy had helped, but the old habit of releasing tension by means of torture had crept in and had me pacing around restlessly in the large foyer.

Glancing up the staircase for the last time, I made a decision.

I walked outside, instructing my guards to keep an eye on Ivy and Cobra, then made my way to the outskirts of the property, the one that bordered the Brennans', and descended into the dungeon.

"You have to let me go or you'll burn in the eternal fires of hell." The local priest I had kidnapped sat tied to the chair, chains shining around his torso, while I examined him like the filthy insect he was.

I flexed my hands into fists. The rage I'd suppressed roared back, drowning out any other feeling.

"The only one going to hell is you, Father. And there's a special place there for pedophiles."

His body twisted in a futile struggle.

"I don't know what you're talking about." The burning flame of panicked resentment flickered in his eyes. "I'm a man of the cloth. I teach Sunday school."

The memories of my own abuse were hazy, buried beneath the weight of the years, but emotional scars were there. They would always be there.

"I know." I bent until we were at eye level. "And you won't be teaching shit by the time I'm done with you."

A bead of sweat trickled down his forehead. Malice mingled with the resentment in his eyes.

"You'll never get away with this."

"Oh, I already did."

Every bottled-up emotion unleashed on this fucker.

I gripped his shoulder and dug my fingers into the pressure points until he squeaked with pain. I slammed my fist into his face, fury darkening the edges of my vision. The air crackled with unleashed violence, and soon, the snap of bone gave way to the wet sound of ripping flesh.

Soon, my heart thundered with adrenaline and tension seeped out of my body.

This was the outlet I needed.

A hand came to my back and I whirled around, ready to punch whoever dared to enter my sanctuary when my hand froze mid-air.

"What the fuck are you doing here?"

"I came to visit your grandpa Brennan and your uncle Liam," she said. "It was a short walk from their property to yours, so I wanted to pop in when I spotted you from the distance." She tilted her chin at the body behind me. "With him." I narrowed my eyes on her and she let out an exasperated sigh. "Christian, I grew up around here. I know every corner of this place. It wasn't hard to figure out where you're dragging a body to."

"That doesn't answer my question, Aisling."

"Your grandpa Brennan and uncle Liam—"

"Please stop calling them that."

"Okay." She sighed again. "Anyhow, they may or may not have been keeping an eye on you and are worried."

I scoffed. "A bit late for them to be worried, don't you think?"

"That's not fair since neither one of them knew I gave birth and didn't know of your existence." She waved her hand, dismissing the topic. "But I'm here for you now and I just want to make you see reason," Aisling said, taking my bloodied hand in hers. "Christian, you have to stop playing the role of judge, jury, and executioner. Instead, talk to your wife. Talk to me. Just *stop*."

I stared at her, then at the bloodied, unconscious body on the ground. Dark liquid pooled around him, and if it weren't for the faint rise and fall of his chest, I would've thought he was already dead.

"I can't," I said. "You should go."

She definitely didn't belong down here. My ragged breaths echoed in the empty space. This stone cellar contained no furniture aside from the chair and a table full of torture tools.

She refused to let go and yanked me with more strength than I'd thought possible.

"Yes, you can. Now listen to me." My heart rate slowed the longer I stared at her. "This... this guy deserves to be tortured and killed. But you don't. Stop staining your soul and live. Move on."

The soft drip, drip, drip of the moisture on the walls pushed away the fog clouding my brain and I was suddenly aware of the blood coating my hands and staining Aisling.

I wrenched myself away from her and stumbled backward, my breathing heavy and my throat raw.

"Please, Christian," she pleaded with a soft voice at my back. "Please let the past go and *live*. For you and your wife. For *me*." Tears burned my eyes. "I don't deserve any reprieve for leaving you, but you do."

I slowly turned around and met my mother's somber

expression, nothing but love in it. No disgust for what she'd just witnessed me do. Just acceptance.

My stomach lurched and I glanced at the unconscious body.

"Let me take care of this," she offered. "Liam can help and we'll be out of here before Ivy even notices us."

I would have laughed if the circumstances weren't so fucked up.

"No. You shouldn't—"

She cut off my protest.

"That's what family's for." To tell the truth, she'd surprised me. It wasn't what I'd expect from someone like her, but maybe she was stronger than she appeared. As if she read my thoughts, she said, "Being with Frank... your father... I've found a strength I never thought I possessed."

She smiled dreamily, the expression out of place here in the darkness of the cellar filled with a coppery scent.

"I guess that's good," I muttered.

"He chases my demons away." My brow furrowed. Aisling's sigh contained multitudes of exasperation. "We all have our crosses to bear, yours heavier than mine."

"I didn't think you were religious."

Emotions slipped into her gaze, an acute sense of guilt turning her eyes a deep blue.

"The point is, Christian, Ivy chases yours away. And when you find someone like that, you hold on to it with both hands and never let go."

"What do you think I'm doing?" I closed my eyes and pressed a fist to my forehead, swallowing the lump in my throat. "But the tighter I squeeze, the faster she slips through my fingers."

The dark cloud that had stalked me for years swirled faster, a thunderstorm in the making.

"You need to talk to her."

Tension zipped down my spine and I cracked my eyes open to glare at her. "I do talk to her."

She pinched the bridge of her nose, and the gesture sobered me. I finally let myself see a part of myself in this strong woman.

"What I mean, son, is talk to her about what you're feeling, whether that be fear, joy, love, passion…"

"And if she—" I searched for the right word and failed. "If she doesn't like what she hears or sees deep down?"

After a long moment of silence, she answered. "It's just a risk you have to take."

Chapter Forty-Six

IVY

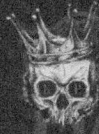

I hadn't seen Christian all day.

Ever since my call with Wynter, I'd spent hours agonizing over how Christian and I could move forward.

Needing a break, I headed to the library. It wasn't as grand as mine back at Murphy Castle, but there were enough Agatha Christie books on the shelves to keep me busy. With Cobra huddled next to me on the loveseat, I read *Murder on the Orient Express,* getting lost in the suspense I knew this old favorite would deliver.

It was well into the afternoon when the door to the library opened. My heart jumped in my throat when I saw Christian walk in, freshly showered in a T-shirt and loose-fitting pants.

He ran a hand through his damp hair as he took the seat opposite of me.

"Hi."

His eyes drifted down my body, then to Cobra.

"Can we talk?" A visible swallow worked its way down his throat. "Maybe without the dog."

I mustered a smile. "Don't tell me you're scared of my bodyguard."

His lips tilted up. "It's her job to attack."

"And you think I'd tell her to attack you?"

"I wouldn't blame you if you did." His eyes flickered with emotion and lines of exhaustion bracketed his mouth, causing my chest to squeeze until I thought it would burst.

I sighed. "Well, I'm not."

Christian's lips curved with a faint hint of bitterness. "Maybe I'll wish for it after this."

The air between us hummed with a lifetime's worth of unspoken words, broken promises, and frustration.

He leaned over, bringing his elbows to his knees. My heart stilled as the eyes of the deep blue oceans looked back at me. Butterflies swarmed my stomach, ready to take flight, right along with all my feelings for this man.

Whenever he was around it felt like free-falling, but in a good kind of way. Most of my anger had dissipated over the past few days, thanks to my conversation with Wynter and a last-minute call with my therapist, and I'd finally let myself work through my conflicting feelings.

Christian opened his mouth, then closed it, and frustration welled in my stomach.

"I'm so sorry, Ivy." He finally broke the silence. "I didn't want to admit it, even to myself, that keeping the truth—"

"Was the same as lying."

"Yes." A grim smile touched his beautiful lips. "I convinced myself I was sparing you, but the truth is, I was being selfish."

"Yes, you were." My hands shook as emotions thundered through me. Cobra raised her head to look at me with alarm, immediately placing blame on Christian, so I whispered a soft command and she bolted out of the room. I twisted my fingers nervously, my pulse accelerating. "My family kept me sheltered, left me in the dark. I don't want that with you. I'm strong; I can take whatever comes our way."

"And you proved that," he said wryly. "The way you handled everything after running into Vittoria, then delivering Father Gabriel to me. The problem was me." He let out a bitter laugh.

I swallowed, knowing it wasn't easy for any man— let alone one ruling a criminal organization—to admit he was wrong.

"The problem has always been me, angel." A heaviness tugged at my chest at the vulnerability in his voice. "I grew up believing I didn't deserve anything good, and then you came along." My breathing slowed, my heart encouraging him to continue. "You're so... good, it felt all along like I didn't deserve you. A part of me thought if you learned the truth about your athair's death, you'd leave me."

I was overwhelmed with what he shared, and I believed him, yet it was terrifying to give him a chance to do it again.

"Were you there?" I rasped. "When Juliette—"

He shook his head. "No, but I knew it was going down, and I didn't stop it. I could have told you—warned you—but I didn't. It didn't matter that we weren't together at that point. I just let it unfold, convinced a person with any connection to Sofia Volkov wasn't worth living."

"It wasn't for you to make that decision," I said, my tone firm, while Christian's gaze bore into me with intensity.

"It wasn't, and while I cannot promise you that I won't make a mistake again, I can vow to you that I'll always be truthful. I give you my word that I'll earn your trust. If you'll let me."

After his betrayal, I'd been scared to trust him again, but maybe that fear was only holding me back. Life was full of risks, and it required a leap of faith to live fully. But I needed him to understand that he couldn't hide things from me.

Just as I opened my mouth, he said, "I'm a fuckup, angel, and my love isn't a fairy tale, but I promise you,

you're it for me. There's nobody that will ever mean more to me than you. You're the only woman for me."

"You hurt me."

"I'm sorry. More than you'll ever know."

"Don't ever do that to me again."

"I won't." Call me foolish, but I believed him. "I love you, Ivy. And I held on so tight, willing to kill, cheat, and steal to keep you with me. It was wrong, especially after all the acceptance you've given me, and I should have... *Fuck.*"

He rubbed the back of his neck, looking uncharacteristically flustered.

"I don't deserve you, but I'm willing to work at it until I do." His jaw tightened. "Please just let me prove to you that I—" He broke off, coughed to clear his throat. "You are my top priority. Your friends are my friends, your enemies are my enemies, and your pain is my pain. I would burn down the world for you."

"Don't break my trust again, Christian," I breathed, slipping off my seat and padding over to stand between his legs. I ran a hand through his hair and he raised his head, pressing his face against my stomach and letting out a sigh.

"Fuck, I missed your touch."

He gripped the backs of my thighs, lifting me to straddle him. Slowly, tentatively, he reached for the hem of my shirt, gauging my reaction.

"Can I undress you?" A shudder rippled through him

under my palms. "I've never wanted anyone," he said, his voice uneven, "the way I want you."

My heart faltered, then picked up again, beating at twice the speed, desire heavy in my veins.

He waited for my permission, and once I gave it, I shifted off him and our clothes began to fall to the floor in a heap.

He gently grasped me by the elbows and encouraged me to climb back into his lap. I put a knee on either side of his hips as he sat back with his shoulders against the cushions.

He crushed his lips to mine in a fierce and desperate kiss.

"Until death do us part," he grunted, his touch hot and possessive.

"Until death do us part," I echoed as we were caught in each other's gazes.

His hot length brushed against my core and my breath cut off. His palm coasted from my elbow up my arm. It traveled over my shoulder, slid up my neck, and continued until his fingers wove into my hair. His head rested on the back of the couch as he stared up at me hungrily.

His other hand was on my waist, guiding me to move. I rubbed my hips against him, the head of his cock right at my entrance, and lowered myself onto him, feeling him deep inside me.

It elicited a sigh from us both. The feeling of him

inside me was so intense, my body trembled with plea-sure. His lips parted so he could drag in ragged breaths as I started to move, and his head tipped further back, his eyes drifting closed.

He lifted his head, opened his eyes, and simply stared at me. Seated all the way, his hand on my waist, he urged me to rock on him. The first stroke wrung a whimper from my lips.

"How does it feel?" he asked.

"So... good."

We found our rhythm, his sensual hands resuming their work. They caressed my breasts, notching over my hardened nipples. They smoothed along my thighs. Slid up my back, tracing my spine.

But it was his heavy-lidded gaze that held all my attention as I rode him, my body threatening to unravel. I had my hands on his chest for leverage, but I lifted them and laced my fingers together behind his neck, pulling him to me.

When our mouths locked together, time suspended. Nothing existed outside of this room. Nothing lived beyond the two of us, our bodies connected as one.

I moved slowly, rocking my hips in a circular motion, grinding my clit against him, trembling with the inten-sity. Sweat dampened our temples and moans drifted from our lips, and he reached forward to tease my breasts with his mouth and teeth. His free hand on my ass pushed and pulled, lifting me to keep up the urgent tempo.

I circled my hands behind me onto his knees and rode him. His gaze caught fire, trailing from my parted lips to my bouncing breasts to where he slid in and out of me. I was so wet it was dripping down my thighs.

His eyes locked there and one of his hands slipped between us to trace my landing strip until he found my clit. He rubbed it in a circular motion, his mouth licking and sucking my nipples. I moaned, every touch feeding the hot buzz in my core, pleasure nearly overwhelming me.

"Fuck, you feel so good," he groaned against my ear, his heartbeat racing against mine.

His hands were everywhere—down my spine, grabbing fistfuls of my hair to angle my head the way he wanted it so he could keep me harder and deeper.

And then he took over completely.

I threw my head back. His deep thrusts shook my body all the way down to my foundation. He grunted and strained as he chased his breath, but he didn't stop driving.

"Oh... God... please... ahhhh."

He swallowed my gasp in his mouth as I climaxed with the force of a category five hurricane. I came so hard spots scattered behind my eyes.

He clamped his strong arms around my body and buried his face in my chest while a series of pleasure-soaked moans fell from his lips. And, with a punishing last thrust and a shudder, he finished inside me, softly nipping my neck in a rough sort of appreciation.

His mouth brushed against me as he whispered, "I love you so fucking much," and warmth filled me like sunlight.

I curled my fingers in his hair as our heavy breaths filled the silence, our naked flesh pressed against together. I was high on a languid post-coital bliss when I rested my face in the crook of his neck.

Christian softened his hold on me, just enough to peer into my eyes. "This is just the beginning of the rest of our lives."

I dropped a kiss on his lips. "Forever."

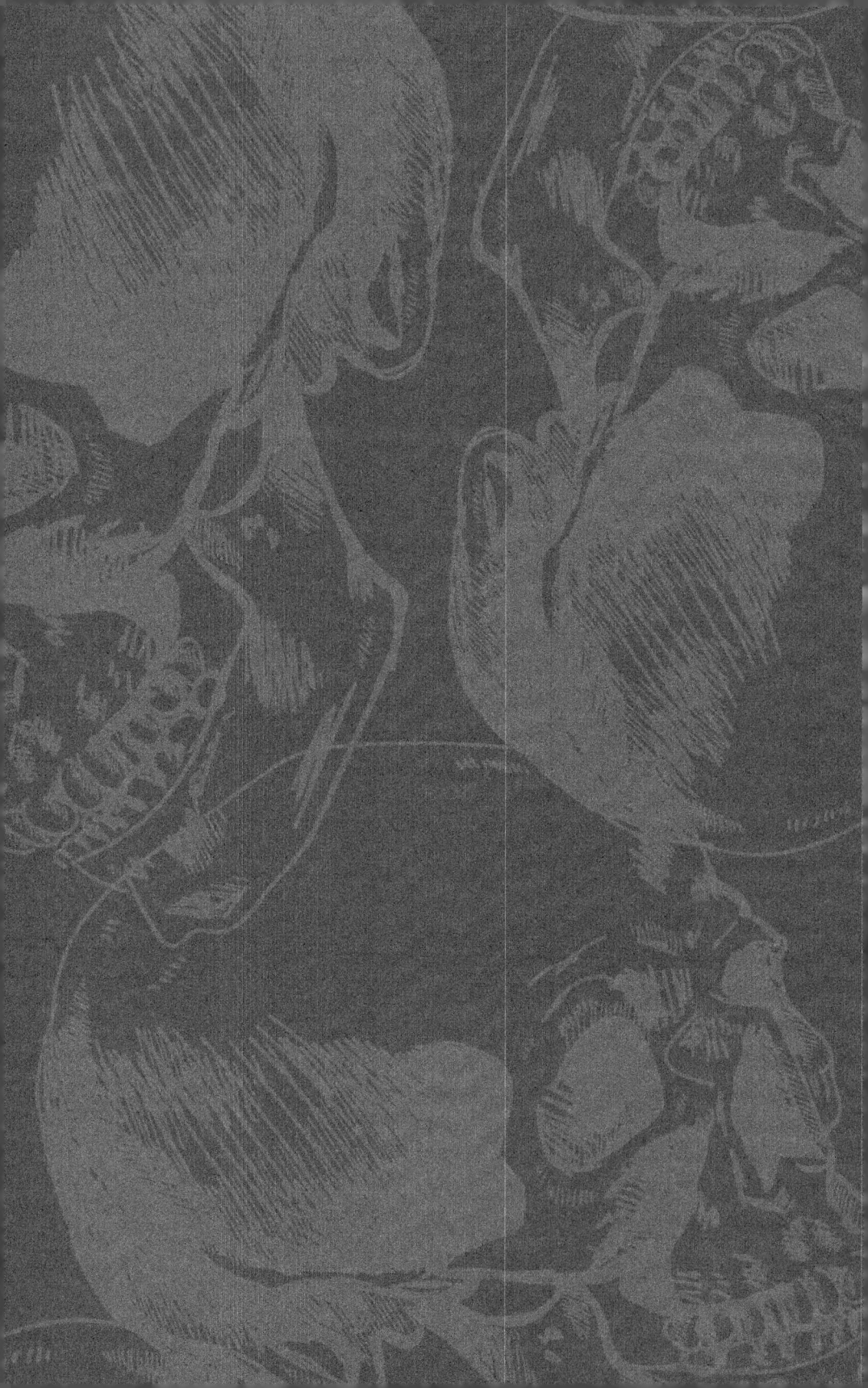

Chapter Forty-Seven
PRIEST

Five Months Later
Ireland

Dr. Freud watched me, her expert eyes giving nothing away.

Life was *good*, and it was thrilling and terrifying at the same time. I'd continued my therapy sessions, sometimes on my own, other times with Ivy, and then there were the ones with the entire family.

"How are things with Ivy?"

A smile touched my lips. "She's doing well. We've settled on living between Ireland and Philly for now, but once we have kids, we'll raise them in Ireland."

She tilted her head. "So you are ready to start a family?"

Four months had gone by since my reversed vasectomy, and although we agreed to wait, I didn't regret going through with it.

"Yes, but we won't rush it." We wanted more time for ourselves. And even now as my wife waited for me in the waiting room, I couldn't help but feel the light beam from my chest.

I'd always struggled with feelings, but never with her. Since I first met her, she understood me before I even said anything.

Together, we were invincible.

I was still working on my negative self-talk patterns, on quieting the voices that told me I didn't deserve her, but I was working on it.

The funny thing was that now that I was happy and had my woman by my side, I wanted everyone around me happy too. I'd been working on building a relationship with Aisling and coming to a mutual understanding with her and my papà.

Dr. Freud's nervous gaze slid to the side as I got to my feet, buttoning my jacket. Taking a step forward across this makeshift office in Dublin, I placed a note on the table next to her, then turned to leave.

"You said I shouldn't look for answers."

I shifted a glance over my shoulder.

"I did."

She raised a brow. "Then why give me this?"

"Because you wouldn't have stopped. Not until you

learned what happened to your sister." I twisted the door-knob, a smile dancing on my lips. "Because you helped me find peace, and I want to return the favor."

I shut the door behind me to the past and smiled at where my future sat, on a rickety plastic chair reading a magazine from 2006. I had everything I needed right here. Now I understood that a child would only enrich us. Our family. Our future.

"How was it?" Ivy asked once we'd stepped out onto the busy Dublin sidewalk where sunrays greeted us. She wore leggings and one of my long-sleeve dress shirts, cinched at the waist with what *also* looked like one of my belts. I'd never seen a more beautiful sight.

"It was good. No groundbreaking discoveries," I remarked. "All those things happen with you." I winked.

She let out a soft chuckle. "Did you give her the note?"

"I did."

My gaze met hers as I opened the passenger door and she slid into the seat. I leaned over and pressed a soft kiss to her lips. "She also prescribed me something."

She stiffened, her eyes snapping open. "What?"

"More sex to ensure the vasectomy reversal was a success."

She chortled, slapping a playful hand to my chest.

"I'm starting to think you're tricking me, husband." Ivy's lips brushed against mine for another kiss.

I nipped her bottom lip lightly while rubbing small

circles over the nape of her neck. "I'm just making up for lost time."

She wrapped her arms around my neck, her touch sending a small shiver through me while I still held the passenger door open.

Her lips parted, a blush rising to her cheeks, and she breathed against my lips, "Then get in the car and drive us home."

I shut the door and walked around the car, getting in the driver's seat.

Her hand came to rest on my thigh.

I hooked my arm around her shoulder, needing her closer. "I love you, angel."

Her eyes sparkled with mischief as she squeezed my thigh. "You better or I'll have Cobra bite your balls off."

I grinned. "I'll show you how much when we get home."

And that was exactly what I did.

Chapter Forty-Eight

PRIEST

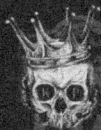

One Year Later

My brother, Basilio, and I, along with our men, were parked a street away from Bogdan's port in my city. After a year of bloodshed, enough was enough. We would take it back today.

I checked my weapons one last time, asking Dante, "Have you checked all surveillance? We know the position of every guard on Bogdan's payroll?"

"Yes."

My phone buzzed, I slid the message open and read it. It was a report on Bogdan's movements.

"He's out of the country," I said. "The Serbian don."

Basilio grinned. "Fuck, that's perfect. This should be easy, then."

Soon, we were out of the car, using the blind spots and cover of darkness to close the distance to the back entrance of the port. Our men trailed behind us, silent as we were. Once we reached it, a rush of adrenaline surged in my bloodstream, my mind craving the violence and bloodshed.

It was just who I—we—were.

I waited a few seconds, then kicked the door with my foot, sending the wood crashing open and the Serbians scurrying for weapons. I killed two before they could reach for them, Dante and Basilio shot others before they could pull their guns out too.

A bullet barely missed me, and I ducked, firing in that direction. Basilio and Dante, and our men, fired at our enemy, eliminating them one by one. There was a lot of shouting, bodies falling with a thud as we made our way from room to room.

It was over quickly.

We had eliminated every single man of the enemy except for one. That one we sent running with his tail between his legs with a message.

The Syndicate took back its port. Step foot on my territory without an invitation and I'll cut your head off.

It was simple and clear. No room for misunderstanding.

That same night we celebrated back in the very same club where I'd first touched my wife.

In the years since my innocence was stolen from me, I'd learned how to turn off dark memories and keep others at bay, knowing that if anyone tried to get physically close to me, the pain would resurface.

And even though we were a family of criminals, I understood there were some actions even criminals didn't condone. I grew up to become a criminal like my father, ruling the Syndicate with an iron fist and turning the likes of Vittoria and Father Gabriel from perpetrators to victims.

Since ruling Philadelphia and the Syndicate, I'd killed many, but I always made sure they deserved it. And my partner in crime—my beautiful wife—stood by my side through it all.

I might sit at the head of the Philadelphia Syndicate, but my wife was my anchor. My strength. Without her, I didn't know what living was, and with her... Fuck, with her, our lives were thriving.

Since I was a boy, I craved a happy home but never actually understood what it meant until Ivy. There was something to be said about having a home filled with love and laughter and seeing the world through your woman's eyes.

To say that I was completely recovered would be a

lie. Ghosts still lurked, but with the work I'd done to keep them at bay, they were few and far between.

Ivy and the girls were camped at the bar so they could *"plan world domination"* with their new project they'd been working on with money they'd stolen. Personally, I thought they were secretly planning how to gang up on their husbands in the future.

I joined my brother by the wall of windows that looked out to the dance floor and bar area where he stood with a pensive expression.

"Are you ensuring they stay out of trouble?" I asked him as I came up beside him and watched them make a toast while laughing.

"Juliette has a knack for getting in trouble," he remarked dryly, a hint of disgruntlement coloring his voice.

My sister-in-law had a tendency to act first and think later, and ever since he learned about Juliette's extra-curricular activities, he was her constant shadow.

"She does, but she also knows how to get out of it."

He let out a small rumble of irritation, but he didn't disagree. After all, we both knew I was right.

"I want to tell you something."

My eyebrows climbed at the unexpected change of subject. "Yes?"

Dante's brows knitted in a frown as he considered his next words. "I want to apologize."

"What for?"

"For failing you. If I knew about Father Gabriel—" His throat bobbed with a hard swallow. "I should have known. I should have protected you." That familiar tightness gripped my chest. "You're my family, my baby brother, and it was up to me to ensure your safety."

"It wasn't your job to protect me." My words came out choked. "Just as it wasn't mine to protect you. But we did it because we're a family. Yes, you're my brother, but you're also my best friend. *You* are the reason I survived Vittoria."

He swallowed hard.

"You're giving me too much credit."

"No, I'm not." He watched me with sharp eyes, his features taut with tension. "It's the truth. I love you, and there's nobody else on this planet I'd rather call my brother."

There was a moment of stunned silence because we weren't in the habit of speaking about our emotions. It was another result of our therapy sessions.

Then Dante's lips curved.

"Ditto." He clapped me on the back as the tightness in my chest intensified. "We're stuck together."

"I don't think Aisling is going anywhere either," I muttered.

"That's a good thing. It would break Papà's heart if she did," my brother pointed out. "And she loves you very much."

I rubbed an exasperated hand over my face. "I have

to admit, her stubbornness and persistence are almost admirable."

"She's nothing like Vittoria."

"No, she's not," I agreed, brushing off the buzzkill of a conversation by switching topics. "Now, go check on your wife to ensure those best friends aren't up to no good." My voice came out scratchy before I cleared my throat. "I promised Ivy I wouldn't spy on them with the security cameras."

He threw his head back and laughed. "Throw me to the wolves, why don't you."

"But first, let's toast." I reached for glasses from a nearby table and poured both of us a whiskey. I lifted my glass and clinked it against Dante's. "To happiness."

"To happiness," he echoed, and we drained our drinks.

A beat passed before we let out awkward laughs.

I threw an arm around his shoulder and steered him out of the office as he held back a grin. "Go and spy on our wives, brother."

Life was made out of chapters. Some were hard, some were sad, and some wreaked havoc on one's soul. But this... it was the start of a new one. The best one yet.

A couple of hours later, I finally had my wife where I needed her. In my office. With me. In my arms.

Hungry for her, I cupped her face and kissed her softly. Soon the kiss turned fierce and passionate, our bodies grinding against each other. She was my other half, the perfect half, and life with her was the most beautiful dream.

"What did I do to deserve you?" I grunted in her ear as I flattened her against the desk of my Philly office in the club where it all started.

"You've ravished me in a dark hallway..." she moaned, her legs opening.

I gripped her throat and slammed into her. She felt like heaven, my salvation. I thought this intense need for her would ease as time went on, but it only intensified.

I pounded into her as her raspy, deep-throated moans filled the air, urging me on. Her fingers gripped the edge of the desk as I fucked her hard and fast, starving for her.

Holding her by the hip, I pushed her long red strands off her neck and leaned over to whisper in her ear. "Best decision of my life."

Her eyes fluttered shut as she came apart around my cock. Unable to hold on, I thrust once, twice, until a powerful orgasm ripped through me and my cum spilled inside her.

"Christian?" As our breathing slowed, she cupped my cheek. "I love you."

My face softened, her lips brushing against mine.

"I love you too. Until death do us part."

"Forever."

This was my life. *Our* life. And I couldn't fucking wait to live it with her.

Epilogue

IVY

Five Years Later

DiLustro-Brennan Estate, Ireland

"Hello, everyone!" Aisling's and Frank's voices reached us before we spotted them. My brothers were right behind them, strolling in like the trouble they were. "Where is the birthday boy?"

They stepped out onto the patio behind our Irish castle where we spent most of the year. Our son, Maddox Jagger DiLustro, wiggled off my lap and ran over to his uncles and grandparents. Cobra, who became my son's constant shadow, followed behind, her tongue dangling and her tail wagging happily.

My brother lifted his little three-year-old body up and

flipped him upside down. He giggled and laughed, thrilled to be dangling by his ankles while Cobra barked at my brother, waiting for a command. If I thought she was protective of me, she was downright vicious in her guarding of Maddox.

"Easy, Cobra," I yelled to calm her down. "They're just playing."

She instantly sat down, her eyes attentive on Maddox and I took the opportunity to snap a photo. I finally got to use my Yale degree in photography when snapping photos of our family.

"Grandma, Grandma," Maddox squealed. "Save me."

"Bren, put my grandson down or I'll have to put you in timeout," Aisling demanded in a stern voice, but the sparkle in her eyes and the curve to her lips gave her away. She was such a softy these days.

"Do it, Grandma," Maddox encouraged, giggling the whole time as Bren flipped him over again and landed him on his feet. "Put Uncle Bren in timeout or Cobra will bite him."

I hid my smile. He was a troublemaker, our son, and the spitting image of his papà.

As Aisling and Bren negotiated his timeout, Maddox ran to his daddy and jumped on him. Christian caught him, his chubby arms wrapped around his neck, and my heart turned over as he squealed.

"You always catch me, Daddy." He wasn't wrong. Christian was a wonderful father and had an abundance of patience for our energetic son who was full of mischief, just like a boy should be. "When can I open my presents?"

"Not yet, buddy, but very soon."

Holding hands, my two favorites made their way to me. Their blond hair glimmered under the afternoon sun, and every time I saw them together, it made me the happiest version of myself.

I loved them so much, and some days I had to pinch myself to believe this was my life. *Our* life.

We spent more time at our Ireland property than in Philadelphia, and I loved every minute of it. It felt like living in a fairy tale.

Green pastures. The cliffs. The ocean waves hit the shoreline, the most beautiful and soothing sounds mixing with the chattering of people who stood by a long table with colorful decorations that had been set up for Maddox's birthday.

The moment he spotted the cake, he let go of Christian's hand and ran over to it, bumping into the table.

I sighed.

"Maddox, you have to calm down," I scolded him softly. "It won't be much of a birthday if you hurt yourself."

"Or the cake," Christian added, his eyes shining with pride.

Maddox didn't like hearing that at all. He was strong-willed and stubborn, much like me, although I refused to admit it. Forevermore, I claimed all our son's good traits as mine, the annoying ones belonged to his daddy.

"But I want cake and presents."

"You have to wait," I told our son. He kicked a patch of dirt, his face twisting with emotions, and I flicked a look at my husband and said exasperatedly, "Make sure your son behaves."

Christian took Maddox's hand again and kneeled to his eye level, then spoke softly but sternly to him. Only a few words were exchanged and instantly our son calmed down.

"When will I have my presents?"

"After the cake," he assured him. "But it's not about gifts, Maddox. It's about seeing all the people who love you."

Maddox's shoulders slumped. "Are Uncle Dante and Aunt Juliette coming too?"

"Of course. They wouldn't miss this for the world, don't worry."

Christian came over and kissed me softly, his palm gently rubbing my belly. "You look beautiful, angel."

I couldn't stop my beaming smile if I wanted to, and I didn't. We took a pregnancy test yesterday and learned we were expecting. But we weren't ready to share it—it was too early, and this was our son's day.

"You're biase,d so you don't count," I murmured.

"I'm hurt." He shot me a feigned look as if offended, but his eyes, sparkling like the entire universe was built for me, betrayed him. "I thought my opinion was the only one that mattered."

I rolled my eyes.

"You know it is, and—"

"There they are!" Maddox's loud exclamation pulled our attention just in time to see him tear past the table, cake and presents, sprinting as fast as his legs would carry him toward my brother-in-law and sister-in-law.

I smiled to see Dante grab Maddox and toss him in the air. "How is it possible it's your birthday? I was just here yesterday yet here you are, getting older and bigger."

Romeo, Maddox's cousin—the only son of Dante and Juliette—had surrounded his father and demanded he pick him up too, and now my brother-in-law was juggling both boys.

Juliette cupped Maddox's face in her hand, kissing him on both cheeks, and then whispered something to him that made him grin ear-to-ear. She probably promised him some adventure. Romeo and Maddox had a tendency to convince Juliette to do the most flabber-gasting things—like water tubing. I feared she was turning them into adrenaline junkies.

But all of this was so much better than the alternative of not having my best friend in my life. It also made me happy to see Christian's relationship blossoming with his own mother. It was far from perfect, but then life rarely was. Although this was pretty damn close.

"Are you okay?" Christian asked, his thumb brushing across my cheekbone and wiping my tears.

I nodded because my voice was lost in the chaos of emotions. Over the years, Juliette and I had come to repair our relationship. It wasn't an easy road, but we'd come to appreciate honesty more than anything.

"You're looking well," was Juliette's greeting as she found her way to me. "But Maddox is looking the best."

Christian went to join Dante and our son, and I was grateful for some alone time with my best friend. She looked good—happy—and the haunting ghosts that plagued her after learning of her birth parents' death had disappeared completely.

"He's a disaster on two legs," I said, smiling. "Every time I turn around, he's getting into something."

She kissed my cheeks and hugged me. "That's a kid's job."

Just when I released her, my nephew appeared, and I pressed a kiss on the top of his head.

"And how is our Romeo doing?"

"Good, Aunt Ivy. Can Maddox and I go see the cake?" Romeo was slightly older than Maddox, but it didn't stop them from being best friends.

"Of course." They were just about to bolt when my voice stopped him. "But first, you forgot something."

His big dark eyes that were so much like his father's found me with a frown when they finally flickered with realization. I lowered to my knees and he pecked me with a kiss, then bolted to a waiting Maddox.

I chuckled. "I feel cheated. That could barely be called a kiss."

"Soon they'll avoid us like the plague," Juliette remarked dryly. "Probably move halfway across the world to avoid us."

"True. Although, with you guys in Chicago and us in Europe, they are left with a lot more playground."

"Asia," she muttered. "Hopefully they stay away from the Yakuza."

I winced. "We better not even introduce that into their vocabulary."

Our gazes traveled over the backyard, our family laughing and hugging. Grandpa Frank was even singing some old Italian song and I couldn't help but feel grateful for the way things turned out. For all of us.

I didn't care about the heartaches we'd had to endure to get to this point.

Maybe it was just a lesson we had to learn.

All that mattered to me was that we got here, surrounded by a loving family and amazing husbands who supported us through our dreams. Family, friends, slightly dysfunctional dynamics—it all reminded me what it was like to be alive and loved.

This was what truly mattered in life. The only thing that mattered.

Epilogue
PRIEST

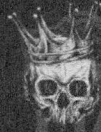

Thirteen Years Later

Children ran wildly over the busy courtyard of St. Jean d'Arc School.

My wife, sister, sister-in-law, and Davina had done a good job with the school, making it a very sought-after place. It wasn't only for the children of the people involved in criminal organizations, but also for the kids of powerful and distinguished families of the political and royal world.

The children, including ours, would be well protected within the lines of this large property. I, along with many of our other associates, had ensured it. I doubted that even the president of the United States was under better protection than the children attending this school.

But as a parent, it still made me nervous not to have my children within my eyesight. My attention darted to my son who was sixteen now, his eyes darting eagerly around, probably already scheming what kind of shit he could get into with his cousins. While protective of his younger sister, much to Poppy's dismay, Maddox certainly didn't know how to keep himself out of trouble.

And that kept me up at night sometimes.

We had been traveling back and forth between two continents for years, but once our son and daughter started school, we intended to stay in the States full-time, close to them.

Yes, both of them were a force to be reckoned with, but so were Dante and I. Morally wrong and wicked people still found our vulnerabilities and used them against us. The truth of the matter was that I would sooner level this earth than allow my children to be touched by such evil.

It was my job to protect them.

Hence the reason for adding several additional surveillance services for security and staying close to the property.

"You have that look on your face," my wife murmured softly, glancing at my profile. "The one that says I'm going to kill anyone who looks at my kids wrong."

I shrugged. "Because I am."

Poppy squeezed my hand. "Don't worry, Papà. If you do kill them, I'll help you get rid of the body."

I glanced at my daughter, the mirror image of my wife. "Thank you, wildling."

Ivy smacked my forearm gently. "You should scold her, Christian, not thank her."

I shrugged. "She wouldn't be the one doing the killing, angel, so we're all good."

Glancing at my daughter, I winked and she stifled a grin.

Was it scandalous that we spoke like that? Maybe, but while protective of our children, I didn't shield them from the ways of the mafia life. I wanted them to be aware, eyes wide open when walking this world, especially the criminal one.

Especially my girl who would one day probably marry a man who was part of a criminal organization. If the fucker did her wrong, I wanted her to know exactly how to handle him. Yes, I'd be there in the blink of an eye to kill the fucker, but if I no longer walked this earth, she would also know how to do it herself.

Poppy spotted her cousins, Wynter and Basilio's Brady bunch, and she shot me a pleading look. "Can I go say hi to Fallon?"

"Sure," Ivy told her. "We're right behind you."

She barely finished the sentence and our daughter was dust in the wind.

Poppy didn't shy away from a challenge and had a

good head on her shoulders which made her get along with Basilio's daughter, Fallon, despite their age difference. Both knew how to rule a room and the people in it. I daresay that my niece was a damn terror. I guess with her big brother, she had to be. Fallon never hesitated to put anyone in their place. After all, she'd had plenty of practice with her siblings.

"There's Romeo," Maddox exclaimed, and without waiting, he bolted to join his cousin.

My wife's beautiful eyes found me and she smiled, sliding her small hand into mine. "Ah, alone at last."

My lips twitched. "Not for long."

She sombered for a moment. "Are you sure you're okay with Maddox and Poppy attending St. Jean D'Arc?"

"Of course," I assured her for the millionth time. "Where else would our children be better protected than in the school that my wife's running?"

I meant it too. Yes, I implemented security measures that would make Rikers Island proud, but that had nothing to do with this school and everything with the ghosts that sometimes still haunted me. These measures would ensure my children would never experience them.

She rose on her tiptoes and pressed her mouth to my lips. It was our favorite way to show affection, kissing, and I could never get enough.

"How did I get so lucky?" she murmured against my lips.

I smiled against her mouth. "I ravished you in a dark hallway, and I got addicted."

"And the rest is history."

"The rest is history." I leaned in and nipped her bottom lip gently. "Which paved the way for our future."

I didn't deserve this happiness or future with a beautiful, loving family, but I'd keep it all anyhow. And I'd end anyone who tried to take it from me.

THE END

What's Next?

*Thank you so much for reading **Scandalous Kingpin**! If you liked it, please leave a review. Your support means the world to me.*

If you're thirsty for more discussions with other readers of the series, you can join the Facebook group, Eva's Soulmates group (https://bit.ly/3gHEe0e).

Next up in the series is Emory and Killian's book, Ravenous Kingpin (https://a.co/d/6bDUWqO).

Did you miss other stories in this series? You can grab them now.

Corrupted Pleasure (Davina and Liam), Prequel https:// bit.ly/3XayjIu
Villainous Kingpin (Basilio and Wynter), Book 1 https:// bit.ly/4dRmqwJ
Devious Kingpin (Dante and Juliette), Book 2 https://bit. ly/3ZMRSpb
Scandalous Kingpin (Priest and Ivy), Book 3 https://bit. ly/3YTAUrU
Ravenous Kingpin (Emory and Killian), Book 4 https:// bit.ly/4dRmqwJ

About the Author

Curious about Eva's other books? You can check them out here. Eva Winners's Books https://bit.ly/3SMMsrN

Eva Winners writes anything and everything romance, from enemies to lovers to books with all the feels. Her heroes are sometimes villains because they need love too. Right? Her books are sprinkled with a touch of suspense, mystery, a healthy dose of angst, a hint of violence and darkness, and lots of steamy passion.

When she's not working and writing, she spends her days either in Croatia or Maryland daydreaming about the next story.

Find Eva below:

Visit www.evawinners.com and subscribe to my newsletter.

FB group: https://bit.ly/3gHEe0e
FB page: https://bit.ly/30DzP8Q

Insta: http://Instagram.com/evawinners

BookBub: https://www.bookbub.com/authors/eva-winners

Amazon: http://amazon.com/author/evawinners

Goodreads: http://goodreads.com/evawinners

TikTok: https://vm.tiktok.com/ZMeETK7pq/

Made in the USA
Las Vegas, NV
07 February 2025

17660742R00256